Assassin's DAGGER

MARINA FINLAYSON

FINESSE SOLUTIONS

Cover design by Karri Klawiter
Editing by Larks & Katydids

Published by Finesse Solutions Pty Ltd
2020/08
ISBN: 9781925607062

Author's note: This book was written and produced in Australia and uses
British/Australian spelling conventions, such as "colour" instead of "color",
and "-ise" endings instead of "-ize" on words like "realise".

A catalogue record for this book is available from the National Library of
Australia

1

———

All morning, I had hunted the golden stag through the forests of Autumn and into Summer. Now he rested, a man again, at the foot of the mighty oak tree, unaware that death perched above him. Hidden among the bright green leaves, I lay stretched out on my stomach on a wide branch, watching him sleep.

How weird was my life? Less than two months ago, I'd been playing in a band with my fae friends, working at a real estate agent's office during the day. I was half fae, but my magic had been so weak it was hardly worth mentioning—and now here I was, one of the most powerful people in all the Realms of Faerie. Sometimes I felt as though my body would split open like an overripe melon from the pressure of all the magic that fizzed inside me these days. It was a dream come true.

Plus, I now killed people for a living. That was a bit of a change from sitting behind the reception desk at Thomas & Granger's, answering the phone all day, smiling at clients until my face hurt, and trying to fend off the more handsy of the agents.

Technically, of course, I hadn't actually killed anyone yet, though it had been three weeks since I became the leader of the assassins known as the Night Vipers. That was why I was hiding in a tree in the magical Realm of Summer, looking down on a deerkin who was soon to become a corpse.

His skin was the same warm gold as the velvety hide of the stag; his eyes, when they had been open, were the rich brown of chocolate, deep and soulful. At the moment, those eyes were closed, his breathing slow and steady. Long, thick eyelashes rested on his golden cheeks, and from his chestnut-coloured hair, magnificent antlers sprouted. They knocked against the trunk of the oak as he shifted in his sleep, but the sound wasn't enough to wake him. He had travelled a long way to this resting spot deep in the green forests of Summer, and he was tired.

Maybe I should have been tired, too, after the chase he'd led us on, but I was fired up with anticipation, eager to claim my first kill as a Viper. To my right, on a branch of his own, lay Ash, my former instructor in the dark arts of assassination. My training as a Viper had barely begun before I'd become his leader instead—the Serpent at the head of the mighty Viper organisation.

Strands of Ash's brown hair fell across eyes the colour of a rain-swept sky. Long and lean, he wore all black—as did I, but he made it look all kinds of lethally sexy. His stillness reminded me of a puma; all that strength coiled tight, stalking his prey with infinite patience.

Sensing the weight of my gaze, he met my eyes, his grey glance cool and controlled as ever. He turned his attention back to the target, but not before I saw the concern that seemed ever-present lately. He watched me as if I was a bomb that could blow at any minute.

That concern had been there ever since I'd taken up mighty Ni'ishasana, Thief of Souls, claiming the magic dagger from the previous Serpent before the man's body had cooled. None of the Vipers quite knew what to make of their new Serpent—a former apprentice, suddenly turned Adept, before I had even made my first kill.

Today, that, at least, would change. My target slumbered at the foot of the tree, almost directly beneath me. He hadn't sensed us as we'd tracked him through the forests. He was deerkin, with the prey instincts of any deer, yet he had run wild and free under trees blazing with Autumn gold, his hooves kicking up a carpet of russet around him, unaware that danger nipped at his heels.

Now the time had come for me to truly join the Vipers, to prove that I was one of them and worthy to wield Ni'ishasana. The blade was a peculiar wavy shape, almost like a lightning bolt, and would have required a wide sheath, but the strange, silvery zigzags of the fae steel were too beautiful to hide away. Besides, I trusted Ni'ishasana not to cut me.

Moving with infinite care, I pulled a tiny vial from my breast pocket and carefully unstoppered it. Inside were a few drops of poison. Night viper venom—taken from the green- and yellow-striped snakes for which our assassins' guild was named. The night vipers were our emblem and our tool. Nowhere else in all the Realms of Faerie did they exist anymore, except in our secret Nest, where we bred them for their venom.

I tipped the vial and let the viscous liquid slide out onto a cushion of Air. Air magic was mine to command now, thanks to the power of Ni'ishasana, along with just about every other magical power there was in the Realms.

It was a heady feeling. My previous life, where even creating a simple ball of faelight had taken effort, seemed like a dream already half forgotten. Now, magic came to me easily, eagerly even, ready to fulfil my every wish.

I blew gently on my cushion of Air, guiding it toward the ground and its target, the precious drops of venom held safely within. Ash lay like a statue on his branch beside me, and nothing disturbed the still of the forest except for the soft twittering of a nearby bird. Everywhere was green and silent, like a great natural cathedral. The sun shone Summer-bright overhead, but it filtered through the massive canopy of the oaks so that the light fell in green sparkles, illuminating the leaves and making them glow like stained glass.

The venom sank lower, glittering in that green light like precious diamonds. My target's mouth was slightly open, relaxed in sleep. All I had to do was guide the venom to his lips and death would follow within minutes.

I held my breath as a soft breeze whispered through the leaves, but my magic had a firm grip on its precious cargo, and the venom didn't spill. It hovered just above his face, and I smiled as I guided it the last few inches toward his mouth. Piece of cake.

As I released the pocket of Air and let the liquid fall, he moved in his sleep.

The clacking of his antlers against the tree disturbed him. The venom missed his mouth and splattered onto his cheek instead, and suddenly he was fully awake, with the instincts of one who knows he is prey. Those liquid brown eyes snapped open, wide and startled.

His hand went to his cheek and found the unfamiliar moistness there. He rubbed it off, then sniffed suspiciously at his fingers. In an instant, he was on his feet and the change shivered over his body. Gone was the golden-skinned man in brown leather trousers and a loose white shirt. In his place stood a golden stag, the powerful muscles of his hindquarters bunched, ready to leap away from danger.

I rolled quickly, dropping from the tree like a stone, but Ash was faster. He landed on the stag's back, knife already in hand. The deerkin reared in fright, tossing back his antlered head, but Ash clung like a barnacle, slashing his throat before his hooves found the earth again.

The deerkin staggered, knees buckling, and Ash slid from his back in a smooth movement. Blood gushed from the gaping wound across his neck, and his eyes rolled in helpless terror.

I closed in, Ni'ishasana in hand, the dagger scenting blood and eager to taste the dying life—but the stag's proud head sagged to the grass before I could obey its wish, and the light went out of his soft brown eyes.

Fury swirled within me as I watched blood spread across the leaf litter, soaking into the forest floor. "Why did you do that?" I hissed at Ash. "He was *my* target. *Mine* to kill."

The dagger in my hand pulsed with fury at being denied the taste of another soul. Every fae it killed, whether it chose to revive them as a mindless slave or leave them dead, fed its power, adding to its stores of magic. Its rage pressed against my mind, pounding and insistent, until my own anger met Ni'ishasana's, spiralling around it. They stoked each other into a roaring fire within me, and my hand shook, barely restraining the urge to plunge Ni'ishasana's twisted blade into Ash's heart instead.

"I was afraid he would get away," he said blandly. "I'm sorry if I have offended you, Serpent. I only did what I thought best."

"*What you thought best*," I repeated with heavy sarcasm. I could tell he was lying. "You're not meant to think; you are meant to obey."

"How was I disobedient? You didn't order me not to kill him."

I ground my teeth, burning with frustration. "You knew I wanted this kill, Ashovar." I found some brief satisfaction in the way he flinched when I used his full name, the way his father had done. Celebrach had wielded Ni'ishasana before me, and Ash had hated him. He didn't like the reminder that *I* now held his reins instead. "This kill was mine, and I didn't need your help."

"I'm sorry."

"Another lie. Why do you lie to me, Ashovar, when you know I can see inside your soul?"

"You're mistaken." His tone was bleak as a winter gale. "I have no soul."

How dared he stand against my wishes? He wanted to play all cold and frozen? I would thaw the bastard out.

I cried out in frustration and hurled a blast of Summer heat at him. I sent the heat spearing into his body, licking along his veins like molten fire. He fell to his knees with a gasp, but made no other sound, though I could see his limbs shudder with pain.

He didn't try to fight back. Though I knew that this was because of Ni'ishasana's nearness—the dagger permitted no treachery against its wielder—it still frustrated me. I wanted him to scream and shout, to *fight* me, so that I could scream and shout back. Find some outlet for the wild fury inside.

But Ash was famous for his icy calm, the way he closed himself off from others. For a while, it had seemed as though I might worm my way past his boundaries, but Ni'ishasana stood between us now, an impassable barrier. I let my power die and watched that proud neck sag in relief.

He remained on his knees for a long moment, bowed over the body of his kill, before he pushed himself to his feet, moving like an old arthritic man.

"All right," he said. His voice was harsh, racked with the pain I had inflicted. "You want the truth? I did it to spare you." His eyes were unutterably weary, as if he knew he was fighting a battle he could never win but still had to try. "You're not a killer, Sage, and killing changes a person. You never wanted any of this. You were never meant to be a

Viper at all. Don't you remember? You took up the burden of the dagger to save your friend, Raven. This isn't you."

Raven, yes. He of the night-dark wings and mocking smile. I could see his face in my mind, but there was no emotion attached to the memory. He was no longer important.

"Not so long ago, you meant for us both to escape the Vipers," Ash went on. "Together."

He moved closer and put tentative hands on my shoulders. His body still trembled with the memory of the pain I had inflicted, but he handled me gently, like the most delicate glass. As if he was afraid I would shatter at his touch.

Seemingly of their own volition, my hands crept up his chest, my fingers tangling in the folds of his black shirt.

Why would you leave the Vipers? the dagger whispered, its myriad voices singing in my mind. *You have everything you want now.*

"We can still be together." I stroked my hand across the firm muscles of his chest. The warmth of his body penetrated the thin fabric, and his heartbeat surged beneath my touch. He was not as cold as he wanted everyone to believe —particularly not where I was concerned. "We have the world at our feet now. There's no need to run."

"The dagger has changed you," he said, "and you don't even realise it. The Sage I knew hated assassins. She would never have stayed once freedom beckoned. You are stronger than this, Sage. But you must give up the dagger while there is still time, before it gets its claws too far into you."

My hand dropped away, and I stepped back. Give up

the dagger? Give up the bottomless well of power that it brought? He was mad.

Mad or treacherous, the voices whispered.

Treacherous? I waited, but Ni'ishasana said no more. I sucked in a breath as it hit me.

He wanted the dagger for himself.

Sudden rage boiled within me, and a red mist coloured my vision. "Do you think I'm stupid? Do you think I can't see what you're doing? You will never have Ni'ishasana."

His eyes widened, as if in surprise. The man was a consummate actor. "I don't *want* it. I hate it. I hate what it does to me. What it's doing to you." His voice rose, and the birds in the trees around us fell silent. "Listen to yourself, Sage. This is the dagger talking. You must give it up, before it's too late."

"I must, must I?"

My voice was calm, but he stepped back. Yes, that was right. He *should* be afraid, with his treacherous talk. He was right to fear punishment.

I raised my hands and sent Summer heat searing through his veins again, but this time, I held nothing back. Power flowed between us, bright and terrible. This time, he didn't suffer in silence. He fell to the ground, a scream wrenched from his tortured throat, and the sound pierced me like a knife.

What was I doing? I couldn't hurt Ash like this.

Yes, you can! the dagger roared. *Teach him his place! He cannot be allowed to separate us.*

A wave of molten rage washed through me, blasting away any other emotion, leaving understanding in its wake. Of course. The dagger was right. Such outrageous behaviour didn't deserve mercy.

"Why do you make me hurt you, Ash?" I crooned, leaning over him. Through our bond, I could feel his agony, and it tasted sweeter than honey. "You know I don't want to hurt you. But treachery cannot go unpunished."

His screams died abruptly as he sank into unconsciousness. I stared down at him dispassionately. In the throes of agony, he had rolled in the blood of his victim, and dried leaves and dirt were stuck to him, smeared across his cheek and tousled through his hair. Rage still burned within me, but the fire was banked for the moment, the need to punish assuaged.

I opened a gate into the Wilds and used my Air magic to flick his unconscious form through the opening in a swirl of scattered leaves. Then, I stepped through behind him, the tickle of threshold magic skittering across my skin, leaving the dead body of the deerkin alone in the silent forest.

Contract fulfilled.

2

The great dining hall of the Vipers was packed to the rafters, the tall stained-glass windows throwing swirls of colour across the grey floors as the morning sun set them ablaze. Everyone seated at the four wooden tables that ran almost the entire length of the room rose in a thunderous wave as I entered with the Adepts, wooden benches scraping back over the stone floor.

I led the way to the high table that sat perpendicular to the long ones in a silence broken only by the occasional cough or shuffle of feet, all eyes on me as I took my seat in the throne-like chair that had once been Lord Celebrach's. Not until I was seated did everyone else resume their places.

The seat on my right was empty. Nuah sat at my left hand. Her bright red hair reminded me of Willow's, although the Adept's was straight and tamed into a neat braid, where Willow's sprang in a riot of curls from her head. One of the silent, grey-clad servants glided over to fill my wine goblet, and I drank deeply. Why was I thinking of Willow? She was in my past and no longer important.

We are your people now, the dagger's many voices hummed in my mind. The shadows in the corners of the large dining hall moved, taking on shapes that had become familiar to me over the weeks since I'd taken up the dagger. There was Umarenthe, the great Air mage. She had been the last wielder of Ni'ishasana before Lord Celebrach. At her side were Utal and Pardiz, both Summer fae.

These three had held the dagger for such a long time that their forms were stronger than many of the others. Celebrach, too, my immediate predecessor, lurked in the shadows. His familiar form no longer sent shivers of fear down my spine, as it had when he was alive. He and his Winter powers were mine to command now, his days of ascendancy over.

I knew from experience that no one but me could see the shadowy souls of the dagger. No one else reacted to their presence. Grey-clad servants brought out the food now that the high table was seated, and a low hum of conversation buzzed through the room. The lower tables were packed, as they had been every night since my ascendancy, and I felt the weight of many pairs of eyes on me.

I didn't flatter myself that this record attendance was any show of solidarity for the new Serpent. I knew my Vipers well. Ni'ishasana compelled their loyalty to its wielder but not their love. Most of them were probably wondering how I had managed to circumvent the dagger's enforced loyalty in order to kill its previous wielder.

Wondering whether they could find the same loophole and use it to gain power themselves.

What they didn't know was that the dagger itself had turned on Lord Celebrach. Without its help, I would have had no chance against him. Now, its love sustained me.

Distantly, I became aware that Nuah was speaking to me.

"What did you say?"

"I said I hoped that your mission was successful," she said, an expression of polite interest on her face.

Nuah was as ambitious as the rest of them, and probably the most powerful Adept after Ash, hence her position at my left hand. She would be leading the charge to unseat me if she could only figure out how it was done. There was no love lost between us.

I cut a piece of beef and chewed it slowly, admiring the scenes of bloody death depicted in the stained glass, before I answered her. It was good for ambitious Adepts to be reminded that they waited on the Serpent's pleasure.

"The target is dead," I said briefly before turning back to my meal. The baked potatoes were particularly good tonight. There was some kind of flavouring I couldn't quite place. Rosemary, for sure, but what was that other elusive taste? Whatever it was, I approved. I gestured one of the servants over and got him to fill my plate.

"Congratulations," Nuah said. "Your first official kill."

My mouth was full of potato, so I grunted. Not that I would have told her that Ash had been the one to make the kill and not me. That was information she didn't need to know.

The noise levels in the hall grew louder as the meal wore on. Beer and wine flowed freely here, and the food was always good, though never quite as good as Zinnia's cooking back in Willow's sith. An odd sensation of loss shot through me at the thought, but I shrugged it away impatiently. I had everything I needed right here.

Nuah chatted with Sharis on her other side for a while, leaving me to enjoy my meal in peace. But as soon as I pushed my plate away, satisfied, she turned back to me.

"Have you given any thought as to who is to replace Evandir?"

There was an empty seat at the end of the high table, which had once been Evandir's. The nine Adepts were down to only eight since Ash had killed him in the battle against Celebrach. The man had been a pig, and I certainly wouldn't mourn him, but his skills were a loss to the Nest.

"Not yet," I said. "Have you?"

I was surprised she'd waited this long to raise the matter. Part of the Adepts' role was to advise the Serpent in matters that affected the Nest, and the rise of a new Adept was a big deal. The choice of who would be elevated to Adept status was a hot topic of conversation at the moment, second only to the speculation on how I had managed to achieve my own elevation. Each of the current Adepts was busy manoeuvring, trying to ensure one of their own followers gained the prize.

"Mezzi has been with us a long time," she said.

That was true. Even without my shadowy associates to advise me of the Vipers' history, I could have figured that out for myself from his seating position in the dining hall. The Vipers were obsessed with hierarchy. The closer you sat to the high table, the more senior you were in the organisation.

At the far end, furthest from the high table, was where the apprentices sat. That had been my place until recently. The only one left was Evandir's apprentice, Atinna—an icy-blond Winter fae with a pointed face and a permanent look of dissatisfaction—though now she was an apprentice without an Adept to train her.

She must have sensed my gaze because she looked up from her meal, favouring me with a glare. She might have to obey me, but she didn't have to like me. If I opened myself to my bond with her, I could feel her hatred pulsing inside her. It would be a cold day in hell before Atinna forgave me for being instrumental in the death of Evandir, her Adept and bed partner.

I turned my attention away from her hot gaze to Mezzi, whose current place was at the very head of one of the middle tables. His dark hair was cut close to his head, giving him a military look that was unusual among the fae.

"He would be a good candidate," I mused.

Nuah shrugged, as if the matter was of no concern to her. "No doubt he would," she said, "but there are several others whose claims are just as good. I'm sure the other Adepts have all made representations to you already."

"Mmm." I wouldn't satisfy her curiosity so easily. If she wanted to know who else was in the running, she would have to find out some other way.

"Saffron is also a strong candidate," she added,

nodding in the direction of the woman who sat opposite Mezzi.

Did that mean Mezzi was only a smokescreen for her real favourite? Which one was her true choice? I probed deeper but couldn't read any emotional clues through our link. The dagger's power allowed me to read strong emotions clearly, even if the person attempted to hide them. Ash was practically an open book to me lately. But either Nuah didn't care much either way, or she was particularly good at controlling her feelings.

"I'm sure there are many loyal Vipers to be considered for the position." I put only the slightest emphasis on the word *loyal*, but I knew she noticed it. Nuah hadn't risen to her current position within the Nest by being stupid or insensitive to nuance. "I'll have no trouble filling Evandir's empty seat."

She glanced to my right. "Speaking of empty seats, is Ashovar not gracing us with his presence tonight?"

"Ashovar is indisposed this evening," I said. She wouldn't be the only one who would have noted his absence. "He finds it unhealthy to disagree with his Serpent."

Nuah sat back, a satisfied gleam in her eye. She was well aware of Ash's favoured position, and any indication that he may have fallen from grace was welcome news. "How very unwise of him."

"Indeed." I pushed back my velvet upholstered chair, causing everyone in the room to spring to their feet. "I hope *you* will remain healthy, Nuah."

She inclined her head in a gesture of respect. "I'm sure I shall, Lady Serpent."

I strode from the dining room and down the long hallway outside it. The carpet was a deep blood-red, patterned with severed hands, eyeless heads, and other miscellaneous pieces of anatomy—a true love song to the assassin's craft. At the end of the corridor, I thrust open the heavy, wood-panelled doors and stepped out into the fresh air.

It was mid-morning. Dinner in our nocturnal world was usually served about nine in the morning. Most of the Vipers would be thinking of their beds soon, but I wasn't ready for sleep yet. I needed some fresh air.

The question of who to elevate to Adept status was an important one, and it should be occupying my mind. There were several deserving candidates, including Mezzi and the woman, Saffron, that Nuah had mentioned. There were many factors to weigh to make the best decision for the Nest as a whole, but I was finding it difficult to concentrate.

A soft breeze rustled through the morning woods as I passed the training grounds and entered the trees. I'd always been comfortable surrounded by nature—it came from growing up in Spring, I supposed, where nature was invited into the home even more so than in most fae Realms. I'd gone to sleep every night for as long as I could remember to the sounds of water trickling, frogs croaking, and leaves rustling in the breeze.

My new chambers, high up in the massive main building of the Nest, were as far removed from nature as it was possible to be in a sith. Siths were little bubbles of the Realms that had been broken off to form their own tiny world, so they were usually full of trees and gardens, since most fae were fond of natural beauty. Some siths were no bigger than a room or a house, and some, like the Nest, covered a vast area, containing many buildings.

Sure, it was no tiny city apartment, but the former Lord Celebrach's rooms still smelled of his scent, mingled with the ashy aroma from his generous hearth. Even sleeping with the windows thrown open, it felt as though I was not quite in the right place, as if things were subtly off kilter.

A tight stand of pines appeared ahead of me, clustered almost completely around a familiar cottage, and my steps faltered. Had my subconscious been leading me here all along? I hadn't set out deliberately to visit Ash, yet here I was on his doorstep.

I had missed his cool presence at dinner. Though most of the time he was no more welcoming than an arctic gale, there was still something familiar about his Winter chill. I trusted him far more than any of the other Vipers in my care. He was the only one that I was confident had any regard for me beyond the obedience the dagger compelled. The others might have to obey me, but I knew they resented my rise.

I pushed open his front door. The short hallway was dark, all the blinds drawn at the windows.

But he's trying to take the dagger for himself, the voices whispered. Umarenthe, Celebrach, Utal, and Pardiz, along with a host of others, their different tones twining together in a jarring chord. I rested my hand briefly on the dagger's hilt, my thumb rubbing reflexively over the egg-sized ruby embedded there. The voices were ever-present, but sometimes when I touched the ruby, I thought I could hear them even more clearly.

I had almost forgotten the reason for Ash's punishment. He had tried to take the dagger, hadn't he? I cast my mind back, but it no longer seemed so clear as it had in the moment.

Guilt nibbled at me, and I frowned as I paced quietly down the hallway. He wasn't in the lounge room. How many times had I found him there, staring into the fire as if its warmth entranced his chilly Winter heart? How many times had I seen him sitting there, gazing into the flames, a glass of spirits in his hand? That chair was practically his spiritual home. But the fire wasn't lit, and the room was dark.

There were only four rooms in the cottage—the lounge room, a small bathroom, and two bedrooms, one of which had been mine. I hadn't been back to that bedroom since I had become Serpent; there was nothing here I needed anymore, not with the resources of the entire Nest at my disposal.

His bedroom door was ajar, and I pushed it gently open. The blinds were drawn against the morning light, and the room was dim. Dark furniture blended into the shadows: a large bed, a chest of drawers, and a massive trunk at the foot of the bed in which he kept his weapons. Two framed photos sat on top of the chest of drawers, but otherwise, the room was empty of personality. Even in his interior decorating choices, Ash played his cards close to his chest.

The room reeked of alcohol. I frowned. He lay sprawled on top of the deep red velvet coverlet, still wearing the same clothes as before, though now they were damp with sweat. He hardly seemed to have moved since I had dumped him here—though the empty bottle abandoned on the floor within reach of his dangling arm suggested that he must have gone in search of a little pain relief in the drinks cabinet.

I moved to the side of the bed and gazed down at him. A light sheen of perspiration covered his brow and beaded on his top lip. His skin was flushed a deeper red than normal, and a dark five o'clock shadow curved around his strong jaw. His eyes were closed, his lashes thick and dark against his cheek, and curls of damp hair fell across his face.

I drew in a breath. He looked unwell, unnaturally vulnerable. The guilt bit a little deeper. Perhaps I shouldn't have told Nuah that he was indisposed. She might very well decide to create another vacancy among the Adepts, since he was clearly unable to defend himself. My own experiences with Evandir had made it clear that, though the dagger enforced loyalty to the Serpent, there was no loyalty among the Vipers to each other.

Fae healing was powerful, and his body was in prime condition—*such* prime condition—but it would still take time for him to recover from the punishment I had inflicted. Perhaps I should have been a little more lenient, considering his record of loyalty.

Lenient? the voices whispered. *Lenient when he meant to separate us? Still means to! How can you call him loyal? He can't be trusted.*

No, I told them fiercely, making an effort to remember exactly what had happened. I remembered explosive rage and a stinging sense of betrayal, but I struggled to recall precisely what Ash had done to provoke those feelings. My response seemed out of proportion to what I knew of Ash's character. *That isn't right. Ash would never betray me.*

He betrayed his father, the dagger reminded me. *Why not you, too? And he was insubordinate.*

It was clear the dagger believed insubordination needed to be punished, yet the feeling lingered that I had made a mistake. Ash deserved better from me. He certainly didn't deserve to lie here like a sitting duck, waiting for the politics of the Nest to take him out.

You can't trust him, Ni'ishasana insisted.

That was *enough*. It didn't make sense. With Ni'ishasana at my hip, Ash *couldn't* betray me. Why was the dagger going to so much effort to convince me he was a threat?

Be silent. A headache began to pound as I struggled against the dagger, demanding room to think in peace.

As you wish. We only seek to protect you from pain. Grudgingly, the dagger withdrew, and I revelled in the sudden quiet inside my head. The damn blade was always *whispering* at me. Pushing me. Insinuating things that made no sense.

Ash stirred, then glanced up at me out of bleary eyes. "Serpent?"

He struggled to lever himself up, but I pushed him back down, which I found easier than I should have. I'd really done a number on him, hadn't I? The niggling sense that I'd treated him unjustly grew into a certainty, and I bit my lip.

"Self-medicating again, Ash? You drink too much." So many times I'd found him with a drink in hand, staring moodily into the fire. Did it help with the self-loathing? In that case, maybe I should take it up—but it never seemed to make *him* feel better. "You use alcohol as a crutch."

"Like you use that dagger as a crutch?"

I inhaled deeply through my nose, fighting the fury that flared at his tone. I'd done enough damage for one night. I clenched my fists until my nails dug into my palms —until I felt sure I wouldn't lash out at him again. Where had all this rage come from? Surely it wasn't normal to feel this angry all the time?

"You can't stay here like this," I said. "You're too weak." I sent out a mental summons for servants.

"I'm fine," he said, and tried again to rise, but his body trembled and sweat broke out on his forehead as he collapsed back on the bed.

"Clearly."

I waited in a fever of impatience until four servants entered the room. They moved silently, a little robotically, in their plain grey clothes. Slaves to the dagger and, by extension, me, they had no life beyond following orders. They'd been brought back to life for that very purpose, in fact. Ni'ishasana could choose, when it killed someone and drank their soul and magic, to leave them dead or make use of their empty bodies. They were zombies that would never rot, and they waited with the infinite patience of the soulless, their eyes dull.

"Take this man to my chambers and see that he is made comfortable there."

They nodded as one and moved forward in seemingly rehearsed synchronicity to hoist him up. Their movements no longer seemed eerie to me but simply a natural part of my new world.

"And make sure he isn't left alone," I added. "I want a guard on him whenever I'm not there. Do you understand?"

"Yes, Serpent," they chorused, their lifeless voices a strange echo of the voices in my head.

I waited until they had gone before resuming my walk. I was mistress of the dagger, not the other way around. I refused to listen to any more of its insinuations against Ash.

3

———

aven came to me in my dreams, his body strong and humming with power, black wings thrusting from his shoulders. Those wings caressed me, so soft I could barely feel their touch on my skin. They enclosed me in a dark, sensuous world where there was only Raven, his hands on my body, his lips on mine. I fell into that warmth, craving his touch, wanting more.

"Where are you, Sage?" he whispered, his breath tickling my ear. His tongue soon followed, and I gasped and shuddered, lost in the sensation of him against me, all around me. His great black wings cupped me with infinite tenderness, shielding us both from the world.

Then the wings were gone, and Raven, too, whisked away in typical dream fashion, and Willow was there instead, her green eyes stormy.

"You killed Rowan!" she shouted at me.

I cringed back, horrified by the hatred on her face. "I didn't! I haven't seen him, I swear."

"You killed him." She shoved me hard, and I sprawled on mossy ground between the roots of a mighty oak. The coppery tang of blood scented the air. "Look what you've done!"

I turned, then scrabbled to my feet with a cry of horror. The deerkin I had hunted lay as I had last seen him, collapsed at the base of the tree, his throat a gaping wound. But now he bore Rowan's face, Rowan's antlers, which I had seen often enough to recognise.

"No! That's not ... I didn't—"

"You did. You're the Serpent; this is your fault. His blood is on your hands."

And just like that, my hands were smeared in bright, sticky blood. I fell to my knees and tried to pull the edges of that gaping wound back together, to somehow keep Rowan alive through sheer force of will. Then I remembered: I *was* the Serpent; I had access to unimaginable powers. Ni'ishasana appeared at my side, and I lay one bloodied hand on the massive ruby, calling on the dagger's powers of healing.

Magic surged within me, rushing down my arm and into Rowan's neck—but instead of the usual blue glow, tiny insects marched over my skin, disappearing into the wound in a black, six-legged tide. I was revolted and fascinated at the same time, watching the creatures roll like a living wave over my arm, their tiny feet tickling. The wound began to close, and I allowed myself to hope.

The tickling turned to scratching, and then to outright pain. Fiery agony blossomed in every nerve ending as the insects rent my flesh from my bones. I screamed, nearly passing out from the pain, but as the world swam about me, I focused all my energy on not letting go of Rowan. I had to save him. The wound was nearly closed now—all I had to do was hold on a little bit longer, bear the torture a few seconds more.

Then it stopped, and the insects all disappeared. My arm was a sheet of blood, dripping gore from the shoulder down. But it was all worth it, because Rowan's wound had disappeared as if it had never been, and his chest moved again as breath stirred in his lungs.

His eyes opened, and I screamed. Black pits stared back at me, and I knew with the strange certainty of dreams that there was no soul behind them. Gone was my laidback friend; in his place, the dagger had left a monster. He sat up, his lips curving into a cruel smile, and I backed away, cradling my savaged arm against my chest.

There was blood everywhere. My head spun as the trees closed in, leaning over me with branches outstretched. The Rowan monster reached for me with hands that had sprouted wicked black claws.

I shuddered awake, my heart racing like a runaway train. It took me a moment to remember where I was and place the familiar surroundings. The bed's enormous canopy stretched overhead, blocking my view of the ornately carved ceiling. I had kicked off the sheet in my panic and lay naked on the soft mattress. The window was open a handspan, the blind rolled up far enough to let some cool air enter the room, and it whispered over my sweat-soaked skin.

All the furniture in the room was dark wood and

ridiculously oversized. The bed could have slept ten in comfort; the table by the window was half the size of the high table in the dining room. I lay on my side, facing the table and the window, and the small rectangle of daylight that shone under the blind reassured me that the dream world was gone. This was real; there were no dream monsters about to rend me with their claws.

Something shifted on the bed behind me, and I sat bolt upright, heart pounding all over again.

Holy Tree! I'd forgotten Ash lay next to me. The bed was so wide I hadn't noticed him at all as I slept. He lay on his side, facing away from me, clad only in a pair of loose cotton shorts. I took a moment to admire the long line of his powerful back, the tight buttocks and strong, shapely legs.

I leaned closer to get a look at his face and saw that his skin glowed a healthy tan colour. That was a good sign. No more hectic red flush. My breasts brushed against his back and his hand shot up. He grabbed my arm, pulling me half across him as he turned toward me.

Grey eyes snapped open, alert for danger. A wary look entered them as he took in his surroundings. "Your pardon, Serpent. I find myself a little disoriented."

He tried to sit up, but I was draped across him, enjoying his hard body under mine. "You've been unwell. How do you feel now?"

"Fine." His gaze darted around the room, then came to rest on my face. "Why am I here?"

"Philosophical questions so early in the day, Ash?" The light at the window had the washed-out quality of late afternoon, just before it shades into evening. Almost time for the fae "day" to start. I slid one leg across his body and felt something stir to attention beneath it, which ignited an answering fire in my core. All I had to do was dispose of the shorts, adjust my position slightly and I could be riding him. I caught my lower lip between my teeth. That was a *very* enticing thought. In fact, all of a sudden, I was having trouble thinking about much else.

He swallowed hard, and I followed the movement of his throat with amusement. Clearly, he was also having trouble focusing. He lay still beneath me, as if aware that one move could spark a fire between us.

"It was more of a locational question," he said, his voice remarkably steady under the circumstances. But his gaze was locked on my mouth, and his breathing was way faster than it ought to be for someone who'd done nothing more strenuous than roll over. "Why am I in your bed? Did we ...?"

"Did we what?" I moved my leg, enjoying the way it made him twitch beneath me. "Enjoy a restful sleep together?"

"Before that." He licked lips that had suddenly gone dry, his desire lighting up the link between us. "Last I remember, we were in Summer with the target."

I rocked my pelvis against him and was rewarded with a shudder through his whole body. My own breath was coming faster now, too. So close. I was *so close* to what I had been craving for weeks. Ever since the dagger had sent me a vision of the two of us together, I hadn't been able to stop thinking about it. The dream about Raven had only inflamed me more.

"The target that you took out instead of me?" I asked. "*That* target?"

I saw the shadow of the memory in his eyes. "Is this my punishment?"

"Does it *feel* like a punishment?" I rocked against him once more, and he groaned. His hands caught at my shoulders, but whether to pull me closer or push me away I wasn't sure. I didn't think he knew himself. "Way to make a girl feel desirable, Ash."

"Sage." He took a deep breath, centring himself. "Did we make love? Why can't I remember?"

I trailed a finger down his cheek, then over his collarbone. "As I said, you've been unwell. *That* was your punishment. I thought it best to keep you here where I could keep an eye on you in your weakened state."

"So we didn't ...?"

"No." I slid the palm of my hand over the tense muscles of his chest, then down his side. "We didn't—but we could always correct that now."

His body was telling me yes, but his eyes said no. "If that is your command."

You are the Serpent, the shadows around the bed whispered. *You could have any man you wanted. Why do you waste time with this one?*

"I *could* command you." But if I was so set on having him, why was I dreaming about Raven? Frustration and confusion warred within me.

"And I would be forced to obey," he said.

Umarenthe's form coalesced out of wispy nothingness in the corner of the room. *Send him away*, she urged.

Begone, I snarled in my mind. Bad enough to be constantly hearing voices without having actual spectral witnesses to my every private moment. At least it had been Umarenthe and not Celebrach. It would have been seriously weird to have him see me naked with his son.

I stared down into Ash's serious grey eyes. His lips were so close. Just one taste? Slowly, I lowered my head and nipped at his lower lip. He shifted a little, and his hands slid down my body to my hips.

Now we were getting somewhere. I kissed him more ardently, and his mouth opened beneath mine, as if he couldn't help himself—but then he lay still, letting me kiss him but not kissing me back.

I lifted my head. "Kiss me."

"Is that an order?"

I frowned down at him, smothering a pang of hurt. "No, it wasn't an *order*."

"Because it sounded a lot like one." He pushed me off him, gently but firmly. "Sage, can't you see how bizarre this is? You nearly kill me with your 'punishment', and you want to kiss me as if nothing happened? It's as if you've forgotten what you did."

"I ..." I began to protest, but the details *were* kind of vague. I could remember all-consuming anger, but not much of the reason. Had I really almost killed him? I stared at him in silence, and he nodded.

"I thought so. The dagger pushes you around like a puppet and you don't even realise it." He reached up and pushed a strand of hair out of my eyes, his touch infinitely gentle. "If we are to be together, I want to know I'm with Sage, not the dried-up spirits of Ni'ishasana. This is wrong."

A moment before, I'd been so sure of myself, but now I felt lost. He was right, wasn't he? I glanced at the dagger where it lay in a pool of sunlight on the vast table, the ruby glinting with inner fire, its twisted blade gleaming. The voices were obediently silent, but anger radiated from it, seeping into my soul until all certainty disappeared.

Red mist coloured my vision, and I clenched my fists. No. He was wrong. How dare he accuse me of being a mere *puppet*?

I rolled off the bed in a temper and shrugged into a silk gown. By the time I turned back, he had covered himself with the sheet.

"I do have an order for you," I said as I belted the gown around my waist. My pulse was still racing, and I was wet with longing, but if I didn't leave now, I was afraid I would lose control again, as I had in the forests of Summer. "Stay there another couple of hours. You could do with the extra sleep."

"I'm fine."

"Do as you're told." I snapped it through gritted teeth, barely holding onto my temper. I was so quick to anger lately, as if the accumulated resentment of centuries kept trying to explode out of Ni'ishasana through me. Sometimes it frightened me—and sometimes it didn't, which was even more alarming. I was starting to see why Celebrach had kept the dagger on a stand in his office so much instead of on his person. Somehow, it was easier to manage my rage when it wasn't physically present.

Ash propped himself up on one elbow, watching as I moved around the room, picking my clothes out of the enormous carved wardrobe and digging out my shoes from where I'd kicked them under the bed.

"Can't you see what the dagger is doing to you?" he said softly. It was as if the bastard could read my thoughts. "This isn't you, Sage. You dreamed of justice and an end to the Vipers."

I stood up straight, one shoe dangling from my hand by its laces. "Is that what *you* want? An end to the Vipers?"

I knew his father had tricked him into joining, that he'd never wanted to be an assassin—but an end to the whole Viper organisation? He'd never admitted to that much before. He was certainly taking a risk admitting it to me now. I was the Serpent—the Vipers were in my care. Ni'ishasana's rage battered against my mind, looking for an outlet. I clenched my fists until my bones ached, fighting for control. Ni'ishasana had brought me unimaginable power, but I was discovering some drawbacks to sharing headspace with a murderous dagger.

"If that's what it takes to free you," he said. "The dagger has polluted your soul, but I know you're still in there. You have to fight."

4

I left my chambers and went to find something to hit. Usually, playing music soothed me when I was mad or frustrated, but I had no guitar here, something that needed to be remedied as soon as possible.

Failing music, I fell back on physical exertion to work out my frustrations with Ash, spending half the night on the training grounds. I no longer had to fear "accidental" damage from my fellow assassins, since Ni'ishasana compelled their loyalty to me, and there were plenty of people willing to go a round or two with me in order to get into my good graces.

I spent some time sparring with Mezzi, sizing him up as a potential Adept. He was a little taller than me and more heavily muscled, but light on his feet. He was also blindingly fast with a knife, though not as fast as the late, unlamented Evandir had been. I was pleased to see that, with my new magically enhanced skills, I was as fast as he was.

See how well you move together, the dagger whispered. *The dance of knives is not the only dance between a man and a woman.*

Not interested, I told it.

You have needs you should fulfil.

Not with Mezzi!

Why not? He is pleasing to the eye.

I couldn't help it; a mental picture of Ash, naked in my bed, leapt into my mind, despite my anger with him. If we were talking about "pleasing to the eye" …

Why him? You think he's special, with his talk of 'being together'? You think he loves *you? The dagger's voices lashed me with scorn. Love is a concept for weaklings, used by the strong to manipulate them. Be wary of the man who comes to you with sweet words—ask yourself what he wants. Because there is always something.*

Ash isn't like that. Distracted by the dagger's talk, I nearly ate dirt, and Mezzi flashed a fierce grin as I dodged out of the way.

Ash is like all the others, only out for what he can get. The only unselfish love is between a mother and her baby, or a father and his child.

I scoffed. *You don't know my father.* There was a reason I hadn't seen him in years. *I might as well have no family.*

We are your family now. We will keep you safe.

A wave of love washed through my whole body, warming me. I signalled the end of the bout to Mezzi, and he bowed and walked away.

But that scheming Viper means to separate us if he can, the dagger continued. *You will have to get rid of him.*

Get rid of Ash? A chill ran through me at the very thought, and I lashed out. *Get out of my head! Leave me alone.*

Silence.

Shaken, I looked around for someone else to spar with. There were too many conflicting emotions inside me. Was the dagger right? Was Ash using me for his own ends, to gain power amongst the Vipers? That didn't feel right, but my head was full of fog, and I couldn't puzzle it out, my brain slow and snarled with anger. So, I sought refuge in action instead.

I trained against Nuah, Saffron, and Sharis over the course of the evening. In between bouts on the training grounds, I met with each of my Adepts, seeking their opinions on a replacement for Evandir. I didn't have the advantage of having known everyone for years as my predecessor had done. I'd spent the past two weeks getting acquainted with everyone under my care, but acquaintance was all it was. I knew little more than names and Realms for half my assassins. Even my Adepts were virtual strangers, and the meetings were a good chance to get to know them a little better.

Not that I meant to unquestioningly follow anyone's advice, not even Ash's, whatever the dagger thought. I was no puppet. I purposely didn't consult him, the only one of the Adepts to be left out, since there was already a perception in the Nest that he had too much influence, having been my instructor. But getting my Adepts' input gave me insights not only into their candidates but into the Adepts themselves. All of it was useful, and could be turned against them if required. Maybe the dagger was right and love was manipulative, but manipulation worked just as well in its absence.

Between the physical exertion of my workouts and the mental gymnastics required to assess not only what was being said in my meetings but what was being left unsaid, I was exhausted by the end of the night. My pillow beckoned, and I fell into bed with a groan, letting my head sink into its cradling softness.

I closed my eyes, shutting out the view of the heavy velvet canopy looming above me. I'd have to get rid of that; it made me feel claustrophobic, like sleeping in a cave where the ceiling was too low. Bad enough to have to sleep in a room with four walls, after years of sleeping in airy Spring pavilions, without closing myself in further with bedposts and drapes. A person could suffocate under the weight of all that velvet.

I drew in a deep breath full of the fresh smell of clean sheets, and ran a hand lightly across the cool linen. No Ash slept beside me today; I had the whole gigantic bed to myself.

The window nearest the bed was open a crack to let in some air, the blind up enough to let it through. The other blinds were completely closed, and the room lay in shadow, cool and dim like a cave. Perfect for sleeping—yet somehow, sleep eluded me.

The air was still, and strands of damp hair clung to my brow. I sighed and opened my eyes again, frowning up at the looming canopy. My body might be exhausted, but my brain was whirring with names and faces. The Serpent's life was a busy one. I'd hardly seen anyone other than Ash when I was an apprentice, but now, my nights were full of people wanting things from me or merely wanting to bring themselves to my notice.

I sighed, willing sleep to come, but apparently a cure for insomnia wasn't among my new magic powers. Every time I closed my eyes, images of people danced behind my closed eyelids. Willow, Allegra, Raven. Even my father, since the dagger had brought him to mind again. I hadn't seen him in years. Not that I wanted to, of course. At our last meeting, he'd been trying to kill Willow, which didn't exactly make him Father of the Year in my book.

The sound of a fae flute drifted through my half-open window, and I resolutely cleared my mind, letting the melody take me away.

Sleep fell upon me at last, heavy and smothering, but the parade of faces didn't end. It was as if my subconscious was determined to show me every person I had ever known, as well as plenty I'd never met, courtesy of the dagger. Ancient mages and proud fae Lords and Ladies competed for space in the dreamscape inside my head.

Ash was there, too, throwing desperate magic at his father in that final terrifying battle in the woods of Spring. Icy winds blasted me, and a storm of black feathers whipped through the air. Raven called my name again as I reached for the dagger, though I knew I shouldn't—and then it was in my hands, dripping with blood. I realised I had just driven it into Celebrach's heart, only this time, as his body slumped, he wore a different face.

Rowan, proud antlers rising from his head, gazed up at me in confusion.

I screamed and hurled the dagger away from me, reaching for my friend with bloody hands. His eyes were open, imploring, and I sobbed as I gathered him in my arms. A river of blood pumped from his chest, more than any body could ever hold, drenching his favourite AC/DC T-shirt, pouring over me until I knelt in a glistening pool of it.

"Sage," he whispered, then he sagged in my arms. I knew he was gone.

I jerked awake, my heart pounding with horror. The room was shadowed, the light shading into dusk. Only a dream. Rowan was alive, safe and well. Probably bumming a free beer off Randall at The Drunken Irishman right now, or perhaps at Willow's place, lumping equipment into her four-wheel-drive, ready for the night's gig.

I closed my eyes again, not quite ready to face my Vipers yet. A pang of sorrow pierced me as I realised that picture of Rowan belonged to another time. Our band had lost half its members. Allegra had become the Lady of Illusion and I was here, Serpent of the Night Vipers. The show couldn't go on without any guitarists at all. With only a vocalist and a drummer, The Outcasts wasn't a band anymore.

That fae flute was still playing somewhere close by. Or perhaps it was a different one, since this flautist had chosen a peculiar tune, quite unlike the earlier sound. The melody slid up and down an atonal scale, strange and hypnotic. I had to admit, I preferred mortal music, though the eerie tune loosened my taut muscles, soothing away the terrors of the dream. It had almost lulled me back to sleep when stinging pain in my foot jerked me alert.

I opened my eyes and yelped. A snake was curled on the pillow right next to my head, its eyes staring into mine. I flinched away, hurling a blast of icy Winter magic out in all directions. It was instinctual—or perhaps the dagger guided me. Either way, the snake flew across the room, hitting the wall with a dull *thunk*.

Other thuds followed, and I sat up, my heart pounding. Two more snakes had hit the floor and lay immobile. Another hung from the canopy of my bed, unmoving, like some obscene icicle.

A thin trickle of blood ran down my foot as I stared in growing horror at the twin puncture marks near my ankle.

I froze, my mind reeling in panic. The bright yellow bands across the snakes' green bodies told me everything I needed to know, as if there had been any doubt. They were night vipers.

One bite meant death. I watched the blood inch down my foot toward the creamy white sheets, my heart pounding.

Their venom is deadly, Ash had warned the day he had taken me to see the vipers in their pits. The day that Evandir had tried to kill me for the first time by throwing one of them at my face. *The victim will die within three to six minutes.*

Three minutes. Three minutes. I had a world of magic at my command, but I was not immune to viper venom. Ash had begun the process of immunising me when I was his apprentice, but it wouldn't be complete for several more months. So now I had three minutes to live.

Unless the dagger's magic could somehow save me.

My heartbeat pounded in my chest, my throat, my ears, so hard I thought I might faint, but I didn't move. I remembered that much from having lived in Australia for the past five years. Despite their country playing host to twenty of the world's twenty-five most venomous snakes, Australians rarely died of snakebite. Most snakes weren't aggressive in the first place, and if they did bite, there was usually time to apply first aid and get the person to hospital, where antivenom could be administered. As long as the victim kept still.

Maybe I'd last a whole six minutes if I didn't move the leg. That was how the poison spread. When the panicked victim ran for help, pumping those arms, moving those legs, they pumped it through the system and killed themselves. But I had no hospital. Bandaging the affected limb and keeping it immobile wasn't going to save me, however much it might help all those Australians. I panted hard, trying to control my panic. *Think.* What could I do?

Suck the venom out? God, no, that wouldn't work. Having it in my mouth would be no better than having it in my lymphatic system.

Magic, then. Wild thoughts of turning my foot to ice and chopping it off swirled in my head. Anything that might save me. With Ni'ishasana's powers, I could probably make myself a new foot, almost as good as the original.

The blood had reached the sheet and stopped. It was

such a small wound it wasn't even bleeding anymore. Crazy to think how something so small could kill me. My legs trembled, despite my best attempt at keeping still. It was hardly surprising, since my whole body was shaking.

Summer magic? Could I burn it out? But that left me with the same problem—a foot that was pretty much destroyed, and no guarantee either that such drastic measures would save me.

It was hard to think. My fingers clutched the sheet, scrunching it in my fists. A searing pain spread from my foot up through my ankle and into my lower leg, like tiny tongues of flame licking at my veins. The skin there had turned a menacing purple. How long did I have left? *Think. Think.*

Beads of sweat broke out on my forehead and in my armpits. Fear sweat slid down my cleavage and tickled at the back of my neck. I swallowed hard, forcing myself to focus on the problem as if it were merely an intellectual puzzle with nothing riding on the answer. Spring had nothing for me, nor did Earth or Air.

Ocean? The dagger's Ocean magic gave me power over water, but liquids were all much the same. I closed my eyes and took a deep breath.

I called to the venom that was inching its way through tiny capillaries beneath my skin. Would it work? Could my Ocean magic distinguish between the lymphatic fluid that was meant to be there and the invading venom? And all without me being able to see either of the substances in question?

It's magic, I reminded myself. Willow didn't have to see

the roots of the trees to call them forth, or the sap within the tree trunks to make leaves grow and flowers bloom. She visualised what she wanted and her Spring magic imposed her will on the world around her. This would be no different.

Clearly, my body didn't believe me, as my heart still pounded, and I was shaking so hard it could hardly be counted as keeping still. I released my death grip on the sheet and flung my hands out towards my foot in an imperious motion. It probably wasn't necessary, but it made me feel better, as if something was being done.

The pale blue glow of the dagger's magic bloomed around me as I envisioned the deadly venom reversing its course, fighting its way back through my white blood cells or whatever the hell else inhabited my lymphatic system. *Exit's this way, guys. Get the hell out.*

Still trembling, I watched the angry purple halt in its advance up my leg. Like the tide going out, the colour receded, all the way back down to the bloody puncture marks on my foot.

Two perfect, clear globes of fluid welled up at the puncture site. As I watched in awe, they rolled down my foot like tiny marbles and plopped onto the sheet next to the small bloodstain.

I jerked my legs away from them and shuddered. Then, I let the magic go, and the two tiny marbles splatted and became nothing more than damp spots on the sheet.

For a moment, I thought I might throw up or even pass out. Hey, why not both? I was still hugging myself and shaking like a tin roof in a category five storm when the door burst open with such force that it banged against the wall and bounced back. Framed in the doorway was Ash, a wild look in his eyes.

"What's wrong? Are you hurt?" And then his urgent gaze left my face and took in the rest of the room, the frozen snakesicles on the carpet and dangling from the velvet drapery over the bed. His face paled. "You've been bitten."

The words came out in a hoarse whisper. In a flash, he was across the room, falling to his knees by the bedside. His eyes were wild and desperate, and for a moment, I was so taken aback by the raw emotion in his face that I was speechless.

Finding my voice at last, I reached out a still-shaking hand and took his. "It's okay. I think I'm okay."

"But you're not—" He cleared his throat and tried again. Horror warred with despair on his face. Every emotion was laid bare, the mask of the cool, unfeeling man stripped away. Now, I saw the heart beneath the mask, and that heart was brimming with terror. This was more than a Viper's fear for his Serpent, but I was too overwhelmed by my own panic and terror to deal with his. "You're not immune yet. There hasn't been enough time."

"I got the venom out." I waved a vague hand at the small wet spot on the sheet. It meant nothing to him, of course. "I used Ocean to draw it out. I think I got it all."

My voice wobbled on the last word, and he surged up from the floor and caught me in his arms. I pressed my face against his neck, feeling the salty sting of tears starting in my eyes. My body shook, but now it was with the aftermath of adrenaline and the heady, unbelievable relief at finding myself still alive.

"How long ago?" His face was pressed against my hair, his arms tight around me. For the first time, I realised he wore no shirt. No shoes, either. Just a pair of loose pants. He looked as though he had leapt straight out of bed and sprinted to my side.

"Five minutes, I think."

He held me away from him, inspecting me intently. "And you feel no pain? No burning sensation? No heaviness in your limbs?"

I shuddered, remembering the fiery pain in my leg. But it was gone now. "No, nothing."

He let out his breath in a long, slow exhalation. "I never thought I would say this, but thank the Lady for Ni'ishasana."

I nodded, fully aware that I would be dead if not for the expansive powers of the dagger. Wiping my face, I sat back, my trembling easing at last. My tears had left a wet patch in the crook of his neck, but he made no move to wipe it away, so I did it for him, brushing it absently until the warm skin beneath my fingers was dry.

"What are you doing here?" I asked.

"I felt your summons."

"I didn't call you." I hadn't, had I? The past few minutes were a blur of adrenaline, but I didn't remember calling anyone's name. I hadn't even thought of Ash. My thoughts had all been in the here and now, trying to solve the immediate crisis.

"Not words," he said. "I felt your fear and knew you were in terrible danger."

He would only have arrived in time to watch me die if I hadn't managed to figure out my own solution, but his instant response filled me with warmth all the same.

"Who did this?" He got up and inspected the snakes on the floor, shoving them with his bare foot. They remained rigid, more like blocks of wood than flesh and blood. I suspected a closer inspection would show that they were frozen solid.

"I don't know. Could have been anyone, I suppose. My enemies are legion."

He cast me a sharp glance. "That may be so, but your enemies here are also compelled by the power of the Blade to be loyal. None of them should have been able to move against you." He grasped the dangling snake behind its head and jerked it free in a violent movement, throwing it down to join the others on the floor.

"Don't stop there." I stood up on the bed and grabbed the canopy and heaved, driven by an urgent need to be rid of the damn thing. It had been bad enough when I only felt claustrophobic with it looming overhead—now that it had proved to be a haven for vipers, my animosity knew no bounds.

When he realised what I was doing, he gave me a hand, and in a minute we had the whole thing down in a shower of dust, complete with another frozen snake that I hadn't known was there. Lucky that my blast of Winter magic had been wide enough to catch them all—although, to be honest, it had probably been more panic than luck.

I jumped off the bed. He was right. Ni'ishasana compelled the loyalty of all the Night Vipers to their Serpent. Supposedly, none of them could harm me. Yet it must have been a Viper—it was inconceivable that an outsider could have penetrated the sith without my knowing it. As the Serpent, I was as aware of the wards as I was of my own hands. If anything touched them, I felt it.

I closed my eyes, focusing on the magical threads that bound me to my Vipers and they to me. The magic appeared like shining blue veins reaching out in all directions from my beating heart. I sent my consciousness darting down the shimmering azure highways, prodding and poking until I found it.

One connection that didn't feel quite right. One connection that led to a heart full of hatred and fierce gloating, a heart that believed me dead.

I opened my eyes and looked at Ash. "Atinna."

5

———

Rage boiled within me. She *dared* raise her hand against me? I would *destroy* her.

I tugged on the thread that bound us and felt a grim satisfaction as shock flooded her, followed by fear. She was right to fear me.

"I will *kill* her." I snatched the dagger up from the table under the window and stormed from the room, Ash hard on my heels. My dignity would have been better served by waiting for her to come to me, but I was too impatient for dignity. I itched to flay her with magic, to watch the fear in her eyes and hear her scream. She deserved to die for what she had done, but I would make sure that death was slow to come. My own terror was still fresh, and I wanted to see her suffer the way she'd made me suffer.

"Perhaps some clothes first?" Ash suggested.

I didn't look back as I hurried down the stairs, the carpet soft under my bare feet. Who was he to criticise? "I should stop for clothes the way you did?"

I was wearing a soft satin nightdress that left my arms and shoulders bare but came down to my knees. Not that it mattered. The Serpent didn't rely on clothes to make her imposing. The ruby in Ni'ishasana's hilt pulsed beneath my grip as if in agreement.

"That was different. You were in danger."

"As will you be if you stand between me and my vengeance."

"Believe me, I have no wish to stop you avenging yourself on Atinna. Obliterate her if you so choose."

I gritted my teeth. Did he think I needed or wanted his permission?

"But," he continued, "may I suggest you first find out how she managed to slip her leash?"

I threw open the door and marched outside into the last glimmers of daylight. The herb garden lay in soft shadow, the wall behind it leached of all colour. Other shadows stirred, and figures coalesced out of the grey dimness. As always, Umarenthe was the most lifelike, and the one who took the lead, though Celebrach, as the last wielder of the dagger, usually hovered at her shoulder. Thankfully, he rarely spoke to me. Considering I had killed him, that saved some awkwardness.

Not that I had wanted to speak to him even when he'd been alive.

I could have used you a few minutes ago. I'd discovered that the spirits of the dagger could hear me just as well if I directed my thoughts at them as if I spoke out loud.

You managed well enough on your own, Umarenthe said, the long hair coiling around her head reminding me disturbingly of the snakes that had just tried to kill me. It seemed to me that she spoke aloud, but Ash didn't hear her. Of course, he couldn't see her either. As real as these shadows seemed to me, they were invisible to everyone else. *And you did say you wanted to be left alone.*

Aren't you supposed to protect me? I was still furious, and the woman's casual attitude made me want to strangle her. Wanting peace inside my head after we'd disagreed over Ash didn't mean I wanted to be so alone that my life was in danger.

We have given you the means to protect yourself. As you did, quite competently. She kept pace with me, though I didn't move over to give her room on the narrow path between the garden beds. It gave me a petty satisfaction to see her shadow form break like a wave over the plants and reform, though if it bothered her, she gave no sign.

But why did I need protection at all?

Through an archway, the path opened up and split to encircle a large fountain. Three stone dolphins leapt up, their bodies intertwined, spouting ribbons of water from their mouths. Here, the herb beds were supplanted by flowering shrubs and small trees. It was one of the few places within the sith that seemed to be purely decorative, and it smelled divine, the heavy perfume of roses reminding me of Willow.

From an archway opposite, Atinna stepped into the courtyard, and my fury spiked. I barely stopped myself from striking her down where she stood. Only my need for answers stayed my hand. Her shoulders were back, and she met my gaze without apparent fear, but our link told another story. Through it, I could feel her terror. She knew she was as good as dead.

She held a wooden flute in her hand, and I remembered drifting towards sleep, lulled by a strange, atonal melody. I glanced sharply at her. Her pale blue eyes held no defiance, only an empty sort of acceptance, as if she knew death was coming and she would rather get it over with.

"Did you use that to work some magic?" I asked.

"I guided the vipers to the right place, then goaded them to attack," she replied. "How are you not dead?"

"How are you not *loyal*?" I bit out, infuriated by her matter-of-factness.

She shrugged, as if the question held no interest for her. "How should I know? *You're* the Serpent."

Figure it out, her attitude said. I snapped, summoning roots and branches to hold her fast. One branch tightened around her neck, dragging her back against the textured trunk of a jacaranda until she was half choked. Her fear surged across our link, and I smiled. Not so casual now.

"Try harder," I said. "How did you know you could work against me?"

When she didn't reply, I tightened the branch until her eyes bulged with terror. Strange how someone so used to dealing death could be so unprepared for her own. She flapped one hand at me. Did she want to talk after all? I loosened the branch, and she drew in a wheezing, gasping breath.

"I wasn't sure I could. But after you took the Blade, I didn't feel the same kind of bond that I had with Lord

Celebrach. It was worth a try. I swore I would get revenge for Evandir."

I clenched my teeth and exhaled through my nose in frustration. Damn Evandir. He was still a thorn in my side even after he was dead.

Is that it? I asked Umarenthe, who had seated herself on the low wall surrounding the fountain and was watching as if this was a spectacle put on for her amusement. Maybe I should offer her popcorn. There was no sign of Celebrach, at least.

Is what it? she asked, trailing her insubstantial hand through the fountain without disturbing the water at all.

Did killing Evandir somehow mess with her bond? It made sense. All the Vipers were sworn to the Serpent, their loyalty compelled by Ni'ishasana. But as I thought back to the beginning of my own apprenticeship, I hadn't been bound to the Serpent, but to Ash, my Adept. My loyalty had been ensured through him. Did that mean that if the Adept died before the apprentice could be sworn as a full Viper in their own right, the bond was loosened or even destroyed?

Given the events of the past few minutes, that seemed likely.

Does it matter?

Of course it matters! My fury found a new target in the shadow woman. *If everyone's bonds of loyalty are broken, I'm a sitting duck. I need to find out how she was able to do it.*

Your other bonds are all healthy. Check them and see for yourself. It is only this one that is damaged.

I let my consciousness flow out through the web that

bound me to the Vipers and they to me, and found her words were true. All was as it should be, the shining blue network intact. There was only that one thread, as I'd already noticed, that didn't shine as bright as the others, that felt subtly wrong. The thread that stretched back to Atinna, awaiting her fate in the embrace of the tree branches.

So, kill her or rebind her, Umarenthe said. *Let's move on to something more interesting.*

More interesting than keeping me alive? Personally, I found that pretty bloody attention-grabbing.

What is your problem? Are you sulking *because I sent you away?*

Of course not. You are the wielder. Her shadow form broke up, dissipating like smoke in the gentle breeze that stirred the leaves. Her voice drifted back to me. *But you need us. Don't forget that.*

I stared at the spot where she had been. Was that a warning? I wasn't getting the slightest hint of emotion from the dagger, even with my fingers touching the ruby in the hilt. But a chill ran through me that had nothing to do with the breeze.

At least the dialogue with the dagger's spirit had cooled my rage enough to consider her suggestion. Rebind Atinna? I supposed she was an asset to the Vipers—an apprentice almost at the end of her seven years of training. It would be a shame to waste that.

And it would be vastly amusing to keep her in servitude, knowing how much she hated me. I'd have to find some particularly repellent tasks especially for her. The idea pleased me so much that I forgot my momentary unease over Ni'ishasana and sent out a silent summons.

In a few moments, Nuah appeared in response, her fiery hair slicked back into an elegant and practical bun. "You wanted to see me, Serpent?"

She was already dressed in clothes for training, but if she found it odd that Ash and I were barely dressed, and Atinna was imprisoned by the vegetation, she said nothing. She didn't look at Atinna, simply kept her gaze trained on me with a look of polite enquiry. She was a cool one.

"It has come to my attention that Atinna is in need of a new Adept to take over her training."

The smallest frown marred Nuah's perfection for a moment. Taking an apprentice was seen as more of a punishment than anything, given the Vipers' peculiar method of acquiring new apprentices.

But she smoothed the frown away and nodded. "And you would like me to be the one?"

"I would. You are one of our best, and I would take it as a personal favour."

I put a slight emphasis on the last two words, and she smiled. Earning the favour of the Serpent was no small thing. Now she would be hoping that I'd choose her preferred candidate as the ninth Adept. Maybe I even would.

She offered me a practised bow. "Of course. You have only to ask. It would be my honour."

"Let's get on with it, then."

I released Atinna, who staggered a little as the plants retreated. Ash stepped forward and took her arm, determined that she would have no more opportunities to harm me. I drew Ni'ishasana, ready to perform the short ceremony.

Atinna glared her hatred as I drew the blade across her forearm, but I only smiled.

6

I stood outside The Lily Garden, the Thai restaurant across the street from The Drunken Irishman, watching people come and go from the pub. The mingled scents of satays and curries had my mouth watering, but I wasn't here to eat. Drink, maybe. Eat, no.

Some music and a little company that wasn't intent on killing me sounded pretty good, but I could have gotten that elsewhere. Ever since Ni'ishasana had reminded me of his existence, my thoughts had been returning to my father. Eventually, almost in exasperation, the dagger had suggested that if I was going to brood about it, I might as well ask around and see if anyone knew what had become of him. Since there wasn't a whisper of him in the Realms, the human world seemed like the logical place to start, and where better to find rumours and gossip than in one of the most popular fae watering holes outside Faerie?

The dagger on my hip thrummed with eagerness. I could feel it but not see it. I'd taken the precaution of attaching an Aversion to it, since I hardly wanted anyone in the pub identifying the famed Blade of the Vipers. For the same reason, I'd Glamoured myself. Not even Willow would recognise me tonight, with my spiked blond hair and limpid blue eyes. She might not even notice the Glamour, since it was a particularly strong one. Ni'ishasana did nothing by halves.

In any case, Glamours were a dime a dozen in The Drunken Irishman. Though it looked like a regular Sydney pub, it was a home away from home for the city's fae, and many of them found it expedient for one reason or another to disguise their appearance before venturing out in public. I would hardly stand out.

I strode across the street to where Tony stood guard at the big glass doors. Trolls made excellent bouncers, and there was definitely some troll in Tony's ancestry. He towered over me, even in my thick-soled boots. I nodded at him and he nodded back, though without the cheery greeting I was used to. Our band had played here so often we were practically family.

It took me a minute to remember the Glamour—he had no idea who I was, and there was a wariness in his eyes that was unfamiliar. Did I look like trouble? I smiled to myself at the thought.

Inside, the familiar smells of alcohol and stale sweat assailed me. The jukebox was pumping out a dance tune and conversation at the tables was at a low roar, everyone trying to be heard over the noise. As I moved further into the dimly lit room, I caught the distinctive click of billiard balls kissing up against each other; a game was in progress at the back, two guys who I knew by sight, regulars.

Hell, everyone here was a regular. It was the place to be for fae living in Sydney, for whatever reason, whether they were exiles as I had been or whether they'd chosen the mortal world.

Making my way to the bar, I glanced around for anyone I knew better. Vague disappointment welled in me when there was no sign of Willow or Rowan. Or even Raven. Allegra, of course, was off ruling Illusion, but I had thought the others might be here. Not that I meant to speak to them. If they'd known anything about my father's whereabouts, I would have heard it already.

The music changed to a new song with a driving bass line, and I smiled. I'd kept the fae flute that Atinna had used in her assassination attempt. Though I couldn't play the flute, it reminded me that I loved music and had barely heard a note since I'd joined the Vipers. That was easily fixed, of course. If I commanded music, there would be music. But I'd developed a taste for human music, and that was a little harder to satisfy in the Nest. This, with the bass guitar and the wailing synthesiser, was what I'd been craving.

Randall was working behind the bar tonight, with one of his human employees. Randall was Tony's dad, and the troll heritage was even clearer in him. Not quite as tall as his son, but built like a brick shithouse, as the Aussies liked to say. Once, Willow and I had made a game of collecting quaint human expressions like that.

"What'll it be?" he asked, flashing me a perfunctory

smile. Again, I felt that same odd let-down. I was used to a warmer welcome.

About to order my usual beer, I paused. "Vodka shot."

"Coming up." He stepped to one side, reaching for the vodka on the shelf behind him.

"She here yet?" the guy on the next stool asked him.

Randall didn't look up until he'd filled my glass. "Not yet. Told you, she doesn't usually get here till around ten or ten-thirty."

"Right." The guy tapped nervous fingers on the bar in a quick rhythm.

He looked about my age, mid-twenties, with light brown hair and the most pitiful attempt at a beard I'd ever seen on anyone older than seventeen. He was also clearly not fae. I wondered what he was doing here. We didn't get many humans in The Drunken Irishman.

He looked at me. "Hi. How's it going?"

"Get lost." I liked my men a lot more hard-bitten and with way better pick-up lines.

I paid Randall and twisted around on my stool, surveying the room. It was only half full, the disco ball doing a slow spin over an empty dance floor. The tiny stage jammed in the corner where we usually played was empty apart from a couple sitting there, engaged in a game of tonsil hockey.

The place was smaller than I remembered and kind of shabby, with its worn carpet and scuffed furniture. Why had I come here? I didn't need this anymore.

Surely there are more exciting places we could go than this? Umarenthe's voice was scathing. *It has nothing to offer you. These people are too weak to be worth the Serpent's time.*

She loomed behind the shoulder of the nervous guy, who was still tapping out a rhythm on the bar, though being careful not to meet my gaze during any of his frequent glances at the door.

I downed my vodka. She was right. The Serpent of the Vipers had no place here.

The door slammed as I slid off my stool.

"That's her," Randall said, nodding towards the door.

The young guy's gaze slid past me, lingering on whatever he saw, and I turned.

Willow had just come in, her bright red curls a fiery halo around her head. I smiled, an unexpected thrill in my heart. She looked good. She said something to the man who had his arm draped casually around her shoulders, leaning in to be heard above the roar of conversation, and I realised it was Raven.

He, on the other hand, did *not* look good. I hadn't seen him since the night I'd been sent to assassinate his father —the night I'd killed Lord Celebrach instead and become the new Serpent. My heart thudded uncomfortably as I took in the changes. Sure, he was still handsome, with his dark hair and even darker eyes—he was fae, it took serious disfigurement to make them unattractive—and he carried an air of wildness that was very appealing. But the blue shadows under his eyes were evident even in this dim light, and there was something off about the way those eyes wandered.

Randall waved them over, and I sat back down

hurriedly, drinking in the sight of Raven. My pulse quickened, despite knowing there was no way they could recognise me.

"This is Christian, the guy I was telling you about," Randall said, indicating the nervous guy on the stool next to me.

Willow's eyes narrowed. "That's an unfortunate name for a changeling. I can't believe any fae parent would name you that."

Christian stood up and offered his hand before appearing to remember that fae didn't shake hands. He grabbed his drink instead, trying to make it look as though that had been what he meant to do all along.

"They didn't. I changed my name when I got back." His chin lifted a little, as if daring either of them to comment.

So, he was a changeling—one of the unlucky humans who were abducted by the fae as a baby, given a taste of the Realms, then thrown back into the mortal world as teens. That made more sense than a random human.

Generally, there were two types of changeling: those who spent the rest of their mortal lives trying to find a way to end their exile and return to the Realms, and those who turned their back forever after on anything to do with the fae. I'd heard of people changing their names once their fae "parents" had thrown them out of the Realms before, but usually those were the kind who wanted nothing more to do with fairies and magic and meant to make a fresh start as a human. It was odd to find one of that type here, in The Drunken Irishman.

I wondered if this one had heard that the king had

recently changed the law that prohibited changelings from staying in the Realms, thanks to Allegra's intervention.

Raven swayed, and Willow tightened her grip around his waist. I realised he was drunk—so drunk he could barely focus, and clearly too drunk to stand on his own. Before I realised what I was doing, I was off my stool, offering it to them.

"Thanks"—Willow gave me a polite smile with absolutely no trace of recognition—"but we're good. We'll be over here," she said to Randall, indicating an empty table nearby. "I'll have a chardonnay. What about you, Christian?"

"I've got a drink."

"Well, I haven't," Raven slurred.

"You've had enough." She dumped him unceremoniously in a chair while I slipped back onto my stool and pretended not to watch them.

He thrust his hand imperiously into the air and clicked his fingers. At least, that must have been his intention, but he currently lacked the coordination to pull it off. "Barkeep! A bottle of your finest."

Randall snorted. "What she said. You've had enough, Raven."

The heir of Spring and a son of Night, Umarenthe breathed in my ear. *These were your friends, were they not? They don't seem too devastated at your loss. Out for a night's drinking. Perhaps they weren't such good friends after all.*

There's no law against drinking, I thought, but I'd noticed Willow's easy smile at the changeling and bit my lip. She didn't look like a person mourning the loss of her best friend.

Raven pasted on what he no doubt thought was a winning smile. "Just one more. How is a man to drown his sorrows without drink? What kind of an establishment is this?"

"The kind that doesn't want to clean up your vomit," Randall said, opening a can of soft drink and pouring it into a glass. "Here, have this."

Raven squinted at it as Christian brought the glass to the table. "Is it alcoholic?"

"Very," Willow said. "Now shush. We're not here to drown anyone's sorrows. We're here to find ourselves a new guitarist."

Christian straightened, slipping into a spare seat at the table with a smile plastered on his face. Seriously? *He* was meant to take my place in The Outcasts? Or Allegra's? This scrawny little changeling with the scraggly attempt at a beard?

I turned away, rapping on the bar to get Randall's attention. Maybe *I* should be drowning my sorrows. There was no way that guy was good enough to replace either of us.

But Willow seemed entranced with him, leaning close and touching his hand occasionally as they chatted, throwing her mane of curls back over her shoulder whenever she laughed at something he'd said. Which was way too often. Surely the guy couldn't be *that* funny. Did it matter so little to her who played guitar, as long as someone did? Was that all our friendship had meant?

Raven didn't contribute to the conversation at all. He

was either bored silly by the talk of a band that had nothing to do with him or he was regretting all the alcohol he'd consumed tonight. He had a brooding look about him that was quite at odds with his usual appearance.

I'd never seen him drunk before. He was usually so charming that I'd imagined he'd be a happy drunk, but apparently that wasn't the case. Why was he even here with Willow? They hardly knew each other. Shouldn't Rowan, as the only other original member of the band, be here if she was interviewing a possible new member?

I was keen to see Rowan, too. Not to assure myself he was safe, of course—that would be silly. I'd only dreamed him dead, and my dreams weren't prophetic. But still, I lingered, watching my former friends from the corner of my eye though I knew perfectly well that this whole thing was beneath me.

So what if Willow was replacing me in her band? What did I care about bands when I had the whole of the Vipers to command, and powers that Willow could only dream of?

And I certainly shouldn't be bothered if Willow was paying attention to some upstart changeling. He probably couldn't play for shit anyway, and she'd be done with him as soon as she heard him play. I glowered down at my drink, wishing I hadn't come. Mortal music wasn't as good as I remembered, either, judging by the crap that was playing on the jukebox.

I cast a sidelong glance at Raven. He looked shocking, but maybe it was only the alcohol. Though those shadows under his eyes looked as though he'd been working on them for a while. It took quite a sustained effort to make a fae look that tired and ... what was the word?

Broken. He looked broken, like a man who had had his dreams snatched away.

I studied his face, noting lines that I didn't remember. But the biggest change was the disappearance of that light that had always danced in his eyes, half mocking and half mischief. He stared down at his glass, shoulders slumped, letting Willow's conversation wash over him unregarded.

Then, he looked up and stiffened, rage lighting him from within as he pushed his chair back and staggered to his feet.

I turned and swore under my breath. Ash had just entered the pub.

7

———

The arrogant bastard hadn't even bothered with a Glamour. What was he thinking? Raven might be drunk, but he wasn't blind. Nor was he likely to forget someone he'd last seen under such ... compelling circumstances. It was sheer madness for Ash to be walking around undisguised. People would recognise him—perhaps others besides Raven. My hand dropped to the hidden dagger at my side, seeking reassurance.

Ash stopped to survey the room, then spotted Raven and strode to meet him. Willow got up, too. Though she couldn't have known who he was, Raven's drunken hostility was clear to see.

I glared at Ash, though he wasn't looking at me, and even if he were, he wouldn't have recognised me through the Glamour. What was he doing here? This was my little corner of the world. I knew perfectly well he had no potential clients to meet here. We had a handful of active jobs, but no new commissions to discuss.

It wasn't forbidden for Vipers to spend time outside the Nest, but it was rare. Once you'd made it through the seven gruelling years of apprenticeship and become a killer for hire, you tended to stick to your own kind. But the way Ash made a beeline for Raven made it look as though he'd come expressly to meet him.

I wasn't the only one watching as he stalked across the room. Randall had been wiping the bar down with a cloth when the door opened, but his hand had stilled halfway through the task. The big bartender had a keen eye for impending disaster.

"What's wrong?" Willow asked, grabbing at Raven's elbow, though whether it was to hold him back or stop him falling over wasn't clear.

"It's him," Raven hissed, in what was clearly meant to be a whisper but came out so loud that half a dozen heads in the immediate vicinity turned toward him. "The assassin."

Oh, great. Half the bar had heard. Ash would never be able to show his face here again. The music was still blaring, but I realised the clicking of billiard balls had ceased. The players had paused to watch this little confrontation.

"I'll have no trouble here, gentlemen," Randall rumbled in warning.

Neither Ash nor Raven so much as glanced at him. Randall locked eyes with his son, Tony, who nodded and left his post at the door, drifting closer in case he was needed. Not that Tony would be able to do much in spite of his size if these two really got into it. Raven was the son of the Lord of Night, and his magic was strong and deadly.

And at his side stood the heir of Spring, who had a few tricks up her sleeve herself.

The use of magic was forbidden in Randall's pub, but convention wouldn't stop either of them if it came down to it. Not that I was worried. I had enough power to rein them in twenty times over if necessary, but first, I needed to know what Ash was doing here.

He shouldn't be here, Umarenthe said. *Didn't we tell you he was false? He comes here to conspire against you.*

The dagger's eagerness for blood thrummed through me, grating against my senses like a stone caught within a shoe. Niggling. Irritating.

I pushed back against the feeling. *They don't look like co-conspirators*, I told her. If Raven could have focused straight, his glare alone would have driven off any enemy. Willow, though less drunk, was no more welcoming.

"What do you want, assassin?" she asked. "Don't come any closer."

Ash stopped, far enough away to please her. Any further and they wouldn't have been able to hear him above the pounding of the music. Willow still had hold of Raven's arm, as if she thought he was the more dangerous of the two and she needed to hold him back from violence. I could have told them that distance didn't make them any safer from a man with Ash's skills.

"I mean you no harm," Ash said. "I only want to talk." He held his open palms out to them, to show his hands were empty.

I took a sip of my drink to hide my smile—as if being bare-handed made him any less lethal.

"We have nothing to say to you," Willow said coolly.

Ash gave a grim smile. "That's fine. I have plenty to say to you."

"Why should we listen?" Raven snarled. "You're keeping Sage prisoner. Release her or I'll kill you."

Tony twitched reflexively at the threat but didn't move forward. Probably his instinct for self-preservation kept him from stepping into the path of Raven's wrath.

His father had no such compunction. Randall came around the bar and moved between the combatants. "May I suggest to you, *most strongly*, that you take this outside?" he said.

More people were becoming aware that something was up. Heads were turning in our direction, people craning to get a look at the two men facing each other, their antagonism crackling in the air between them. Christian had slid down in his seat, as if he would have liked to slide right under the table, and was watching the scene unfold with a horrified fascination that I recognised all too well. It was the look of someone who knew they were outgunned and outclassed, wondering if they would survive a clash of titans.

I finished my drink and set the glass back down on the bar, leaning forward in my seat.

Order him back to the Nest, Umarenthe said. *Will you sit here and do nothing?*

If he conspires against me, he seems doomed to fail, I pointed out. *And if he succeeds, I would rather know of his schemes.* I wasn't going anywhere until I found out what this was all about.

"Perhaps it would interest you to know that I'm here to help you get her back," Ash said.

Willow sucked in a breath and glanced at Randall. "There's no problem here." She tugged on Raven's arm. "Let's sit down and discuss this like reasonable people."

"I'm not reasonable," Raven said, "and *he* barely rates as a person. He's a soulless killing machine."

Willow bundled him back into his chair, despite his protests, and they all sat down. I fiddled with my empty glass, feigning lack of interest, though I had a ringside seat to this little drama.

Christian looked as if he would rather be anywhere else but trapped at a table with an assassin—he must really want that guitarist job. When Ash sat down beside him, he scooted his chair over until he was practically in Willow's lap. Perhaps he thought that death was catching.

"What have you done with Sage?" Willow asked, her gaze like flint.

Ash met the challenge in her eyes coolly. "I've done nothing with her."

"Then where is she? Why hasn't she come home?"

"You're keeping her prisoner," Raven said, leaning forward aggressively. He looked ready to hurl himself across the table at his enemy—if only his head would stop spinning.

Ash permitted himself a small smile. "Trust me, she is no one's prisoner."

"Then what has happened to her?" Willow asked.

"She saved my life," Raven said, "and then left me for

dead. Sage would never have done that of her own volition."

"Sage has ... different priorities now."

"I don't believe it," Willow said flatly. "Sage doesn't turn her back on her friends."

No, I didn't. Did I?

These people aren't worthy to be the friends of the Serpent, Umarenthe soothed. *You have achieved a higher plane of existence than they could ever understand.*

That was true. My hand rested briefly on the invisible dagger, drawing comfort from its presence.

"What was that dagger that Sage picked up after she killed the assassin?" Willow asked. "When she saved Raven."

"You didn't want her to take it," Raven added.

Ash frowned. "That was the root of our current problem. An enchanted blade."

"An enchanted blade known as the Soul-stealer?" she pressed. Ash said nothing, but she took his silence for assent. "I thought as much." She glanced at Raven. "There were rumours that it was in the Vipers' possession."

"What do you know of the Thief of Souls?" Ash asked.

"Plenty. I *am* the heir of Spring." A shadow crossed her face and she stared down at the table for a long moment. "So she is gone."

"No." Ash sat forward, making Christian flinch. "Sage is strong, and she hasn't held the dagger long. There is still a chance to save her."

"Sage is more stubborn than a cavalcade of mules, but

no one escapes once the Soul-stealer has them in its clutches."

"You are her friends. If I arrange a meeting, you could persuade her to give it up."

I breathed in sharply, fury rising within me. Now I saw his game. He thought if these people could persuade me to give up Ni'ishasana, he could take it for himself.

I told you, Umarenthe whispered.

Be silent! I screamed inside my head, and the shadow woman obediently dissipated into thin air. But I couldn't unhear her words, and crushing disappointment added fuel to the fire of my rage.

I had dared to hope that he actually cared for me as a person, not merely as the means to an end. All along, the dagger had been right, and he meant to betray me. Thank the Lady for Ni'ishasana. Without its power, I could not have been here tonight to discover his plan.

"Persuade her?" Raven's face twisted into bitter lines. "She walked away and left me bleeding on the ground. You think she cares for me anymore? For us?" he corrected himself.

"That was when the dagger first seized her," Ash said. "I can only imagine how overwhelming its power must have been in that moment. It was a wonder she could walk at all. But it can't keep up that level of control all the time, and she fights it. I know she does. Sometimes she seems almost like the old Sage."

"What do you know of the old Sage?" Willow asked bitterly. "You only ever saw her as a prisoner. You don't know anything about what she's really like."

"I know she is brave—braver than any of us. She picked up that dagger, knowing full well what would happen. I didn't understand it at the time, but I've thought about it since, and the only way she could have defeated my father was if the dagger helped her. She must have promised herself to it in exchange."

"But why would it want her?" Willow asked.

"That, I don't know, but I know Sage is the most loyal friend a man could wish for. She took up that dagger to save *him*." He levelled a steely glare at Raven, who looked away guiltily. "And I know she hasn't given up—so we can't, either."

8

I couldn't listen to this anymore. Briefly, I entertained a fantasy of blasting Ash with flame, setting the whole place alight. Burning away my hurt feelings with cleansing fire. But then I remembered that Fire was the only Realm whose magic I didn't possess. None of the previous wielders of Ni'ishasana had come from there, nor any of those whose souls it had stolen, leaving them mindless servants to the dagger. I could sear him with Summer heat, but that wasn't quite enough to satisfy my craving for fiery vengeance.

He glanced my way, a startled look on his face, as I stood up and stormed for the exit, brushing past Tony.

The night air cooled my temper somewhat, though visions of bringing the whole place down on his scheming head with Earth magic still tempted me. A motorbike roared past as I stopped on the pavement, waking a sudden yearning in me to ride away and forget everything. Funny, I hadn't thought of my bike in weeks, and now I missed it—

missed that freedom it gave me, that state I achieved where I thought of nothing but the road, leaning into the turns with my whole body, feeling the power in my grip, the purr of the engine vibrating through me.

The door behind me banged shut.

"Sage."

I whirled on him at the sound of his voice, fists clenching. Maybe I couldn't ride right now, but pounding the shit out of Ash would probably be almost as satisfying. "You dare conspire behind my back?"

"It *is* you. I felt something through our link just now, and I knew you were close by. That Glamour is good."

I huffed out a breath, a little taken aback at the lack of reaction, and groped around again for my outrage. Something about the concern in those grey eyes of his made it hard to stay mad at him.

"Do you deny that you're planning to take the dagger for yourself?" I asked. "Why were you meeting with those people?"

He flinched as if I'd struck him. "Take the *dagger*? I'd take my own life first." His eyes blazed down at me. "You know me better than that. I was talking to *those people* because they're your friends."

"And you want them to persuade me to give up the dagger so that *you* can have it." Even with Ni'ishasana grating against my mind, pushing me to righteous anger, something about that sentence sounded off the moment it left my lips.

"I want them to help me save you. You're not an assassin."

"You think I'm not good enough."

Frustration ruffled his calm, before he drew in a deep breath. "On the contrary, I think you're too good for my world. Go back to your old one while you still have a soul to save."

"I would be an assassin already if you hadn't stolen my kill from me," I snapped.

His face hardened. "You have the Blade with you, don't you? You're wearing it on your body."

"What if I do?"

"It twists you. The closer it is, the more it controls you, but you can't leave it alone, can you? You're like an addict. You can't bear to—"

He broke off, his attention caught by something on the other side of the street. I followed his gaze, wondering what had caused him to stiffen like that, but all I saw was a man coming out of The Lily Garden with a plastic bag of takeaway Thai, and another waiting to cross the street.

Ash caught my arm and hustled me toward the opening of an alley just down from The Drunken Irishman. "We need to gate out of here."

I dragged my arm free, checking back over my shoulder. The stranger was crossing the road, angling in our direction, but he didn't look particularly threatening. "What's your problem?"

"Can't you feel it?" We stepped into the mouth of the alley. It was poorly lit, but that was no deterrent for magic-enhanced eyes. "There's something—"

Suddenly, we were no longer alone in the alley as several figures emerged from the shadows. Ash stepped in front of me, letting loose with a blast of Winter magic that left icicles dangling from an overhanging balcony and filled the air with the rainy scent of his magic but had no apparent effect on the people in front of us.

Finally, a chance to vent some of my anger. "Get out of my way." I sidestepped neatly around my would-be protector.

"Stop," a voice behind us said.

Ash whirled, placing his back against mine, a knife appearing in his hand as if by magic.

It was the man who'd been crossing the road, and now I knew what Ash had been staring at. He looked like a regular human, if a little pale in the dim light of the alley, but something about the way he moved was subtly wrong, as if he'd forgotten how to walk, or had learned how to do it from watching someone on TV. And there was something about that voice ...

"Who are you?" I demanded. "Call off your men or prepare to say goodbye to them all."

He gestured at the shadowy figures in the alley and they halted in their advance. "We mean you no harm. We've come with a message."

I caught my breath, shocked to the core. I knew that voice—but I'd never seen this man before in my life. A faint whiff of magic clung to him, a bitter scent that I'd only ever smelled once before, the night Willow had almost been murdered in front of me. This was all wrong —was that what Ash had sensed?

I eyed the man suspiciously. He was wearing a Glamour. Could it be ...?

Shifting to keep the man and his companions in view, I laid a hand on Ash's knife arm, urging him to stand down. I wanted to hear this. "Who's the message from?"

"Your father."

I knew it. Fallon Domani stood before me, disguised by Glamour. "Show me your real face," I managed.

"You don't want to see that."

"I'll be the judge of what I want."

"Very well."

For an instant, the Glamour fell away, revealing a rotting corpse underneath the facade. His eyes and most of his nose were gone. Only scraps of flesh clung to the skull underneath. I shuddered in horror. But he wasn't my father, unless my father had taken to dyeing his hair since I'd last seen him. And died.

Ash leapt forward and drove his knife into the creature's heart, but he didn't fall.

"I'm already dead," he said, gazing down dispassionately at the knife protruding from his chest. The Glamour was back, and it looked odd to see no blood flowing from what should have been a mortal wound on a seemingly healthy person. The corpse pulled the knife out and politely offered it back to Ash hilt-first. "You can't make me any deader."

"Why do you speak with my father's voice?" I burst out.

"He wanted to make sure you would listen to his message. He has spent years trying to contact you, but Willow blocked him at every turn."

Willow wouldn't do that. Would she? Sure, he'd tried to kill her, but she respected me enough to allow me to make my own decisions about who I did and didn't want contact with. At least, I had thought so.

"Maybe he should have thought about that before he tried to kill her."

"He wants to tell you how sorry he is for that. It was a moment of madness, and he is a changed man. He is devastated at the rift that has opened between him and his only child."

I stared at the corpse, thinking. A moment of madness? A very well-planned moment, if so. Could the man who had done that really have changed?

But, then again, he'd never exhibited homicidal tendencies before that night. Not that he'd been the world's greatest father. He'd wasted little time in offloading me to be brought up by strangers in the Court of the Spring Lord after my mother had died. His infrequent visits had been the highlights of my childhood, whenever he'd returned from his mysterious travels long enough to remember that he had a child.

Maybe he'd heard I was now the Serpent of the Vipers. Maybe he was proud of what his half-fae offcast had become.

Of course, the voices of the dagger sang. *Who would not be proud of a child such as you? You have scaled heights that few have dreamed of.*

"This is a strange messenger to send," Ash muttered, still holding his clearly useless knife in readiness.

"We are dealers of death," I said. "Perhaps he thought it appropriate to send the dead to speak for him."

It was certainly impressive. I'd never heard of anyone

who could reanimate the dead to this extent—to have them walking around under their own steam, without the necromancer being present. Except for Ni'ishasana, of course. But even the dagger could only do it if it had dealt the killing blow. I'd thought I had every power apart from Fire, but I couldn't do that.

"Then speak your message and be gone," Ash told the creature in harsh tones. Considering how many dead bodies he'd seen—and created—it was strange how unsettled this one was making him.

The dead man turned dark, expressionless eyes on me. Now that I knew what lay beneath the Glamour, I could understand why that gaze seemed subtly off. His fake features were perfectly lifelike but lacked the spark that animated living beings. "Your father wants to see you."

"Can you trust a man who speaks through dead lips?" Ash asked. "Don't go. He wants something."

The empty eyes turned to Ash. "He wants to see his daughter."

Perhaps I should say no. I would have, but I couldn't deny that my initial reaction to the shock of hearing his voice again had been joy. And what did I have to fear? Even if Ash was right and there was something sinister about my father's motives, I had more power in my little finger than he had ever dreamed of. I had no reason to fear him. And I killed people for a living—I could hardly be put off by a corpse messenger.

"How did you find me?" I asked.

"All will be revealed at the meeting," the corpse promised.

"Where and when?"

"At a time and place of your choosing. Tell me, and he will be there."

Ash shook his head, but I ignored him. Where would be a good place? Somewhere in the Realms?

Perhaps the human world would be better. I was comfortable here, whereas my father might not be. It would give me an advantage in the meeting, and he would be less likely to try using magic against me, if his intentions were sinister.

So where would be a suitable place for the meeting of a dangerous necromancer and the leader of a gang of ruthless assassins? A coffee shop hardly seemed appropriate.

I smiled as the perfect location occurred to me. "Midnight, Sunday, at the Tower of London."

9

It was nearly dawn by the time we returned to the Nest. I'd hardly spoken to Ash on the way back, my head spinning with thoughts and memories.

My father wanted to see me again. My father, who had tried to kill my best friend. My father, who was also the man who had given me my beloved Lightning, the beautiful mare who had made my teenage years bearable. It was hard to reconcile the two men; even harder to put aside my anger at the man who had abandoned me.

I owed that man nothing. I barely remembered the father of my childhood, the Papa I had adored. And yet ... that father had been the sun our lives had revolved around, my mother and me. It had been a long time since I had felt as loved by anyone as by that long-ago Papa.

As the first pink glimmerings of dawn appeared on the eastern horizon, Ash and I strode down the path toward the magnificent main building of the Nest.

"Make sure you're there for dinner," I said. Ash had a

habit of eating in his own little cottage instead of joining the rest of the Nest in the great dining hall. "I'm going to announce the new Adept."

I was almost used to eating dinner in the morning light now. Willow and I had kept a schedule that was characterised by having basically no schedule at all. On weekends, we had been fully nocturnal—playing in the band or partying with friends until the wee hours of the morning, then spending most of the day asleep before rising in the late afternoon to do it all again. During the week, however, I'd had my job to go to. Office work wasn't something you could do in the middle of the night.

But since joining the Vipers, I'd had to shift to a fully nocturnal schedule, with breakfast after sundown and dinner at what should have been breakfast time.

"I'll be there," Ash said, then hesitated. "Your father's overture was suspiciously timed."

"Oh?"

"He's had no contact with you since you left the Realms and yet, as soon as you become a person of power, he decides to take notice of you."

"The messenger said that he had tried to contact me before, but Willow prevented him."

His eyes searched my face. "And you believe that?"

I shrugged irritably. I wasn't sure if I believed it or not, but I didn't have to answer to Ash. "If I want to see him, I will."

"You arranged a meeting."

"I arranged a meeting, but I may not go. I haven't made up my mind yet."

In fact, I was leaning towards a no, for the very reason Ash had just pointed out. However, it wasn't his place to say so. He was annoyingly forward with his opinions.

Which reminded me of something else he'd done that had annoyed me. "You can stop trying to protect me all the time. There's no need to leap in front of me like a bloody knight errant at the slightest sign of danger. I'm far more powerful than you. If anything, *you* should be ducking for cover behind *me* and letting me take care of any threats."

His eyes darkened. I could tell he didn't like that. "If that is your command, I will of course obey it. I live to serve." That reeked of bitterness, but his next words were sincere. "I would give my life for the Serpent."

"For the Serpent, or for Sage?"

"At the moment, they are one and the same," he said, then strode off toward his cottage, leaving me to enter the main building alone.

It was dark inside, the faelights turned low, each illuminating only a small circle of dark wood panelling and blood-red carpet, leaving long stretches of shadow between. From the shadows between the islands of light, a figure coalesced. This time, it was Celebrach rather than the dagger's usual spokeswoman, Umarenthe.

He fell into step beside me, though he glided rather than walked. *Ashovar urges you to caution*, he said. *I did my best to make a leader of him, but I fear his thinking is too small.*

I glanced sideways at the shadow's indistinct features. "You think I should see my father? That's a surprise, coming from you." Celebrach had been a terrible father, trapping his son into a life he didn't want.

Though perhaps, on reflection, his motives had been purer than I'd first thought. It had seemed to me that he delighted in torturing his son. Now, it occurred to me that he had hoped to raise Ash to a position of glory. From that perspective, I could see how Ash might have been a disappointment to an ambitious father.

Think how much your father has to offer, the shadow said. *He has delved into corners that no one has dared to in hundreds of years, perhaps mastered arts that were thought lost to Faerie. He could make the Vipers great.*

That was true. I hadn't considered that aspect of it, too focused on my own familial dramas. But Celebrach was right—what had Fallon learned on all those mysterious trips he had taken through my growing years? Clearly, he had learned the secret of reanimating the dead, which was no small feat.

That could be a problem for us, if he chose to share that knowledge with the wrong people. After all, who would pay for an assassination if the victim could be brought back to life to accuse their killer? Most of our targets were probably well aware of who had paid for their sudden exit from the world.

Seen in that light, as Serpent of the Vipers, it was practically my duty to speak with my father and explore these matters. How strange that Celebrach should be the one to make me see that.

Back in my room, I removed Ni'ishasana and laid it on the bed while I considered my wardrobe. A sea of black greeted me, of course—it was rare to see a Viper dressed in any other colour—but I needed something a little more upmarket than my current ensemble of black jeans and T-shirt for the coming ceremony. This morning, I needed to look the part of Serpent, commander of the most feared force in the Realms.

I picked out a long black dress. The bodice was studded with emeralds, and the silken skirt flared out from my hips to the floor. I chose a silver belt, slung it around my hips, and shoved Ni'ishasana through it. I studied myself in the mirror for a moment. Brown eyes looked back at me from underneath a short crop of dark hair. I looked almost as tired as Ash did.

At least no one would be sending vipers after me in my sleep today.

The dining room was already full when I joined the Adepts waiting for me outside the smaller door at the back of the room. Word had gotten out that I would be announcing the new Adept, and the large space buzzed with excitement. It wasn't every day that a new Adept was created—I hadn't been born when the last one had ascended—and no one wanted to miss it.

Ash waited among the other Adepts, wearing a tight-fitting silken shirt. His belt buckle was silver, in the shape of a snake curled around itself. I was pleased to see that he'd made some effort to dress up for the occasion.

Nuah also wore a dress, though unlike mine, hers was moulded to her body like a second skin and required a slit up one side almost to her hip to allow her to move freely. A gold pendant swung between her breasts, and a dagger gleamed at her side. All the Adepts wore that same dagger tonight. It was the symbol of their rank.

She nodded as I arrived. "Serpent."

"Nuah." I gestured for her to lead the Adepts into the room.

Benches scraped back as everyone stood, watching in silence as we entered. I glanced at each candidate for Adept in turn as I strode to my seat at the centre of the high table. All stood with their heads respectfully bowed. They looked calm, but I could feel excitement, anticipation, and nervousness thrumming through my links with them.

I stopped behind my chair, hands resting on its high, carved back, and surveyed the room. "Sit."

More scrapings and rustlings followed as they obeyed; then, all eyes turned attentively to me.

"You all know what this is." I picked up a long black box that lay on the table in front of me and flicked it open, revealing a dagger nestled on the blood-red silk within.

It was beautiful, made of faerie steel, of course, but with more of a silvery sheen than most blades. A snake wound around the black hilt, worked in inlaid bands of gold and silver, its eyes two glowing green emeralds. I tilted the case, displaying the dagger to the room, and a soft sigh greeted it. Every last Viper seated at the long tables dreamed of one day possessing such a dagger.

"We have a vacancy among our Adepts," I continued.

Many of those assembled glanced at Ash, some with hostility and others more thoughtfully. Everyone had heard that he had created the vacancy by killing Evandir, though it was not as well known that he had done it to stop Evandir from killing me. There would probably have been even more hostility directed at him if they had known that.

"Tonight, it is my pleasure to announce our newest Adept, a Viper who has killed more than three hundred targets since rising from the ranks of the apprentices. He is a worthy Adept indeed. Mezzi, come forward and receive your reward."

Applause filled the hall as Mezzi stood up and strode toward me. Saffron and the other possible candidates clapped with as much enthusiasm as anyone else, carefully hiding the disappointment I knew they felt. It was a strong enough emotion in all cases that it was easy to pick up through our links.

Surprisingly, the strongest emotion came from the usually controlled Sharis, standing on Nuah's other side. I glanced at him in surprise, wondering if I had imagined that flash of pure rage. He gazed back at me, brown eyes impassive, the link between us empty of any hint of emotion, but I caught the movement of his jaw and realised he was grinding his teeth.

Sharis had championed Saffron's cause, and I had chosen Nuah's candidate instead. I stared at him until he lowered his gaze respectfully. The blond assassin would have to get used to disappointment with me in charge. I didn't care to have my decisions questioned.

Mezzi bowed deeply to me, a gleam of triumph in his eyes as I removed the dagger from its case and handed it to him hilt first.

Ni'ishasana had no part in this ritual, since anyone rising to the rank of Adept was already firmly bound to me and to the Vipers. But there was blood involved—it seemed as though blood was involved in all our rituals. Perhaps it was to remind ourselves that we did, in fact, bleed, the same as those whose lives we ended.

Mezzi took the dagger reverently, bowing again, then opened a careful cut across his thumb. Some Adepts made a dramatic slash. One had even been killed by the Serpent of the time in a manoeuvre that had taken everyone by surprise. But Mezzi was careful, as any good Viper should be, and only drew the requisite amount of blood. Then, he closed his bleeding hand around the blade, letting it drink. In moments, a green glow burst from his clenched fist, illuminating the front of the hall.

"You are accepted as an Adept of the Vipers," I said. "Wield this blade forever more in their service or face the consequences."

"I dedicate my life to the service of the Serpent and the Vipers you lead," Mezzi replied, completing the short ritual.

The other Adepts stood and bowed as one as Mezzi walked to the end of the table to take his seat as an Adept for the first time, waiting until he was seated before resuming their own seats. I sat, too, and the servants took this as a signal to bring in the food. As a special mark of honour, Mezzi was served before anyone else at the high table.

"A wise choice, my lady," Nuah said, a satisfied smile on her face as she watched her favourite tuck into his meal.

"I'm sure he will make a fine Adept."

Our eyes met, and she inclined her head toward me. "As you say."

This was how the game was played: she took on an unwanted apprentice and I rewarded her by choosing her candidate for the Adept's position.

And speaking of her apprentice: "I see Atinna is elsewhere." Atinna's place furthest from the high table was empty. "Or was she not interested in seeing who became Adept?"

"I'm sure she was, but I didn't consult her preferences." Nuah's tone was cool. "She is spending these hours polishing all my blades and reflecting on the wisdom of her past choices."

I wasn't entirely successful in hiding my smile. "You make an excellent instructor."

"That is my hope."

We ate in silence for a while. I watched the unsuccessful candidates carefully, noting who they spoke to and whether they made an effort to appear undaunted. Disappointment radiated down every link toward me, which was only to be expected. It was resentment I was on the lookout for.

"We received a message while you were out, from a new client seeking our help," Nuah said.

I frowned. Viper policy was to bring such messages immediately to the attention of the Serpent, and if the Serpent was absent, to that of the highest-ranked Adept. That would have been Ash, but he had been with me.

The situation hadn't arisen for years, since Lord Celebrach had so rarely left the Nest. As a result, I hadn't considered the possibility, but I found that I didn't like being in the position where an Adept knew more than I did about Viper business, even though Nuah was second in line after Ash. Perhaps it was time to change the rules.

"Oh? Who is the client?"

"Lord Eldric's brother, Jaxen."

I raised my eyebrows at that. What little I knew of Jaxen I had learned from Allegra, and her opinion wasn't flattering. Jaxen was a wastrel, the younger brother of the Lord of Autumn, and did little other than drink his brother's cellar dry. Where would a man like that have found the coin necessary to order an assassination?

"How curious. I wonder if Lord Eldric knows?"

Nuah laughed. "I suspect not, since he is the intended target."

10

I walked into The Lord Nelson, motorcycle helmet under my arm. I was now the proud owner of a brand-new Kawasaki Ninja in black and fluoro green. My first bike that wasn't secondhand and on its last legs. I mean, what was the point of power and wealth if you didn't enjoy the perks occasionally?

The Lord Nelson was a quaint old pub at Miller's Point in Sydney. The area was mostly residential, with some old warehouses converted into smart new office spaces. It had a great view of the harbour, but it was nowhere near as busy as The Rocks, just down Argyle Street, where you could hardly move for tourists.

I scanned the tables until I found the lone fae in the pub. An opened bottle of wine sat in front of him, and he was scowling down at his glass. Probably annoyed that I was late. That was another perk of power. Everyone had to wait on your timetable, then act as if it didn't irritate the living shit out of them.

He looked up as I slid into the seat opposite him. He was blond, but then, I was a redhead for this meeting. I could tell it was a Glamour. I caught a glimpse of wings rising behind his back when I glanced at him from the corner of my eye, and remembered Allegra saying he was a Jumper, one of those few fae who could move between this world and the fae one without having to navigate the vagaries of the Wilds in between. A useful person to have around. I assumed that was why Lord Eldric put up with him.

Jaxen studied me for a long moment. "You're not what I was expecting from an assassin."

I set my helmet on the chair beside me. "Did you think I'd walk in carrying a scythe?"

"You look too pretty to be a killer." He flashed a practised smile. "Can I get you something to drink?"

Tonight I sported a red-haired, green-eyed look that reminded me of Willow, and my face was soft and rounded. Glamours were usually meant to persuade humans that we were no different than them. Occasionally, as now, they also served to disguise our true appearance from other fae. He must be able to see that I was wearing one, which made his comment ridiculous.

"If you thought that only men could kill, think again. The females of our species are far more deadly."

"Like black widows?"

"And praying mantises." They tore their partners' heads off after mating. I could tell already that that would be an excellent idea in his case.

He indicated the Hello Kitty backpack on the chair

beside him. "I brought the money. Do you want to count it?"

"That won't be necessary."

"Aren't you afraid I might have ripped you off?"

"It wouldn't be me who would need to be afraid in that scenario."

His smile faded. He looked down at his drink, as if suddenly remembering it was there, and took a swig from the glass. "So, how does this work? I must admit I'm curious. I've never ordered an assassination before."

"You must have been saving up for a long time." The price for the elimination of a Lord of the Realms was immense, and it astonished me that a man such as this had managed to find the money.

He smiled. "I have generous friends."

I gave him the usual spiel. He had three days' grace in which to change his mind, and after that, the process would begin; it could take up to a month; there was to be no further contact between us unless he had a change of heart within the prescribed time, yada yada yada.

"And how you do it?"

I paused. I'd never actually been to one of these meetings before. Usually, the Adepts handled them, but I'd been annoyed at Nuah's intrusion into my territory and had decided that, as a new Serpent, I needed to experience all the facets of our business. I hadn't been expecting such a question. "Do you have any preferences? We will, of course, accommodate them where possible."

His eyes gleamed with delight. "I can order anything I wish?"

"Within reason. We prefer to work in the shadows, but if you wish to make a statement in public, we could arrange something."

"But I could choose something lingering? Something excessively painful?"

"If that is your wish."

What had Eldric done to engender such hatred? From all I'd heard, he'd been a reasonably good brother. Allegra liked him, though perhaps more now that she was a Lady and not a changeling of his Court. Before her elevation, he'd been more inclined to use her than help her. Still, I could hardly hold that against him. That was practically the definition of fae.

If I had had a sister, I would have stood by her through thick and thin. How could someone hate their own flesh and blood so much? *Excessively painful.* What a charmer this guy was.

It occurred to me that I *had* had a sister, even if we weren't blood relations, and tried to imagine hating Willow so much that I wanted to give her a lingering death. My imagination wasn't up to the task.

Jaxen refilled his glass and smiled again. It was not a pleasant expression. "Oh, yes, that is indeed my wish."

"Then perhaps one of our more slow-acting poisons would be desirable."

He sat back in his chair and beamed at me. "That sounds perfect. I shall leave it in your capable hands."

"Then our business here is done." I grabbed my helmet and stood up, indicating the backpack, eager to be rid of Jaxen's company.

He rose and passed it to me with a slight bow. I threw a Glamour over it as I shrugged the heavy weight onto my back. I refused to ride around Sydney sporting a pink backpack. It didn't go with the riding leathers at all. When I strode out of the pub, it was plain black.

I dispelled the Glamour disguising me as I put my helmet on, then straddled the bike and kicked the engine into life. Its throaty rumble made me sigh with pleasure. I'd been riding motorbikes ever since I'd left the Realms, finding them a more than adequate substitute for the horses I used to love. It was one of the best uses of iron that humans had come up with. There was something about the noise, the rumble of the engine beneath you, and yes, even the occasional splattering of a bug on your visor—it was all part of the experience. Of course, the speed didn't hurt either.

I roared down Kent Street and took the ramp to the Harbour Bridge. The great steel arch loomed overhead as I joined the traffic streaming out of the city. I wove in and out of cars on my way across the bridge, just because I could, delighting in the agility of the bike. I'd missed this. The lights of Milson's Point and the grinning face of Luna Park beckoned me across the water.

I peeled off at Miller Street and headed into North Sydney. The roller door to the parking garage clanked upward as I gained the driveway of a perfectly ordinary office tower, no different than any of the other buildings that lined the street. This was where the gate to the Nest was currently located, although I'd been considering moving it.

Siths could be anchored to any point in the mortal world, and some featured an entry point to the fae Realms as well, though that was rare. The Nest had one, though no one but the Serpent knew of its existence.

My former friends already knew that the mortal-world entry to the Nest was located somewhere in Sydney, which was something of a security risk. As the Serpent, the safety of the Nest was my responsibility, and that included ensuring its location was a closely guarded secret.

I parked the bike and took off my helmet, running a hand through my short hair. A flash of movement caught my eye as the roller door rumbled its way down, like the portcullis on a castle. Something small and black had swooped underneath it, and I held up my hand, halting the door's grinding descent.

I scanned the gloomy interior of the garage. Parking was at a premium in North Sydney, and the place would be full in the daytime, but now only two cars remained, parked close to the lift. At this time of night, most office workers had gone home.

My boots thudded on the concrete as I strode for the lift, a prickle of unease running down my spine. Could it have been a bat? It was too late at night for birds. Of course, there was one other possibility, but how could he have found me?

A whisper of magic brushed against my skin, and I spun in its direction, bringing my own magic to high alert, ready to release. A black-clad figure who was decidedly not one of my Vipers strode out from behind a pillar, confirming my worst suspicions.

It was Raven.

~

"It's good to see you, Sage." He stopped a fair distance away, though if he thought that made him safe, he was kidding himself.

"What do you want?"

Power bubbled inside me like fizzy wine, and the voices of the dagger whispered, urging me to violence. He had tracked me. He was a threat that needed to be dealt with. My hand drifted to Ni'ishasana's hilt. Of course, I had concealed it with an Aversion for my interview with Jaxen, but the feel of the enormous ruby there under my thumb settled me, even if I couldn't see it.

"You used to be a little ... friendlier than this," he said. A mocking grin curled around the corners of his mouth, and I recalled the sensation of those lips on mine. As he had no doubt intended I should.

I dragged my gaze away from his lips and met his eyes again. This was not the Raven I'd seen in The Drunken Irishman, so full of drink he could barely stand. This was the Raven I was used to, in control of himself and with that mocking edge that suggested nothing really mattered to him and everything was a source of amusement. The dream hadn't done him justice. He was a head-turner even among fae, with those laughing dark eyes and silken black hair.

"How did you find me?" Surely he couldn't have spotted me in that instant between removing the disguising Glamour and putting on my helmet? The odds against him just happening to be in the right place at the right time were astronomical. Now, I had inadvertently led him right to the building that housed the gate to the sith. Moving its location became even more urgent. "Are you working with Jaxen? Is this fairy gold he gave me?"

Jaxen had paid me the fee for Lord Eldric's assassination, but if he was working with Raven, the assassination was only a scam—the same scam that Raven and I had once pulled, pretending to want the Lord of Summer killed in order to trace the assassins back to their lair. That was what had started this whole thing and led me to the place of power I currently occupied. But if Eldric's killing was only a ruse, then shortly, the heavy gold that weighed on my back would turn into leaves or flower petals and the deal would be off. Lord Eldric would be spared.

"Why would I work with him? I can't stand the man." Raven glanced at the backpack and frowned. "I assume Jaxen is doing his brother's bidding. I wonder who the Lord of Autumn wants assassinated?"

I smiled. "Perhaps you'll find out soon."

He shoved his hands in his pockets, feigning a lack of interest. "Perhaps I will."

"So how *did* you find me?"

As I spoke, I ran spells through my mind, looking for one that would wipe his memory of this meeting. I would move the entry to the sith as soon as possible, but it would take some hours. And who knew what cavalry Raven had waiting in the wings? The king probably hadn't changed his mind about subduing the Vipers just because I'd disappeared.

"Maybe a little bird told me." He shrugged carelessly and grinned. That grin did strange things to my insides, things that brought that desperate moment in his arms alive again. "A guy can't share all his secrets. Gotta keep a little bit of mystique."

Raven and his damn birds. But wouldn't I have noticed something as odd as a raven out at night?

Kill him, the voices of the dagger whispered in my ear. *Forget wiping his memory, just kill him. This devil-may-care attitude is an act. He's dangerous, more dangerous than he appears.*

I was well aware of that. "What do you want, Raven?"

He shrugged again, the grin fading. "I'm not sure, anymore. I thought ... But then I saw you tonight." His expression hardened, became accusatory. "I can't believe we've been frantic with worry, and here you are, parading around Sydney actually arranging your sordid little murders."

"Frantic with worry?" Because the memory of being in his arms made me feel things I didn't want to feel, I snapped back at him, "You didn't seem so worried when I saw you dancing in Spring that night."

His coal-dark eyes sparked with anger. "You think I wanted to be there, or took any pleasure in it? My father dragged all three of us there."

"Who? You and your brothers?"

Raven was the youngest of three brothers, which was a positive embarrassment of riches in the fae world. Children were rare, and three strong sons was almost unheard of. Other Lords changed wives as fast as they changed clothes, in search of one who could give them an heir, but Lord Nox had been married to Lady Fiana for an eternity because she had given him three. But I couldn't see what kind of business the Lord of Night would have in Spring that required the presence of all three sons.

"Yes. My father is angling for a match with Spring. He wants Paxyl to marry Willow."

I raised an eyebrow, my interest caught. Did Willow know about this? There hadn't been a whisper of it before I'd left her, and she wouldn't take kindly to the knowledge that her father was entering into talks involving her future without consulting her. "That's a step up for a mere second brother. Why not Quinn?"

"Because Quinn is Father's heir and will be Lord of Night one day after him. If he and Willow married, their Realms would ultimately be combined. We're already down to nine Realms—no, ten, now that's Illusion's back— out of the original thirteen. It would be a shame to merge any more. We've lost enough of them." He gave a rueful smile, though it seemed a little forced, as if he'd just remembered he wasn't supposed to care about anything serious. "But thank the Lady in all her goodness that it's Paxyl and not me who has to marry Willow."

A perverse desire to stand up for my former best friend filled me. "It would be the making of you. You could do a lot worse than marry Willow."

"I'm not the marrying type."

In my previous life, it might have bothered me to hear

him say that, to have him confirm that he wasn't the kind of man to settle down with one woman. I'd been right to fear for my heart where he was concerned. But it didn't matter now. What did a Serpent want with a Lord's layabout third son when I could have my pick of Vipers?

A particular Viper sprang to mind, one with cool grey eyes instead of mocking black ones.

"Well, then, you'd best be on your way, then, hadn't you? If you've quite finished expressing your disappointment in me?" I turned away, heading for the elevator.

He covered the distance between us in a heartbeat and caught at my arm. I barely managed to hold back a killing blast of magic.

I glanced pointedly down at his hand, then back up. "If you don't move that hand, you'll lose it."

He let go but didn't back up. There was a hint of despair in his expression now, and he looked more like that Raven who'd been attempting to drown his sorrows at The Drunken Irishman the other night.

"*Sage.* I didn't come here to talk about my father's dynastic ambitions. Come back with me! All I've heard is some story about a dagger, but I can't believe anything could change you so fundamentally. You're the strongest person I know. They've got some hold on you, haven't they? Did they threaten to hurt us if you didn't cooperate?"

He had moved his hand, but I could still feel that desperate grasp on my arm. Something strangely like regret fought for acknowledgement inside me, but the dagger was howling it down.

Kill him now! it demanded in a chorus of voices that swelled until I could barely think.

I felt pulled in a hundred different directions, stretched thin. I didn't want to kill him, did I? And yet Ni'ishasana's power flooded me, demanding release. My body trembled with the need to strike out at something, anything.

"You think the Vipers had nothing to offer me?" I ground out between gritted teeth, fighting the urge to lash out and show him exactly what the Vipers had done for me. "I'm happy where I am."

Stop fighting it, the voices urged. *Kill him.*

He stepped back, disgust written plainly on his face. "You were like family, Sage. How can you turn your back on us like this? Don't you know how important family is?"

"Maybe I've found a new family." I glanced at the shining silver doors of the lift. A red mist was filling my vision, and I had to get to the lift before the whole world went red or I would strike out.

Yes, the voices chorused. *Strike him down. You know you want to.*

And that was the thing. I *did* want to.

"You need to go," I told him, clenching my fists as if I could hold in the lethal power that threatened to burst from me.

"Then at least grant me one favour. Please, Sage. I'm begging you." There was desperation and real fear in his eyes. "Call off the hit on my father."

I nodded brusquely, unable even to speak for fear that opening my mouth would unleash a storm of killing magic. His eyes searched mine for a moment; then, he bowed his head and dissolved into bird form.

I managed to hold it until the raven had flown from the garage, but then the power blasted from me. The two parked cars flew in opposite directions, smashing into the walls in a thunder of twisted steel and broken glass as I stalked towards the lift.

11

I was late to the training grounds. Not only had I had my excursion to the human world, but I'd had to spend three hours on my return in relocating the Sydney entry to the sith. Ni'ishasana had walked me through the process, but it was tedious—plus, to add insult to injury, the dagger had informed me that we shouldn't open gates directly into the Wilds from inside the sith for a couple of weeks. Apparently, moving the main entry meant that the Nest's boundaries became a little unstable until it had settled into its new location properly, and using anything other than the main gate for a while could be a problem. The Vipers would be simply *thrilled* to hear that they would have to come and go through the human world for a fortnight. I raged at the necessity. How had Raven been able to find me?

Jaxen and his stupid pink backpack had been an annoyance, but Raven's appearance was a threat to the Nest. By the time I'd changed into workout gear and made my way to the training grounds, I was in a foul mood. Punching someone sounded like the ideal way to work out my frustrations.

That turned out to be harder to arrange than it should have been, which didn't improve my mood. The problem was finding anyone prepared to take me on when I was so clearly seething. They were all too scared of attracting my ire if I lost, and I suffered through a series of short matches that were over almost as soon as they'd started, with me invariably the victor. I rose from my third bout, after slamming Saffron's head into the ground, more on edge than when I'd started.

If only Nuah was around. I had the feeling she would give me a fair bout. Or better yet, Atinna. She'd like nothing better than to smash me in the face.

"Mezzi," I said, seeing he was between bouts.

"Yes, Serpent?"

"Spar with me."

"Of course."

He finished wiping his face with a towel that was already damp with his sweat and put it down. His short dark hair gave him the look of a soldier, and I knew from our previous bouts how strong he was. Keeping up with him should give me a real challenge, as long as he put his heart into the match.

We circled for a moment, sizing each other up. A small smile played about his lips, then he struck without warning. I evaded his fist and landed a blow of my own, then danced back out of reach, watching his eyes.

He seemed content to circle, waiting for me to make a

move. His smile widened into a grin, and his glance swept my body in a look that was more admiring than assessing. I responded with a flurry of strikes and kicks. That would teach him to keep his mind on what he was supposed to be doing. He retaliated, but his blows landed softly, his kicks only glancing across my hip instead of nailing me in the solar plexus.

I growled. "Stop playing and fight me."

In response, he swept my legs out from under me, then offered his hand, all solicitude. The hand lingered on my skin longer than necessary after hauling me to my feet. He'd be in my bed faster than a speeding bullet if I gave the word. Shame he wasn't the one I wanted.

I brushed his hand away and attacked with renewed vigour. He was actually an excellent fighter—his defence was good enough to look genuine, but not strong enough to cause me any real problems. That took real skill, but it only made me more frustrated. Our dance ended with him face down on the ground, my knee in his back and his arm twisted up behind him, yet it gave me no satisfaction.

By the time Ash arrived at the training grounds, my temper was a fragile thread indeed, ready to snap at the slightest provocation. I knew my Vipers well enough to know that most of them would kill me if they only could, yet they didn't have the balls to spar with me.

Ash joined me as I slugged water from a flask and mopped my sweaty face.

"He thinks to curry favour by letting you win," he observed with a frown. "What more does he want? He's already an Adept."

I gave Mezzi's retreating back one last frustrated glare, then raised my eyebrows at Ash. Honestly, men were so slow sometimes. "He wants to sleep with me, of course, and become the favoured Adept."

Something glinted in his eye. Was that anger? But it was gone so fast I couldn't be sure.

"None of these bastards will give me a proper bout for fear of offending, and I've just spent three solid hours relocating the entry to the Nest. I'm not in the mood for pandering."

He stilled. "Why did you move the entry?"

"Our security was compromised." I wouldn't say more with a dozen other Vipers within earshot.

Something flickered in his eyes, and I drew in a shocked breath at a sudden rush of comprehension. The odds of Raven randomly stumbling upon me in a city of five million people were absurdly small, so he must have followed me from my meeting with Jaxen.

Which meant he must have known in advance about the meeting. That crack about a little bird telling him where to find me had been a smokescreen, because he knew I'd assume he meant the actual flesh-and-blood birds he used as spies. But he'd meant an informer. Someone had tipped him off.

And who would have betrayed the Vipers like that? Only someone who wasn't as devoted to the organisation as everyone assumed. Someone who I'd found consorting with my former friends only days before. Someone who was standing right in front of me, considering me warily.

"Train with me," I said abruptly.

"You look angry," Ash replied. "I'm not your punching bag."

"You're whatever I say you are." How *dared* he?

"As my Serpent commands." He bowed his head, and a quick burst of temper flooded me.

"You are *so* full of shit."

"I beg your pardon?"

My fists clenched as magic surged within me. Hadn't he learned from his last punishment? "Yes Serpent this; no Serpent that. So obedient and devoted. You talk the talk, but you don't walk the walk."

He stared at me, his expression calm. "When have I ever done anything against your wishes?"

My frustration was growing by the minute. There was an inner core of steel in him that simply refused to bend.

"I think we both know the answer to that," I growled. I wasn't spelling it out for him in front of the keen-eared Vipers all around us, who were all politely pretending they couldn't hear a thing but were probably hanging on every word. "Choose a weapon, arsehole, and prepare to defend yourself."

"Unarmed, then."

He still had that wary look in his eyes. Who could blame him? My whole body glowed an icy blue from all the magic I was leaking. I needed an outlet for my rage before it tore me apart. I could barely contain the fury that heated my blood. I was always angry lately, but this was more than the usual slow burn. This was white-hot heat that threatened to melt my very bones.

I lunged forward, raining a flurry of blows on him. The

few that connected glanced off him as he dodged and spun. He was insanely fast—there was a reason he was the preeminent Adept among the Vipers, and it wasn't only that he was his father's son. Despite his distaste for the work, he was damn good at it.

I let the magic flow where it would, and shadows grew around me. Not the shadows of Ni'ishasana, but those of Night magic. The faelights over the training grounds dimmed, the darkness around me thickening. He stepped back, trying to see what was happening, but my darkness foiled his efforts.

Launching out of the Night like a striking snake, then darting away again, my blows began finding their target. I grinned, the pressure inside me easing as I kicked him in the side of the head and watched him stagger.

"Are we using magic, then?" he asked, a note of challenge in his voice.

Magic wasn't permitted on the training grounds, but I was the Serpent. I could do as I pleased. Still, I was feeling magnanimous after landing a few good blows. The killing fury had died down, so I let the magic fall away.

I managed to dodge the next punch, but it left me open to a solid kick that slowed me down. I fought back even harder—he was stronger than me, but I had moves that could still surprise him, human moves I'd learned in my time in the mortal world.

I landed in the dirt more times than I could count, but he ate as much dirt as I did. I found myself grinning as we fought, despite the fact that my body was one giant ache. Perversely, I was almost happier when he was the one grinding my face into the dirt. Not that I liked losing, but it proved to me that he was holding nothing back. Finally, a decent fight! He wasn't interested in currying favour. He was as honest in his throws and punches as he was in the rest of his life.

An honest assassin. It sounded like an oxymoron.

Well, except for telling Raven about my meeting. But I found the physical exertion had calmed my rage about that. He was still wrong, but I knew why he'd done it—this ridiculous notion of his that I must somehow be saved from the very desirable position I occupied. It could even be seen as a sign of his affection for me, in a warped sort of way. Still, we assassins were nothing if not warped. We didn't think like other people.

I threw him over my hip, then stopped him rising with a foot on his chest. He watched me from the ground, breathing heavily.

"Enough," I said, admiring the bruise on his cheek with great satisfaction, though it was already fading due to his fae healing.

He got up, and I wiped myself down with a towel. My body ached from the number of times I'd kissed the dirt, and I was covered in sweat and dust, but I felt loose and relaxed. It made me realise how much meeting with Raven had destroyed my peace of mind.

After a shower, I walked back along the path with Ash, enjoying the cool night air on my still-heated skin and the soft sighing of the wind in the trees. I was more inclined to forgive him for his betrayal of my meeting place since he'd given me such a thorough workout. If only I could tempt him to some physical exertion of a different kind. Why did he fight so hard to save me from a situation that so thoroughly suited me?

He smelled of clean skin and wet hair, with an underlying hint of ironbark forests and cool, green spaces. We walked so close together that his arm brushed mine occasionally and I wanted to take his hand and turn him towards me. *Force* him to admit that those "accidental" brushes of skin against skin were no accident. That right here, right now, we had all we needed to be happy.

"You told Raven where to find me," I finally said.

"I did."

"You don't sound particularly repentant."

He stopped and faced me. "I'm not. Why should I be sorry for doing what's right?"

"*What's right*? Working to undermine your own Serpent is right?"

"You would be the first to agree with me if the dagger wasn't polluting your thinking. You were the one who taught me hope, Sage." A shiver ran through me at the intensity in his eyes. He looked at me as though there was nothing else in the world but the two of us. "You taught me to fight for what's right. And I'll never stop fighting for you."

"I ..." I started walking again, confused. I should be angry—he'd outright declared he intended to continue defying me. And yet ... I wasn't. My hand crept to my side, searching for the comfort of the dagger at my hip, before I remembered I had left it on its stand in my office. I chewed my lip. Why were we arguing, again? "I don't need anyone to fight for me."

"That's where you're wrong."

I sighed. This argument could go round and round in circles forever.

"Have the Vipers ever returned the fee and cancelled a job before?" I asked in an effort to distract myself from the heat of his body next to mine and the confusion of my emotions.

He gave me an odd look. "Lord Celebrach cancelled the hit on your friend Allegra after our client was revealed to be a servant from Illusion and not the Lord of Summer he had been posing as. My father didn't care to be deceived. However, he stopped short of returning the money. Cancelling and returning the fee is rare. As far as I know, it's only happened once or twice. In Lord Celebrach's time, a husband ordered a hit on his wife at the same time the wife hired us to kill him."

My eyebrows shot up in disbelief, and he grinned in a sudden release of the tension between us. The grin was a rare expression on him, and I liked it more than I could have thought possible. It stirred something deep inside me, an attraction that was more than mere lust.

"How could that happen?" I knew what careful records the Serpent kept, since I was now the keeper of them.

"Two different Adepts had arranged meetings with the two clients for almost the same time without realising the identity of the other client. And then they both accepted money for the job at those meetings. It wasn't until they reported back to Lord Celebrach that he realised there was a problem."

"So, what happened? Which hit did he fulfil?"

"Neither. He gave them both back their fee, though he refused to tell them why."

"I'm surprised he didn't just have them both killed." It was what I would have done.

He gave me a reproving look, as if he were still my instructor and my lack of proper Viper ethics disappointed him. "Killing a current client is unthinkable. How many people would deal with us if they thought they might not survive the transaction?"

He had a point, I supposed. "I bet Celebrach was still tempted."

"Why are you asking about this?"

"I've decided to cancel the hit on Lord Nox. I'll meet with Sir Ebos myself and explain. I'll need you to set up a meeting."

"May I ask why?" He looked surprised. Sir Ebos was clearly a traitor, betraying everything he was meant to uphold as a Knight of the Realms by ordering a hit on one of its Lords, but that was no concern of the Vipers'. Assassination was a business: we took the money, we performed the hit. Businesses didn't generally turn clients away.

"No, you may not."

If he was going to continue trying to undermine me, then I had no compunction in keeping my conversation with Raven to myself. Not that I wanted to share it anyway. Raven's final words had stirred something in me that felt like ... shame? Guilt? It was odd and disturbing, and not something I wanted to discuss, even with Ash. I couldn't understand it. I owed Raven nothing. He wasn't a Viper.

But it did make good political sense not to completely destabilise the Realms. Assassins didn't thrive in total anarchy—people did their own killing when things got too bad. An all-out war in the Realms didn't benefit us, and we had a contract to take out Lord Eldric. Two dead Lords in the space of weeks would bring the Realms perilously close to war as everyone looked around for someone to blame. One major hit was more than enough. The fact that I'd picked Lord Eldric to die over Lord Nox had nothing to do with the look in Raven's eyes as he'd begged for his father's life. It was a simple, random choice.

Thinking of Lord Nox brought my own father to mind. They were similar in build and colouring, both tall men whose pale skin contrasted sharply with their dark hair, though Lord Nox's eyes were the same coal-black as his son's, whereas my father's were green, like those of so many Spring fae. My own brown ones were a gift of my mother's part-Maori heritage. I hadn't seen Fallon in five years, and only sporadically for years before that, so he was virtually a stranger.

Not even a stranger I particularly cared to become better acquainted with. He would have taken Willow's life to fuel some dark spell if I hadn't stopped him. At the time, Willow had been important to me, and the incident had left me with a bad taste in my mouth. I'd all but decided against seeing him again, despite the meeting I'd arranged —he was undeniably dangerous, and the more I thought about it, the less likely it seemed that his desire to see me was motivated by anything pure.

But Raven's desperation had shaken me more than I'd realised. Clearly, he loved his father very much, and something inside me yearned for that Papa I had loved so freely as a little girl. He and my mother had been my whole world. Raven's words still echoed inside my mind: *Don't you know how important family is?*

Perhaps I could risk a meeting, to see if there was anything there, any possibility of rekindling that relationship I still longed for despite the years and the betrayal. After all, we weren't so different anymore, he and I. Both killers, both powerful, though my powers far outclassed his. It wasn't as if he could harm me now.

The meeting was set for Sunday night. It couldn't do any harm to hear him out long enough to see if his desire to reconnect was genuine, and, as the shadow of Celebrach had suggested, to see what advantage for the Vipers I could wring from the relationship.

We stopped outside Ash's little cottage, tucked away behind its shield of pine trees. Even the location of his home spoke of his desire to hold himself aloof. I studied his face in the moonlight.

"You look tired."

For someone who kept everyone at a distance, he was standing very close, his eyes on my lips. "I am perfectly well."

I leaned toward him, and he didn't pull away. Emboldened, I moved closer, until we were almost touching, the heat of his body warming me. Perhaps tonight was the night I would break through his shields.

Our lips drifted closer as he stood frozen. I laid a hand on his chest and felt the tension in his body, as if he fought a furious battle with himself.

If so, he lost. My lips brushed his, the touch as delicate as a butterfly, and he growled. I felt the reverberation in his chest. Then, his arms snaked around me, pulling me closer, his lips pressing harder, his tongue searching eagerly. I slid my arms around him and tugged at the back of his shirt, longing for the feel of his skin under my hands. Finally, he had given in, and my long wait was rewarded.

It was as if my touch burned him. His whole body jolted, and he stepped away from me, breathing hard. I could only stare, bereft, as his iron control reasserted itself.

"I'll arrange that meeting and let you know the time." He strode away up the path and slammed his front door behind him.

12

London wasn't so different from Sydney. Bigger, of course, but full of the same skyscrapers and traffic, and people who rushed through the grey streets, intent on their own business. Until you came across some ancient building or other glimpse of its long and varied history, you could have been in one of any number of major cities around the world.

Ash led me to the meeting site, since I wasn't familiar with London. That was the disadvantage of having to move the entry to the sith: I'd known Sydney well. I could have shifted the entry to another part of the city, but this seemed like a good opportunity to make a change and a complete break with my old life—especially if Ash was going to try to force my old life back into the new one. This would make it harder for him.

We could have walked through the Wilds to get to the meeting place, but I'd wanted to experience the Tube. We joined the stream of people gushing out of Tower Hill station, buffeted along by the current. It was dark already outside, since it was winter here, and freezing cold—cold enough that I missed the heat of Sydney.

"This way," Ash said. He wore a Glamour tonight that mainly consisted of a short beard, which somehow made him look even hotter than usual. I'd spent more time sneaking glances at him than I had admiring the London scenery.

Across the road, the Tower of London bulked against the sky. Tomorrow night, I'd be meeting my father there.

Right outside the station stood a section of wall built in Roman times, still preserved. In a small grassed area in front of it, a classical statue loomed larger than life. Emperor Trajan, armoured and with a cloak draped artfully over one arm, stood with the other raised, as if caught in the middle of addressing the Roman senate.

The bronze statue was much newer than it appeared, but the wall had been there for over two thousand years. Such a span of time wasn't so impressive in the Realms among the long-lived fae, but here in the human world, that was a hell of a long time. Having been used to Sydney, a relative newcomer on the world stage, it was strange to think that people had been building walls in this same spot for over two millennia.

A tall, dark-haired man stood with his back to us, reading one of the information signs to one side of the ancient wall. An aura about him suggested fae, and when I squinted, I could see a vast scaled form in his place, a winged terror that was rare even in the Realms and hadn't been seen in London since long before the Romans had built that wall. This was our man.

I moved to stand next to him. "Sir Ebos."

He glanced sideways at me, then turned back to his study of the sign. Irritated, I used my Night magic to darken the air between him and the sign to make it unreadable. He might be the Dragon, one of the King's Chosen and therefore one of the most powerful people in the Realms, but I was the Serpent of the Vipers and I wouldn't be treated like some lackey with a message.

"Assassin," he said, turning to me with a sigh.

If that was meant as a put-down, he'd missed his mark. I was proud of what I was. Ash had disappeared, leaving us alone in the small garden, but I knew he hadn't gone far. The bond that connected us told me he was close by. He would want to be close enough to "protect" me, despite the fact that Ebos had no hope of harming me even if he wanted to make an enemy of the notorious Vipers. But Ash's withdrawal had given us the illusion of privacy despite the steady stream of people flowing past. None of them showed any interest in the old chunk of wall or the two people apparently admiring it.

"I have paid your fees," Ebos said. "What is the purpose of this meeting? I thought there was to be no more contact between us. It's risky for me to be seen with you."

"That's why I chose a meeting place in the mortal world, far from fae eyes," I said. That was a lie; I'd chosen to meet here rather than in the Realms because I knew that the older fae, like Ebos, felt uncomfortable in the iron-laden mortal world. It pleased me to put him off-balance.

"Why am I here? Your first attempt on Nox failed. I hope you don't imagine I'll pay you more for another. I paid for a death, not a mere attempt at one."

His contemptuous tone riled me, but I didn't let it show. Let him bluster; he had no power over me.

"Your gold has been returned," I said coolly. "You'll find it in your chambers when you return to the palace."

That had been dangerous to achieve, especially since security had been tightened at Whitehaven owing to the last Viper incursion within its marble halls. But Mezzi, ever eager to impress, said he had a contact in the palace, so he had handled it for me. It looked more professional than expecting the client to lug a bag of gold home. It also subtly pointed out that we could enter his rooms if we wanted to, even with all the security of the palace. Nowhere was safe from the Vipers.

"I don't want a refund," he said, exasperated. "I want the job done."

"I'm afraid that won't be possible."

"Why not?"

A pigeon fluttered down onto Trajan's shoulder and sat there, gazing off into the distance as if it were thinking deep pigeon thoughts.

"No reason that you need to concern yourself with."

Ebos scowled. "He's paid you off, hasn't he? You fumbled the kill, so he knows he's a target and he's paid you off."

"The Vipers don't operate like that."

"The Vipers don't take a man's money and then give it back to him and wash their hands of the job, either. What are you playing at?"

"No one's playing at anything. This is not a game."

"This is *preposterous*, is what it is. I want to speak to your leader."

I smirked at him. "I assure you our leader is fully aware of the situation. You won't get a different response from anyone else."

"Lady's *tits*," he swore. He flung out a hand, and the pigeon that had been sitting on the statue abruptly disappeared in a sizzle of flame.

He wasn't even looking, but the bolt of fire was laser-targeted, tight and gone so fast that I almost doubted the evidence of my eyes. Envy welled inside me. That was some power—and the only one I didn't possess. Dragons tended to keep to themselves and were rarely found outside the Realm of Fire. Nor did they encourage visitors. As a result, no one from Fire had wielded Ni'ishasana in all its long history. Nor had the dagger had the opportunity to kill anyone from that remote Realm and take their magic into itself.

He stalked away with a snarl, leaving me to watch the breeze pick up the tiny flakes of ash on the statue's shoulder and gently waft them to the ground.

The Tower of London loomed on the other side of the road, its forbidding battlements floodlit from below. I gazed across at it, leaning my elbows on the stone wall in front of me. Tomorrow night, I would be inside those battlements, meeting my father for the first time in five years.

The Tower was no Whitehaven. The faerie king's palace was a thing of beauty, its delicate towers defying gravity, whereas the Tower of London squatted on the landscape like a bulldog, solid and oh-so-British, its hodgepodge of towers rising from within the circling wall.

It had a certain grandeur, but its purpose was not to awe with its beauty. It was a working fortress, historically a place of imprisonment and execution. Gazing across at its heavy towers now, I began to wonder if it had been the appropriate place to suggest for such a meeting. I felt a foreboding I couldn't explain.

Ash appeared at my elbow, gliding soundlessly out of the night. "How did he take the news?"

"Not well." I shrugged. "But what can he do?"

"The Dragon's cunning. Perhaps he'll arrange an accident for Lord Nox."

"Perhaps."

It was nothing to do with me if he did. I hadn't promised to protect Raven's father from all harm. I had done what I could in breaking the contract to take his life; the rest was up to the forces of Night to protect their Lord.

"Where did you disappear to?" Our bond had told me that he was still in London and relatively nearby, but he'd kept me waiting for longer than I had expected.

"I was scouting out the local pubs." When I glanced at him in surprise, he added, "I thought you could probably do with a drink after your meeting with the Dragon. And you did say you wanted to experience more of the city."

"Then lead on."

Perhaps we should have gone straight back to the Nest. There was plenty to do, and Lord Celebrach had rarely ventured outside it, from what I'd heard of my predecessor. But I wasn't ready to shut myself away from the world as he had done. The dagger hummed its approval deep in the recesses of my mind. It seemed that Ni'ishasana was also keen to get out into the world again, now it had a new wielder.

The pub Ash had chosen was disappointingly modern —I'd been expecting some quaint olde worlde English pub, full of dark wood panelling and heavy exposed beams. Instead, glass doors slid automatically open at our approach, revealing décor no different than that of The Drunken Irishman. The familiar smell of beer and cooking meat wafted out to greet us. That smell was probably the same in every pub.

I slid into a booth while Ash went to the bar to order. The mirrored wall behind the bar reflected the hundreds of shimmering bottles lined up along its length. I could see Ash's face with that gorgeous beard in the mirror as he spoke to the bartender. In a moment, he was back with two beers.

He slid onto the bench opposite me. "I ordered you a meal. Chicken schnitzel."

It wasn't that long since I'd eaten, but it had been many weeks since I'd tasted something as mundane as chicken schnitzel, and my mouth watered in anticipation. It wasn't a meal that was generally found in a fae dining hall. Perhaps I should change that.

I smiled down at the table as I realised I could, but when Ash asked why I was smiling, I only shook my head. Being excited about chicken schnitzel seemed a little beneath the dignity of the Serpent of the Vipers.

We discussed Viper business while we waited for our meals to arrive. The hit on Lord Eldric was exciting, even if I was still annoyed at Ash for revealing my meeting with the client to Raven. The prospect of food had mellowed me to the point where I didn't raise that issue again. I'd certainly made my displeasure well enough known already.

"I'm going to take this hit on personally," I told him after some discussion of what we already knew of Lord Eldric's habits and the surveillance that would be necessary.

"Then I'll do the surveillance for you," he said.

"You misunderstand me. When I say I'm doing this hit myself, I mean the whole thing. Surveillance, planning, everything."

"Then let me—"

I cut him off. "No. You will not be involved." The memory of my last supposed hit still rankled. He had stolen that target from me at the last minute, and I was having no repetition of that fiasco. "How can I ask my Vipers to go out and risk their lives when I've never done the same? How can I win their respect when I'm not a true assassin myself?"

"There's no question of winning their respect," he

protested. "Ni'ishasana compels—"

"Ni'ishasana compels their loyalty, yes. But respect? I want more than courtly bows and lip service. I will be the most feared Viper of them all. They will bow to me because they fear *me*, not the power of the dagger I wield."

The waitress's arrival with our meals prevented him replying, but I could read the resistance in his eyes and feel his frustration burning down our link.

I caught his eye. "Stop trying to save me, Ash. You're wasting your time—I don't want to be saved."

He speared a piece of potato and shoved it in his mouth without saying anything. That wasn't agreement, but I was more interested in my chicken than managing his emotions. In time, he would give over this ridiculous notion of liberating me from the Vipers. How did he even think it could be done? The dagger had only ever been passed on through the death of its wielder before, which made perfect sense to me. Who would voluntarily give up this bond and the power it bestowed?

I turned my attention back to my meal, savouring every mouthful. The cheesy, tomato-y goodness exploded on my tongue, rich and savoury. When I was finished, I set down my knife and fork with a sigh. Definitely something to add to the menu at the Nest.

I sat facing the doors, and I stiffened as they slid open and three people I knew very well entered the pub. I cast a sharp glance at Ash, who was still eating with an air of innocence that I now realised was rather studied. Their presence here couldn't be a coincidence.

Ash had set me up. Again.

Now will you act? the voices of the dagger asked, sharp as knives. *How many more times does he have to demonstrate his treachery before you end him?*

Hot anger pulsed through me. I'd have to punish him, hard enough to finally get through to him. Whatever his intentions—and however cute he looked with a beard—this behaviour could no longer be tolerated. It was underhanded, it bordered on the traitorous, and above all, it was annoying the shit out of me.

At that moment, Rowan's questing gaze met mine across the room, and his eyes lit up with hope. My own heart beat a little stronger to see him standing there in the flesh. He was real and whole, perfectly unharmed—as strong and healthy as ever. Perhaps now the nightmares of the dead deerkin and his sightless, accusing eyes would cease to plague me.

He wore a T-shirt with a skull and crossbones and had his long hair pulled back into a messy ponytail. With a few tattoos, he could have matched several other patrons already seated in the large room, and no one gave him a second glance.

That wasn't the case for his companions. Willow walked on one side, her fiery red curls cascading freely down her back, her tight jeans drawing admiring glances from just about every man with a pulse. On Rowan's other side strode the Crown Princess of the Realms, Lily Brenfell, and my mouth tightened at the sight of her. *Not* one of my favourite people.

"It seems we have company," I said to Ash.

He set down his knife and fork and pushed the plate

away. He'd barely touched his food, and it suddenly occurred to me that his suggestion of eating here had simply been a way to delay our departure until these uninvited guests arrived. Uninvited by me, at least. Clearly, *he* had issued an invitation. To his credit, he didn't bother pretending to be surprised.

He deserves no credit, the dagger hissed.

"You and I need to talk about this later," I warned him.

He moved over to make room as they arrived at our table. Lily glared at him, then jerked her head at Rowan, indicating he should go into the booth first. Did she think, having invited her here, he would stab her if she got too close?

Easygoing as ever, Rowan slid into the seat next to Ash, leaving Lily to settle herself on the edge of the bench seat. Some things didn't change. Rowan was still letting himself be pushed around by the women in his life.

I met his soft brown eyes, and he gave me a tentative smile. "It's good to see you, Sage. I've been worried about you."

I almost replied that I'd been worried about him, too, before recalling that he didn't know about the deerkin Ash had killed and my subsequent nightmares. Willow sat down next to me and wasted no time getting to the point.

"You need to come home." She glanced at Ash, a look full of icy hatred. "I don't care what these people have promised you; this is insane."

These people was spat out as if the words tasted bad. Willow could be as imperious as the princess when she chose.

"No one has promised me anything. They have already delivered." I set a mild Aversion around our booth. None of the onlookers had lost interest in these two stunning women and several men had drifted closer, close enough to be an annoyance. The Aversion gently suggested that they would be better off elsewhere and they began to drift away.

Willow felt my use of magic, and her eyes narrowed. "Did *you* do that?"

"I did," I said calmly, my hand falling to caress the ruby-studded hilt of the unseen dagger at my side, hidden under its own powerful Aversion.

Her gaze sharpened, and I could feel her magic probing the edge of that Aversion. "What have you got there? Is that it? Is that the dagger?"

I smiled. Why not let her see? Ni'ishasana was glorious indeed and deserved admiration even outside the Nest. I let the Aversion hiding it fade away, since the larger one around our booth would keep any prying mortal eyes from seeing what they shouldn't.

Rowan flinched back as Ni'ishasana was laid bare, his doe-like eyes startled. "It has a strange sheen to it."

Lily spoke for the first time, her face pale but her voice steady. "The infamous Thief of Souls, I presume?"

Rowan edged closer to her, as if he wanted to move further away from the dagger, but she blocked his exit from the booth.

She laid a hand on his leg to reassure him. Interesting. Were they friends now? Who would have thought the haughty Princess of the Realms could unbend far enough to befriend a lowly Autumn deerkin? Maybe she was just really into drummers, like half the girls that turned up at our gigs.

Rowan's troubled eyes rested on her face. "The Thief of Souls? It has a name?"

"It is a storied blade, although the stories are all dark ones. It is said to contain the souls of all those who have ever wielded it."

"And it bestows their powers upon its current owner," Willow added slowly. "How can you bear to touch such a thing?"

I laughed. "Very easily. Didn't you hear her? Those souls belong to some of the greatest mages the fae Realms have ever known. And their power belongs to me."

She couldn't have looked more horrified if I'd confessed to eating puppies for breakfast. "You have to fight this, Sage."

She sounds exactly like Ashovar, the dagger hissed. *Why do you waste time with these fools? They are beneath you.*

"But..." Rowan shook his head, frowning in confusion. "I don't understand. If this dagger is so powerful and important, why do *you* have it? No offence, but I thought it belonged to the assassins."

No offence. He meant, why was a powerless half-fae in possession of one of the world's most powerful artefacts? But for once, I wasn't offended. After all, I was no longer that girl looking in from the outside at all her fae friends and their casual use of the power they took as a natural birthright. Now, I could grind Lily into the dust, even with all her Brenfell strength. I could beat Willow at her own Spring games, overwhelming her with the power over plant life that she had always wielded so much better than everyone around her. And as for Rowan—he had no more power than the average fae, and wouldn't come anywhere near to testing my strength.

The fact that I could destroy them all without raising a sweat put me in such a good mood that even Lily couldn't dent it.

"The Thief of Souls belongs to the leader of the Vipers." The princess eyed me with suspicion, as if she thought I'd stolen it.

"And so it does," Ash said, entering the conversation for the first time.

Lily started, as if she'd forgotten he was there. "You made Sage your leader?" Her tone, so incredulous, would once have stirred resentment, but now it made me want to laugh.

"She made *herself* our leader."

"But that's ridiculous." Willow glared at him, outraged. "Sage is no assassin." Then, she transferred the glare to me. "Killing that one guy to save Raven doesn't make you an assassin."

"I also killed those Vipers," I reminded her. "When they attacked us in the sith."

What a long time ago that seemed now—and how odd it was to say that *the Vipers attacked us*. There was no such *us* anymore, no siding against the Vipers.

"That doesn't make you an assassin either," she insisted. "That was self-defence. You're not a killer."

"My point exactly," Ash said. "Listen to your friends, my lady."

His easy use of the honorific shocked Lily, and seemed to drive home the truth more than any argument. "A month ago, you were begging my father to destroy the Vipers, and now you're *leading* them?"

I shrugged. "People change. Even you, Princess."

It hadn't escaped my notice that she still had her hand on Rowan's leg, and I wondered, now, if that was more of a proprietary grip than a comforting one. If a princess of the Realms could become so friendly with a lowly deerkin, anything could happen.

Rowan was a great guy, but he didn't have an ambitious bone in his body. He'd be content to be the drummer in a third-rate pub band for the rest of his life. Hardly the kind of person you'd expect to attract a woman like Lily. And yet there she sat, snugged up nice and tight against him. There was even what looked suspiciously like cat hair on the sleeve of her dark blue shirt. That probably belonged to Kel, the cat that Allegra had foisted on us after its previous owner had died—and then she'd gone off to rule Illusion, leaving Kel behind to terrorise the birds of Willow's sith.

Yes, the Lily covered in cat fur instead of precious jewels was a far cry from the one who had first arrived in the human world.

"Raven said you'd changed," Rowan said sadly, "but I didn't want to believe it."

"People change," Willow said. "But not that much. Not on their own. That dagger is poisoning you."

Poisoning, the dagger sneered. *Poisoning, she says, when we have given you everything. No one understands the bond between us.*

"Where *is* Raven tonight?" I asked. I would have expected him to be part of this delegation, or whatever it was. Unless ... I eyed Ash thoughtfully. Could there be some rivalry there? That was a pleasing thought. Maybe the Lord of Night's third son *hadn't* been invited.

"He's given up," Willow said. "I've never seen him in such a funk before."

"He said you were going to cancel the hit on his father," Lily added. "Did you?"

"You can assure him that the Vipers will take no further interest in Lord Nox."

Lily leaned forward, her face lit with interest. "Who ordered his killing?"

"That's Viper business."

"That's *kingdom* business," she said sharply. "If someone wants one of the Lords of the Realms removed from the picture, my father needs to know who it is."

"That's Viper business," I repeated lazily. Her expression of frustration was enormously satisfying.

"At least tell us why," Willow urged. "Lord Nox isn't even aware that he has any enemies."

I snorted. "Everyone has enemies." I thought of Jaxen, happily laying down a king's ransom in exchange for the murder of his own brother. "It's merely that some people's enemies are wealthier than others."

Willow grabbed my wrist, giving my arm a little shake. "Come on, Sage, you know that's not true. What about my parents? They've ruled Spring for almost three centuries with never a hiccup, never a border dispute, hardly even a cross word with another Lord or Lady. All their subjects are content. You can't possibly believe this 'everyone has enemies' crap. Why would you say that?"

"It's the dagger talking," Ash said, as calmly as if he wasn't betraying me and the Vipers in one short breath.

Lily nodded. "It has its claws in your soul already, Sage. One day, you'll join the others trapped inside it. There's no escape."

Willow's hand tightened on my wrist. "Not if I have anything to do with it. Give him the damn dagger and come with us. You are *not* a Viper."

"She can't." Lily's eyes never left mine. "The Soulstealer doesn't wait until they're dead to claim its victim's souls. She's dependent on it already—she has no will of her own."

"Yes, she does," Willow insisted. "You don't know her the way I do. She's a fighter."

"You argue over me as if I'm a piece of meat that has no say in this discussion," I said, suddenly bored with the whole thing. This evening had been a lot more fun when it had only been Ash and me and a plate of chicken schnitzel. I looked down at Willow's hand on my wrist, then back at her face, ice in my gaze. "Let go."

"Never," she said. "You're my best friend, and no friend of mine would willingly choose this."

I let Summer heat dance over my skin. Willow let go with a gasp, shaking her burned hand, and the dagger purred with pleasure.

"Then perhaps I'm no longer a friend of yours."

13

Everyone seems convinced that you won't make a Viper, Umarenthe said. *Your choice of friends leaves much to be desired.*

Still seething, I strode down the frigid streets of London with Ash beside me. Unseen by him, Umarenthe walked on my other side, her shadow self boiling and reforming as she moved.

They're wrong, I told her in the privacy of my own mind.

That's because they don't know you the way I do, she said. *They have only seen a tiny fraction of what you are capable of. You will be so much more than a Viper one day.*

Yes, one day I would be a soul trapped within Ni'ishasana, just like her, according to Lily. Then I, too, could appear at inconvenient moments to harass the new wielder.

Is it true that I will become like you in the end, existing inside the dagger?

Of course, she said, sounding surprised. I guess I had thought, since I had no magic of my own, that it wouldn't work the same way for me as it had for the previous wielders. *But that day is a long way off yet, and you have much to do. Starting with dealing with* him. She jerked her shadowy head at Ash.

A new shape formed in the darkness between two streetlights and matched Ash's pace on his other side. It was Celebrach. Ash would be horrified if he knew that his dear departed dad stalked the streets beside him.

You can't allow him to continue like this. Celebrach's face was stern. *His weak nature leads him to betray you at every turn. You must act before he grows any bolder.*

Why keep him around at all? Umarenthe asked. *He seems to be nothing but a thorn in your side.*

Arrange an accident for him if you don't want to kill him yourself, Celebrach suggested.

I missed a step, shaken by surprise. In life, Celebrach had delighted in torturing his disappointing son, but he would never have wished him dead. But the shadow of Celebrach's soul that inhabited the dagger had no such compunction.

I don't want him killed. Best to get that straight immediately. I wasn't sure if Ni'ishasana could arrange an accident without me, but I wasn't taking any chances. *I only wish him to be as obedient as every other Viper.*

Umarenthe's elegant shoulders disappeared as she shrugged, then reformed from the coiling shadows. *I don't know what you see in him. You could take any other Adept as your lieutenant. Mezzi seems eager to please. Nuah, too. Any of them would be better than this one.*

We arrived back at the new entrance to the sith. It had amused me to attach it to a blue police box in the street outside Earl's Court station. Not the most discreet choice, perhaps, considering the number of tourists who flooded the area in the daytime looking for photo ops with the iconic box. If any of them saw us coming and going, they would wonder if the TARDIS had landed for real. But it was only for a few days, until after the meeting with my father. After that, who knew where I might anchor it? The world was truly my oyster.

"You go ahead," I said. They were the first words I'd spoken to Ash since we'd left the pub. He could be in no doubt of my displeasure with him.

He paused with his hand on the door, the arched windows of the Underground station glowing behind him. "Where are you going?"

"To begin my surveillance on Lord Eldric. Since no one seems convinced that I'm a real Viper, it's time I laid their doubts to rest. Including yours."

He reached out and cupped my cheek in his hand. "Sage, don't."

"Don't what? Don't do what any Serpent must? You forget yourself, Adept."

I was still angry at him, but his hand was so warm against my skin, and the unexpectedly tender gesture eased the knot of anger in my chest. Somehow, my own hand crept up to cover his.

He moved closer and gazed down at me with all his

usual seriousness. "I forget nothing; it's you who has forgotten." His hand slid from my cheek and through my short hair to cup the back of my head. My breath hitched at his nearness. "Send Nuah or one of the others to do that. Come back to the Nest with me."

"And what?" Bitterness tinged my voice. This softness wouldn't last. "Bid you good night as you go back to your cottage to drink alone again?" I could read the answer in his eyes. "Do I repulse you that much?"

"You don't repulse me at all."

"The dagger, then? It's ruled your life for decades. Why is it any different now?"

He shook his head. "You know why. Because we were so close. *Freedom* was so close."

That again. Annoyed, I stepped back, and he let his hand fall away. "You'd better get back to the Nest, then."

He nodded but made no move. "Are you going to stand there and watch me?"

"Absolutely. Clearly, you can't be trusted to follow simple instructions. So let me spell it out for you, Ash. Go back to the Nest immediately. Do not leave it again until I return."

I could tell from the way his glance slid aside that he had only intended to go to the Nest long enough to say he'd obeyed, and then he'd meant to come after me. Now, he had no choice. His bond with the dagger would compel his obedience.

"What if you never return?"

"Then you'd better learn to love the Nest, I suppose." I

folded my arms and tapped my foot in an obvious signal for him to hurry up.

He gave me a mocking half-bow that reminded me unexpectedly of Raven, opened the blue door, and stepped inside. I gave him a moment, then opened it myself to check that he had actually gone through the magical gate into the sith and wasn't just standing inside the small wooden box in the human world. But he had obeyed; clearly, he couldn't disregard such a direct order. I'd have to remember that and make sure to be specific in future.

I headed off to find a gateway into the Wilds, and ended up in a little park, using a gap in a hedge. Mist swirled briefly around my feet as I stepped through, and a tingle of threshold magic rippled over my body, like tiny insect feet on my skin. Trees rose around me as I kept walking, and a path unspooled at my feet, shining in the moonlight. I didn't bother looking back; I knew the park was gone, and I would only find more trees at my back.

Crickets chirped beside the path, and a light breeze rustled the leaves, but those were the only sounds other than the quiet thud of my boots on the dirt. I placed my feet with care—I had no desire to stray from the Greenway.

At my current level of power, that might not be quite the disaster that it would be for anyone else in this strange place between the worlds, but it would certainly be an inconvenience. So, I followed the path through the dark tunnel of trees, holding my destination in the forefront of my mind, and was pleased when an arch twined with leaves of red and gold appeared ahead.

I took a moment to wrap the night around myself. I'd never tried shadow-weaving, though I had used an enchanted candle for light-weaving once, the night I'd stalked Ash through Sydney and sneaked into the Nest behind him. How long ago that seemed. At the time, it had felt like a disaster, but I wouldn't be where I was if that little excursion hadn't turned out the way it had.

No such problems faced me now, of course. I was in full command of the Night magic that Ni'ishasana had given me, not using borrowed magic tied to such a weak tool as a candle. Night magic allowed me to move unseen through the darkness, as invisible as I had been in the daytime while using the enchanted candle.

Stepping through the arch, my boots tapped on wood. I stood on a small bridge, barely wide enough for one person, that bent in a gentle curve over a stream. There were no handrails, but since the stream was no more than knee-deep, that was hardly a problem. Behind me, there was no sign of the arch I'd stepped through; no sign of the dark trees leaning over the path I'd travelled. On both sides of the bridge, soft grass studded with tiny white flowers formed a lush carpet underfoot.

In front of me reared the massive trunks of the Hall of Giseult, Lord Eldric's forest home, their tops crowned in leaves of russet and gold. It was lit from within so that light shone through the trees and illuminated the silks hanging everywhere, making them glow like lanterns.

This was no stone castle like the king's home at White-haven; this blended into and celebrated the forest around it. Inside, I knew, the floor was grass and staircases had been built into the trees, leading to upper floors that twined around the trunks of the great structure. Two guards were stationed at the entry, but there were no gates to keep out the unwelcome, only a wide swathe of bronze silk, which rippled in the slight breeze as if it were alive.

I headed toward that bronze drapery, keeping to the shadows of the trees that edged the wide expanse of lawn. The grass was thick and spongy, and my footsteps showed as momentary depressions that a keen eye would notice.

Fortunately for me, the two guards seemed more focused on the preparations that were going on in front of them. Servants were setting up for some kind of picnic, though I couldn't see why the Lord of Autumn should choose to eat on the grass outside his home rather than in his perfectly good dining room. But more silks were being scattered across the lawn, and low chairs carried outside by an ever-changing parade of people. The door guards' main job seemed to have changed from one of protection to merely holding aside the hanging drapes to allow the people to pass through more easily.

That would certainly help me. I stopped under the trees and watched the comings and goings for a few moments. The same five men kept reappearing, carrying the heavier items, and two women seemed to be in charge, directing them where to place everything. As well as these, several women came and went with assorted baskets and armloads of flowers, plus trays heaped with delicate cakes and tiny tables on which to place them.

I moved out from under the trees, intending to follow hard on the heels of one of the workers. If I stayed close enough, my presence wouldn't trigger the wards. I tucked in tight behind a short girl with a tumble of golden curls down her back and slipped right under the noses of the guards.

Inside, the grandeur of the Hall was laid bare—but, to my horror, so was I. There was too much light in here for shadow-weaving, and my form became faintly visible. Not fully, more like a shadow than a true flesh-and-blood person, but more than enough to give away my presence. Abruptly, I eased behind one of the great trunks holding up the leafy roof before someone caught sight of me.

Damn it. Light-weaving had been more reliable than this. I trembled with the jolt of adrenaline and drew in a deep breath. This was ridiculous. I had more magic in my little finger than anyone else in the Hall had in their whole body—what did I have to be scared of? It infuriated me that habits of a lifetime still chained me.

If light-weaving would serve me better, then all I had to do was change to light-weaving. There was no reason to hide and shiver. I straightened, letting the Night magic dissipate. For a brief instant, I was fully visible. I almost hoped that someone *would* see me. They wouldn't live to draw another breath if they did.

But the handful of people in the Hall were gathered at the far end, near the large dining table on its dais. One servant was polishing it to a mirror shine; another staggered under the weight of a box he carried. A little knot of women—higher-born, judging by their clothing—walked slowly across the Hall, chattering all the way, and disappeared through one of the arches on the right-hand side.

None of them noticed anything amiss before the Day magic filled me and I winked out of sight again.

I took the stairs that led to Eldric's rooms. I'd been here before, with Allegra, not so long ago. That had been the day the king had saddled us with the care of his arrogant daughter. My lip curled at the thought of Lily, and my hand crept to Ni'ishasana's hilt.

She has no will of her own. How dared she? What did she know, anyway, of the bond between me and the dagger? She had no idea what it meant to be powerless in the fae world. She couldn't understand the gratitude I felt.

My fingers stroked the enormous ruby in Ni'ishasana's hilt as I passed a man at the top of the stairs, stepping neatly aside so he had no idea I was there, close enough to kiss. Or kill. The liquid notes of a harp drew me to a doorway, where I paused and watched the harpist for a moment. Her head was bent, watching her hands on the strings, long hair the colour of straw hanging free. A man sat in an armchair watching her, a wineglass dangling from one hand, his chin propped on the other.

In the next room, a child played on the floor with antlered toys that had too many legs to be deer, and rather too many fangs, each detail carefully carved from golden wood. A woman sat at a table behind her, the bright green feather of her quill bobbing as she wrote a letter. The scene was so domestic, so peaceful. A thrill surged through me.

I was the storm that could destroy that peace, the dagger that struck without warning out of the night. I could do anything I wanted to and no one could stop me.

No one knew I was there. Wards and guards were useless against me.

I stopped opposite Eldric's rooms. The door was closed, and two guards stood outside, loosely at ease, their swords sheathed. I could be through that door with Eldric dead at my feet before they realised there was a problem. They couldn't stop me. No one could.

A deadly glee bubbled within me. I could kill Eldric. Here. Now. Surveillance be damned. I was untouchable. Why should I bother with surveillance? I was already here, through the wards, the guards helpless against my power. Why wait?

As if he'd heard my thoughts, one of them straightened, suddenly alert. His companion glanced across at him with a grin as the golden-haired girl I'd followed in approached.

"Here comes trouble," the grinning guard said.

The first guard acted as though he hadn't heard him, though a slow colour crept up his neck and into his cheeks. His sharp, pointed face and russet hair made me wonder if he was foxkin.

The girl paused. Her knowing smile told me she'd noticed the blush, too. "I hope you've got your dancing shoes on, Pettis. The musicians are warming up."

The blush deepened. "I'm on duty."

"Well, I can see that—and what a fine job you're doing of it, too." She exchanged a grin with the other guard, then seemed to take pity on the blushing Pettis. "Come and find me when you're off duty. I've saved you one of the blueberry tarts. I know they're your favourite."

Both men's gazes followed the wiggle of her hips as she walked away.

"Blueberry tart means she fancies you," Pettis's companion said. "Just be careful of those teeth of hers."

Blueberry tarts were one of Zinnia's specialties, and I had a sudden memory of Nevith biting into one of the delicate pastries in a flash of white teeth, steam rising from the deep purple filling. He and I had spent many happy occasions in her kitchen, persuading her to part with just one more.

I hadn't thought of him in ages, and a weight of sadness settled over me that he was gone. It was strange to recall how angry I'd been about his death, and how determined I'd been to make the Vipers pay for it. Those emotions felt like part of a story I'd heard, something that had happened to someone else, not me.

Soon, a man approached with a message for Lord Eldric, and I slipped into the room on his heels.

The Autumn Lord was seated at a desk beneath a wide window that showed leaves in russet and gold, lit by faelight, outside. The room wasn't as big as I remembered it being when I'd met with the king here. Perhaps the occasion had overawed me.

Message delivered, the man left again, and Eldric bent his head back to his work. It would be so easy to circle around behind him. All I had to do was take a handful of his auburn hair in my fist and drag his head back. Ni'ishasana would slit his throat from ear to ear and drink his soul down like wine. His powers would be mine.

Yessss, the blade hissed.

It was so quiet in the room that I could hear the faint scratching of his quill over paper as he wrote. He didn't hear Ni'ishasana's voice, of course. That was only for me, the wielder of the dagger.

Then you will know you are truly alive, Ni'ishasana said, shadows springing to life in the corners of the room. Umarenthe was there, and Celebrach, plus a handful of others. Their voices hummed with power. *Nothing makes you feel more alive than the warmth of hot blood spurting over your hands, watching as someone takes their last breath. Do it, and fully join the ranks of the Vipers. Then you can show them all who is the Serpent.*

The voices were right. I stared at the gold highlights in his hair as my hand tightened on the dagger's hilt. Thirst for blood filled me, a terrible anticipation that could only find completion in an act of violence. I could feel my blade bite into his throat already, picture the blood. There would be a look of shock in his dying eyes as he understood that safety was only an illusion—that even here, in the heart of his own home, his life was mine to take. His power mine to wield.

I moved closer. Only the length of the carpet lay between us. The span of his life was now measured in seconds. The dagger urged me on, thrumming with eagerness beneath my hand.

The dagger.

Again, I heard Lily's words, her tone laden with contempt. *She has no will of her own.* I stopped halfway across the warm autumn tones of the carpet, my feet glued in place as the bloodlust drained away, its heat replaced by ice.

Move, the voices insisted. Umarenthe swirled closer, her insubstantial touch on my arm. *Do it. Do it.*

The dagger's insistent whisperings beat against my mind, but I couldn't move, caught again by the pity and horror in Willow's eyes. *No will. No will.* The carpet had expanded into a vast territory, impassable.

Pettis knocked and poked his head in as I struggled. "The feast is ready, my lord."

Eldric shoved back his chair and stood, stretching the kinks out of his spine. "Finally! I've been smelling that roast pork for hours."

He crossed the room on quick feet, passing so close I could have touched his mustard-coloured coat. Or slashed his throat with my blade.

Instead, I simply stood there and watched him go. Slowly, I pushed Ni'ishasana back through my belt and flexed fingers that had been clenched so tight around its hilt that the shape of the massive ruby was imprinted deep in my palm. Outside the door, footsteps strode away, Eldric followed by his guards, and the corridor fell silent.

Eventually, I moved again, as if waking from a dream.

Well. I was only here for surveillance, anyway. There was no rush. I had plenty of time to fulfil my contract with the Lord of Autumn's duplicitous brother.

14

———

The next night, I stood outside the Tower of London again, with Ash at my side once more. Its crenellated walls were floodlit so they glowed in the dark. The wide plaza where we stood, now empty of tourists and vendors—even of pigeons—was dark by comparison. A lone, old-fashioned lamppost stood straight as a spear at the entry to the bridge leading to the massive arched gate.

Nothing stopped anyone walking across that bridge, right up to the iron gates barring the way. Down below, the moat—a wide stretch of grass—shone under the bright lights. I contemplated the thick, brutal walls. They weren't high enough to keep me out, no more than they could pen the ravens who lived here, or the pigeons that were everywhere during the daylight hours.

I had a good look around for ravens, just in case. The famous Tower ravens should be safely locked away for the night, so any I saw would be Raven's spies—and I'd had enough of "accidental" meetings with my old friends lately.

I risked a glance at Ash's stern profile, but it told me nothing of his thoughts. He'd been avoiding me. The only time I'd seen him had been at dinner, when he'd been forced to take his seat at my right hand. He hadn't asked how my little expedition to Autumn had gone, and I hadn't volunteered any information either.

One thing that wasn't at my side this time was Ni'ishasana. I'd left it in my rooms back at the Nest, where no one who wasn't bound to it could access it. Lily's words had been going round and round in my head ever since I'd seen her. *She has no will of her own.* That wasn't true. I was no thrall of the dagger. I had taken its powers, but it hadn't taken my soul. I didn't need to carry it everywhere, like some junkie that couldn't bear to be parted from her fix.

It has its claws in your soul already, Sage. She thought so, did she?

It was complete and utter bullshit. My soul was my own, and it was one hundred per cent claw-free. Did she think she could scare me into giving up the dagger? Had Ash put her up to it? It sounded like the same muddle-headed thinking he'd been doing since I'd become Serpent.

"Wait out here," I told him. "Let me know if there's any danger."

"Are you expecting trouble?" He seemed pleased. "I thought you were convinced your father's motives were as pure as the driven snow."

That was another reason for leaving the dagger

behind. The thought of anyone trying to take it from me caused a hot spike of rage. It was *mine*. And I wasn't stupid, whatever Ash seemed to think. I wouldn't trust my father until Fallon had proven himself. Ash was right—it seemed a little too coincidental that Fallon should suddenly come over all paternal once the dagger had come to me.

I would be cautious and wait to see what my father wanted before I decided whether to renew our relationship. And if I did, it would be on *my* terms, because it suited my goals. His were of no interest to me. Fallon might be an infamous necromancer, but *I* was the Serpent of the Vipers.

Feeling strangely light, as if this were a holiday and not an important and potentially dangerous meeting, I called my Night magic to make me invisible, and Air to lift me over the ramparts of the Tower's walls. My head was clearer than it had been in weeks, without the stifling rage that had been dogging me lately. Strange, but welcome, nevertheless.

From above, I could see the odd layout inside. "The Tower" was a misnomer, as there wasn't a single tower, but several. A higher wall loomed inside the outer one, and there were buildings of different styles, all boxed in by the massive walls. The walls were so thick that houses were built into them, and window boxes full of flowers and front doors painted in cheery colours made odd neighbours against forbidding architecture and businesslike battlements.

There must be people living here—perhaps the famous Yeomen of the Guard. I'd never been here before, so I wasn't sure. There were no lights on in the houses at this hour—it was almost four in the morning—but I kept the Night magic wrapped around me anyway. I didn't want anyone who happened to be looking out their windows to raise the alarm.

Hovering in the air, I checked carefully for any sign of betrayal, but no one lay on the steep roofs or hidden behind the ancient battlements to ambush me. Even so, I stayed invisible until I'd reached the ground again, glancing around as I settled onto the grass. There was no sign yet of my father. I'd come early deliberately, to check out the lay of the land first.

Several buildings bulked against the walls, but only one stood in the centre of the grounds. It was tall and turreted, square, and its pale stone gleamed under the floodlights. Some kind of repair work was going on, as one side was blanketed in scaffolding. Was this "the" Tower? It was in a different style than the outer walls, newer-looking, though not new. It was still probably several hundred years old.

I walked around its base, checking in all the shadows, a little nervous hollow opening in the pit of my stomach as I waited for my father. What should I call him? Not Papa, like a child. But "Father" didn't feel right, either. He hadn't been much of a father to me. It would have to be *Fallon*, if I called him anything other than *you bastard*.

I wandered over to a discordantly modern shape cordoned off from the lawn by a low metal fence. It was a wide circle of what looked like glass or Perspex, encircled by a larger circle of shining steel. In the middle of the

Perspex circle rested what looked like a cushion made of the same substance. I almost expected to see a glass slipper resting on it.

On closer inspection, the whole thing turned out to be a memorial to Anne Boleyn and others who had lost their heads within these walls, which gave the cushion a much less fairytale vibe. I was reading the names inscribed around the circumference of the circle when I caught movement out of the corner of my eye.

Fallon strolled across the grass towards me, a long cape of dark green swirling around him in dramatic style as he moved. He always had had a tendency towards drama. A welter of emotions rose within me: anger, hurt, love, betrayal, and a strange longing. All at once, I was seven years old again, watching him walk away from me the night he'd dumped me on Lord Thistle and Lady Feronique.

Being fae, of course, he looked no different than he had that night. His hair was still black without a single grey despite his age, his skin pale and smooth as porcelain. He had the vivid green eyes so common in Spring. I'd inherited my brown eyes from my mother, along with her darker skin. His rosy lips would have made a lipstick manufacturer sigh with envy; that and the cape, combined with the pallor of his skin, made him look more like your stereotypical vampire than a fae.

Not that I had ever thought that when he'd been my darling Papa. I guess I'd gotten cynical in my old age.

He smiled. No fangs, so the vampire image slipped a little. I wasn't sure what a necromancer was supposed to look like. If he'd paid a price for his forbidden knowledge, it certainly didn't show in his face.

"At last," he said, spreading his arms wide. If he expected me to run into them, he had sadly misjudged the situation. "It's been too long, Sage."

I folded my arms and gave him a chilly look. "You knew where I was. You could have visited any time." Or not left me in the first place.

"Well, then." He let his arms fall and fussed a little with his cape, as if this scene wasn't playing out the way he'd imagined. Had he pictured it with him as the magnanimous star at the centre of the drama, and me the grateful child hurling herself into his arms? "We're not always free to follow the dictates of our hearts, however much we might like to. There are duties and responsibilities attached to any position of power, as you are no doubt discovering."

"Dictates of our hearts, my arse," I said, and saw a flash of temper in his eyes. "Last I heard, there were duties and responsibilities attached to being a parent, too, which you seem to have conveniently forgotten."

"I left you with friends highly qualified to give you the best upbringing," he said stiffly.

I snorted. "They did their duty, but no more." Their love had all been for Willow, their real child, not the one foisted on them.

He spread his hands in a gesture of helplessness. "I had no choice. I had a higher calling."

"What could be more important than caring for a child

who had so recently lost her mother? Why did I have to lose both of you?"

My voice cracked, surprising us both. Strange how this ancient history still had the power to hurt me.

Many fae adored children. That was why there were so many changelings, human infants stolen away because the fae birth rate was so low and any child was better than none. There were quite a few of us half-fae, too, despite the social stigma of sleeping with mortals.

But looking in Fallon's hard green eyes, I could see that he wasn't one of those who melted at the sight of a child. His real love had been for Anita, my mother, and his love for me had been conditional on that. The child she'd borne had been acceptable as part of a package, but once his wife had died, that had been it for him.

"Sometimes we have to make hard choices in life," he said. "Other priorities take us away from those we love. You, of all people, should understand that. Who did you leave behind to take up your current position?"

Willow. Rowan. Even Raven, confusing as our relationship was. Zinnia and Yarys in the sith, and Randall and Tony at The Drunken Irishman. Allegra and the Hawk. Even the king, I supposed. Hell, the whole human world. When you looked at it like that, it was a lot to give up. I felt a momentary pang of sorrow as I contemplated the roll call, but it passed. I had so much more now.

"What's done is done," I said, and surprise rippled across his face before his expression smoothed over again. "Whatever your past failings as a father, that still leaves us with the question of why we are here now. What do you want?"

However unexpected his approach after all these years of silence, I had to remember that he was a powerful man, and this could be an opportunity for the Vipers.

"What any father wants," he replied smoothly. "To know his child."

I cocked an eyebrow at him, and he smiled.

"I can see you find this hard to credit, but indeed, it's not new. I have been trying to contact you for several years now."

"You couldn't have tried particularly hard. My whereabouts were no secret."

"No, but you had a powerful protector guarding you more fiercely than a dragon guards its hoard. Willow foiled my every attempt to get a message to you."

"You could have come in person," I said. To the pub, to my work—there were plenty of places he could have seen me without Willow coming between us.

"I tried that, too. Every attempt was met with threats and even violence." He rubbed at his neck, where a small scar marred his smooth, seemingly poreless skin. He met my eyes and smiled ruefully. "I assumed you wouldn't take kindly to my hurting your housemate, so I left it alone, confident a better opportunity would one day present itself. And here we are."

The wind stirred his cloak and ruffled his dark hair. My hand crept to my belt, but the reassuring shape of Ni'ishasana's hilt wasn't there. Ash wasn't far away, though; his concern radiated through our link.

"You weren't always so scrupulous about hurting Willow," I said.

He looked away, as if embarrassed. "That was a dark time. I can hardly remember what I was thinking then—a kind of madness overtook me."

I raised both eyebrows in an openly sceptical look.

"Oh, you have every right to doubt me. I don't blame you one bit. All those years I spent searching for a way to bring back your mother, forgetting that I still had you. I turned my back on my living family and spent all my time with the dead." He met my gaze squarely, and I saw pain and regret in those brilliant green eyes. "I know that must have been hard on you, and I'm sorrier than I can say. It took facing death myself to make me see the error of my ways."

"What happened?"

He waved a hand dismissively. "That's a story for another time. But words are cheap. I can tell you until I'm blue in the face that I've accepted that your mother is gone and nothing I can do will bring her back, but it will take time for you to believe me." His voice softened. "She's immensely proud of you, you know. We both are."

The way he spoke of her, in the present tense, as if they'd been chatting over a cup of tea ... it made my spine tingle.

"What do you mean, she's proud of me?"

"I've spoken to her. She wanted you to know that she misses you."

I swallowed hard, unnerved. I was an assassin—death was my job. And, as wielder of the Thief of Souls, I was hardly unfamiliar with the concept of being able to communicate with the dead. And yet the idea of being able to speak to the mother I could barely remember was so alien.

Raw longing filled me. He could hardly have said anything better calculated to entice me.

I couldn't even remember the sound of her voice, though I'd fought to hold on to the scraps of memory that remained. I'd been seven when she died, and all I could recall were impressions, little vignettes: the smell of her rose perfume, the feel of her arms around me, the warmth of her laughter.

"She wants you to be happy," he said. "As do I. Let me be part of your life, Sage. Even if it's only a little bit."

I swallowed around the painful lump in my throat. He sounded so sincere, and his eyes held such warmth. But what was the saying? *Fool me once, shame on you. Fool me twice, shame on me.* I was no child to be taken in by a pair of smiling green eyes and a few empty words.

But I *was* the Serpent of the Vipers. As such, it was my responsibility to wring any advantage possible from this encounter. So, I would be cautious, but I wouldn't reject him yet.

"If you're such a reformed character, why are you still a necromancer?"

He smiled. "I rather thought that would weigh in my favour, instead of against it, considering your own position. However, it's hardly my choice at this point." He sighed. "Once a necromancer, always a necromancer, it seems. I have powerful enemies now, like Spring. If I gave up my powers, they would fall on me like a pack of dharrigals. I find that keeping a few revenants around engenders the proper amount of wariness in one's enemies."

He clicked his fingers, and the shadows at the base of the tall central tower stirred. Three men—no, not men, though once they had been—stepped into the light, walking with that same unnatural gait as the messenger who'd accosted us outside The Drunken Irishman. Empty eye sockets gaped, and their teeth were exposed in permanent, ghastly grins. They wore the clothes they must have been buried in, tattered and rent by time. Rotting flesh and glimpses of pale bone showed through the holes. I wondered why Fallon hadn't bothered to dress them in something better—his messenger had worn ordinary clothes.

Probably the graveyard clothes were meant for effect, to put me off. In which case, it was working. I shuddered. There was something unnerving about their eyeless gaze, too. They lurched to a halt a comfortable distance away. They didn't move fast, but they'd already proven hard to kill, and presumably, a necromancer had an endless supply of them. It would make anyone think twice before attacking him.

I regarded Fallon steadily. He had given a reasonable explanation, but I wasn't going to make this easy for him. "I don't know if I can forgive you."

"Then let's not talk of forgiveness. Let me start instead with an apology and a gesture of my good faith." He slipped a heavy gold signet ring from one finger and held it out to me. "Do you recognise this?"

I shrugged. He'd often worn rings or other jewellery when I was a child, as vain about his appearance as most other fae. A small emerald was embedded in the flat upper surface of this ring, but it seemed otherwise unremarkable.

"I've been wearing it since you were three years old," he said. "I've never taken it off in all that time. Do you know why?"

"I feel sure you're about to tell me."

He pushed the ring towards me. "I'm sorry, Sage. I thought I was doing the right thing. Protecting you. And I know you suffered for its lack. Take it. It's yours."

"The ring?" It certainly wasn't mine. Apart from the fact that I didn't recognise it, I could see without trying it on that it was too big for my slender fingers. Confused, I took it from him.

"No," he said. "The power. It contains your magic, Sage."

15

"You're upset," Ash said when I reappeared outside the Tower of London. "Did he hurt you?"

His eyes raked me, checking for injuries, but there weren't any for him to see. The pain was all on the inside. Pain and fury and gut-wrenching betrayal. I'd gone through my whole life with barely more power than a fae child, being looked down on and dismissed, for nothing. My own father had stolen my power from me.

"I don't want to discuss it. Let's get back to the Nest."

I stalked through the dark streets, the signet ring crushed in my fist, the pain of it digging into my flesh a welcome relief. At least it was a clean, physical sting, unlike the storm of hurt and fury raging inside me. Ash walked beside me, but for once, I barely noticed his presence, my awareness all turned inward as I reeled at the enormity of what had been done to me.

"But the meeting—what did he want?"

"To play happy families."

His eyebrows shot up. "A little late for that, isn't it?"

"You'd think so, wouldn't you?"

"Did you find out how he tracked you down?"

"Oh, yes," I said, gritting my teeth.

Yet, angry as I was, there was still a little girl inside me that thrilled at this attention from her beloved Papa. I couldn't decide if that made me angrier, and wrestled with it all the way back to the Nest.

Once I was inside, my fury leapt up like a fire stirred with a poker. Ash followed me into my suite, and I slammed the ring down onto the small table in the sitting room where I'd left the dagger. I trailed my fingers lovingly over the twisted blade, head still spinning, the hurt and anger a physical lump in my throat.

"What's that?" he asked sharply, coming to my side.

"*That* is how Fallon managed to track me. Apparently, it links to the tiny amount of Spring magic in me—because it contains the rest of it. This ring is full of power. *My* power, that he stole from me when I was little."

The words tasted bitter in my mouth. Ash drew in a shocked breath.

"Did it seem odd to you that the child of such a powerful fae should have so little power of her own?" I seethed. "People have found that surprising all my life. But he always told me it sometimes happens like that, that the human blood overwhelmed the fae somehow, as if it was a goddamn virus. And, like a fool, I believed him."

Ash laid a hand on my shoulder. "You weren't a fool.

You were a child. Of course you believed him—it's natural to accept what your parents tell you as truth."

"I even parroted the lie to everyone else, despite their doubting looks. Talked them into believing it, too. Why didn't I question it?"

"Would it have made any difference? You couldn't have forced him to give it back, even if you'd known. I'm surprised he gave it back now. Did he say why?"

"As a gesture of his *good faith*." I shrugged Ash's hand away and strode restlessly to the window. Good faith, my arse. If he'd dealt with me in good faith, he would never have stripped a trusting child of what was rightfully hers.

It was still a couple of hours until dawn. Outside, a servant crossed the lawn towards the lake and the dark bulk of the forest beyond it. A glow of faelights behind the roof of the stables marked the training grounds, and I could hear the faint crack of wooden weapons striking each other.

"Good faith," Ash repeated, his tone sceptical. "I see. And has it made you trust him any more?"

I pictured myself on those training grounds, sword in hand, and my fists tightened. "It's made me want to rip his head off his shoulders."

The corner of his mouth quirked. "Why did he take it in the first place?"

"He said he did it to protect me. Apparently, I showed early promise." Fae children grew into their power bit by bit over the years. Usually, there was a surge around puberty, and another when they reached full adulthood, around twenty or twenty-one. But at three, mine had already been as strong as a ten-year-old's. "He could tell I would be stronger than many full-blooded fae, which he put down to his own strength—"

"Modest of him."

I bared my teeth in a humourless smile. "There was already tension between him and the Spring Court because he'd married my mother instead of simply bedding her and taking off with the resulting child like any decent fae would do. He was afraid I would become a target if my power exceeded what was socially acceptable for a half-fae, so he removed most of it and hid it in the ring."

"That doesn't make a lot of sense to me. Wouldn't you be more of a target if you were weak?"

I shrugged. "I'm only telling you what he said. He also said he had always intended to give it back to me when I was old enough to understand such things, but circumstances prevented him."

"Circumstances."

Our eyes met, and I saw a fury in his to match my own. Strangely, knowing that someone else shared my feelings eased them.

"You know, the circumstance where he abandoned me to be brought up by other people while he went wandering off learning how to create zombies instead. That was a much more worthwhile use of his time."

"And now he gives it back, when you no longer need it."

"The definition of irony. My life is an Alanis Morrissette song."

Ash looked confused. He probably hadn't spent enough time in the human world to get the reference. Then, he picked up the ring and examined it more closely. The emerald flashed in the light from the faelamps.

"He may be lying," he said. "The ring could be a trap."

"What kind of trap?"

"You could fall under his control if you put it on. If your father is as powerful as you say he is, it's possible he could craft such a spell into the ring."

I supposed I should have thought of that, given the fae reputation for deception. But I'd been too shocked by what Fallon had said to consider that it might all be a lie.

And if he *was* lying, he was a master at it. Going to the meeting, I'd been sceptical as all hell of his motives, but he'd managed to convince me of his sincerity. I held my hand out for the ring, and Ash dropped it into my palm, the metal warm from his touch.

"No." I shook my head. "It feels true. I can sense the ring calling to me."

"That could be part of the trap," he pointed out dispassionately.

"I know what my own power feels like."

"Half an hour ago you didn't know you had any."

Is he afraid you will become more powerful? the dagger whispered. *Does he* want *you to remain incomplete, forgoing the power that is yours by right? See how vehemently he argues against accepting your father's gift.*

I glared at Ash. "My father has given me a priceless gift."

"Which has made you furious because he stole it from you in the first place."

"Yes." I put the ring back on the table next to the dagger and took a deep breath, trying to get my seesawing emotions under control. I was simultaneously elated at knowing I had strong Spring magic after all, furious that my father had taken it from me, and thrilled that he'd given it back. I wanted to deck him and hug him at the same time.

My head throbbed, and the ruby in the dagger's hilt pulsed in time with my heartbeat. I'd felt so much more myself tonight out in the streets of London, but now that I was back in the Nest, I could barely think for the anger that once more simmered beneath the surface, colouring everything I did and thought. If only Ash didn't *argue* all the time.

"So Fallon isn't a great judge of emotional reactions," I said. "But he meant well."

"He *meant* well? Are you hearing yourself?"

"Can't you consider for a moment that my father could genuinely want to reconnect with his daughter?"

"Have you forgotten what your father is, Sage? You and I, we don't have fathers like other people's. They don't do things out of the goodness of their hearts. Fallon is not the kind of man to do anything that doesn't benefit Fallon."

"Perhaps it does benefit him. Perhaps even necromancers need their families."

Ash made a sound of disgust. What did he mean, *we don't have fathers like other people's*? This wasn't about him.

Red mist crept into the corners of my vision and I itched to lash out at something. Anything.

"Are you sure you're not just jealous that *my* father seems to care about me, when yours could only plot and scheme to trap you into the Vipers?"

"I'd hardly call it plotting and scheming. He took advantage of a situation, that's all."

"You thought it was a coincidence that your girlfriend got sick with something so rare that the only hope of saving her was to take her to your father?"

He went perfectly still. The ticking of the clock on the far wall sounded loud as a hammer on wood. "What are you saying?"

"That Celebrach had one of his Vipers administer a slow poison."

I watched him cast his mind back over her symptoms, and my anger abruptly cooled at the devastation that bloomed on his face when he realised I was right.

"I sometimes wondered if ... but I hadn't seen him for years—I thought we were so well hidden. *I* sought *him* out, looking for a cure. How do you know this?"

"I wield the dagger now," I said gently, wishing my urge to hurt him hadn't led me to this point. Wishing I wasn't so *angry* all the time that I lashed out at the closest target. How could it help him to know this? "I know things about its history."

Not everything the previous wielders had done, of course. There was way too much history there for that. But Celebrach was my immediate predecessor, and that knowledge hadn't been buried too deep—he was actually proud of how adroitly he'd played his son.

His son, who was looking so gutted that it tugged at my heart.

"So, you see," I said, "you shouldn't blame yourself for not being able to save her. There was never anything you could have done to alter her fate."

He looked down, his hair falling across his face and hiding his expression. I resisted the urge to comfort him, sensing that sympathy from the person who'd dumped this news on him wouldn't be exactly welcome.

"Well, that's ancient history now," he said at length, his voice as calm as ever. "The more pressing issue is whether or not your father is sincere." He looked up, a determined expression on his face. "But whatever you believe on that point, don't be in a hurry to put on that ring. Lady alone knows what will happen, and you don't need the power anyway."

See? He does *mean to deny you. Always he tries to influence you, to keep you dependent on him.*

"But this magic is *mine*. You've always had magic, so you can't understand. The fuss that the purebloods make about power, who's got more and who hasn't ... you wouldn't believe the trouble it's caused me. He stole a part of me, and I'm mad as hell about it. He had no right." I struggled to hold onto that new sense of gentleness, but outrage threatened to overwhelm me again. All this time, trying to get the fae to acknowledge I even existed, when I could have been wiping the floor with them. "I will have what is mine."

"You're impossible."

On this point, I wouldn't be shifted. "Go and work out your frustrations on the training ground, Viper."

He stiffened, then swept into a deep bow. "As my Serpent commands."

He strode from the room without looking at me again, and I could tell from the way he held his jaw that he was grinding his teeth. I sighed as I closed the door behind him.

He grows more insolent by the day, Umarenthe said. The shadow woman hovered by the table, leaning over the ring, inspecting it as carefully as Ash had done. *He will have to be brought into line soon.*

Perversely, when she criticised Ash, all my own irritation with him faded away, and I leapt to his defence. "He's only trying to protect me."

The wielder of Ni'ishasana needs no other protection.

"True." I stood next to her and contemplated the ring for a moment before picking it up again and focusing my magics on it. What I'd said to Ash was true—the magic within it felt familiar, and it tugged at me. "I can't sense anything wrong with this, despite Ash's dire predictions."

She shrugged, a ripple of shadow in the dim room. *It is exactly what the necromancer said it was: a ring containing a great deal of Spring magic. If he's telling the truth about the origin of that magic, all you have to do is destroy it and the power will return to you.*

"And if he's not?"

Then you've lost nothing anyway.

I toyed with the ring, admiring the emerald. "How was

he able to draw it out of me and into the ring in the first place?"

It's not easy, the shadow woman said. *Only those with great power can manage it, and even then, they need to be intimately familiar with the victim and their magic if they wish them to survive the experience. The process itself is similar to a fae giving some of their power to a changeling, only in reverse. It's usually only possible among family members.*

"So Fallon couldn't have stolen anyone else's?" He'd been gone so long, who knew what he could have been up to? And I already knew the lengths he was prepared to go to—he'd been willing to kill Willow for more power.

Unlikely. And it would have to be someone from Spring. It's not possible to steal power in this way from a Realm other than your own.

"He seemed so sincere. The last thing he said to me was a promise that there would be no more secrets between us."

Secrets aren't always a bad thing. This secret was about protecting you.

I raised an eyebrow, pleased to find that someone, at least, didn't think I was mad for believing Fallon in this.

But then, Umarenthe was part of Ni'ishasana, and the dagger was my greatest ally.

16

———

A Serpent's work was never done. Life at the Nest didn't stop because my father had reappeared; I was still the new Serpent with a million things to wrap my head around, and over a hundred Vipers to get to know. I trained daily in sword and knife work, and spent time on my studies. Ash was no longer technically my trainer, but I had a lot to learn yet about the arts of the assassin.

Much of the business of the Vipers happened automatically. Assignments had already been given out before I took over, and several hits were in the planning or execution phase. I had to approve new ones that came in and assign them, either to Adepts or regular Vipers, depending on the expected complexity of the operation.

I instituted twice-weekly meetings with my Adepts, partly to help me stay on top of things and partly to keep an eye on them. Other than Ash, I barely knew any of them. I had a nodding acquaintance with Nuah and Mezzi. Nuah and I had begun our acquaintance on the training grounds with threats on her part, which had swiftly escalated into attempts to kill me. That was when I'd been a powerless apprentice. She was all smiles and cooperation now, but I hadn't forgotten.

Though she was no longer a danger to me, I didn't trust her, and I had no doubt that the other Adepts were just as frustrated at finding themselves answering to a woman who'd barely begun her apprenticeship. The fact that they couldn't move against me directly didn't mean that they weren't capable of causing me trouble. Ash, for instance, could be vulnerable if they all united against him, and I had no desire to lose the one Adept I could actually trust.

And so, I watched them all carefully, noting body language and using my links with them to probe beneath their calm surfaces for hints of their true feelings. I searched for flashes of emotion, whispers of intent, anything I could use, all while keeping up a confident exterior of my own. In time, they would learn not to defy me, but I was prepared for a rough ride through the getting-to-know-you period.

All nine of them sat in a semi-circle in front of my desk. I had considered the idea of a more human-style conference, where we all sat around a table together, but quickly discarded it. We weren't work colleagues or equals. Better to remind them of that.

I leaned back in my chair, Ni'ishasana conspicuously placed in its stand on the bookshelf behind me, and listened to Nuah's report on Atinna's progress. The girl was working on surveillance for Nuah's next hit, and apparently proving herself to be a model apprentice. I was happy to have her out of the Nest for a while. She had even less chance of doing me harm than the Adepts did, but having her glare at me while I ate dinner in the hall every night had been getting a little old.

"Where are we at with Eldric's assassination?" Sharis asked, once Nuah was finished.

I contemplated the fair-haired Viper. He had big brown eyes and a rounded face that made him look harmless, almost childlike. But there was a glint in those eyes that was anything but harmless. Saffron had been his preferred candidate for Adept, and I suspected he wouldn't be forgiving me any time soon for elevating Mezzi instead.

Our bond gave me no hint of his emotions—another sign that he was one to watch. Few people, even among the Vipers, had that kind of self-control.

"You needn't concern yourself with Eldric's assassination," I said. "I'm handling that personally."

"Excellent." He inclined his head in the shallowest of bows. "Do you need anything, or will Ashovar be assisting you again?"

Yes, definitely one to watch.

"Do you think me incapable of managing without assistance?" He was a Summer fae, so I sent a Winter chill around the room. The temperature dropped ten degrees in a heartbeat as the flames in the hearth flickered and shrank.

"Of course not." He even managed to sound genuine. "You are the Serpent."

"I am," I agreed blandly. Watching him try not to shiver warmed the cockles of my heart.

"I'm moving on the Spring minstrel tomorrow," Mezzi said, giving Sharis a disdainful look.

"Tomorrow night?" I asked.

"No, during the day. I'll hit him while he's asleep."

"This is the one whose wife ordered the hit because he was sleeping with her best friend?"

"Yes. She wants him taken out in bed, while the friend is there." He grinned, clearly relishing the thought. "As messily as possible, so the friend can wake up to it."

"Bloody vengeance is always so satisfying," Nuah said with a cool smile.

I dismissed them all soon after and sat staring into the flickering flames, which now warmed the room as normal.

I hoped for his sake that Sharis was smart enough to take the hint. Looking through Celebrach's ledgers, I could see he'd performed more than his share of hits in the last decade or so, second only to Ash. Either he was particularly good at his job or my predecessor had favoured him —in which case, he might need some extra encouragement to accept the new status quo. And it would be a shame to have to break such an efficient assassin.

At least I would have no problem in that regard with Mezzi. He was the first beneficiary of my reign and seemed pretty pleased with his new status. He also clearly enjoyed his work. The Spring minstrel's death would not be an easy one.

Mezzi would be there in daylight. It was a long time since I'd seen the beauty of Spring in full sunlight. I'd lived nocturnally under Lady Feronique's rule, and she had encouraged an early bedtime for Willow and me. Especially me. She said it would make me grow taller, but I suspected it was only to limit the number of hours she had to put up with me.

The sun was one of the main things my mother had missed when she'd moved to the Realms to be with my father. I remembered that much of her, because she'd often let me stay up late so we could walk in the garden together in the early morning. I didn't have many memories of our time together now, but most of them were from those garden walks—images of her smiling face turned up to the sun, of her hands planting seeds and the rich earthy scent of the soil, of the feel of her arm pressing me close to her side, the sun warm on my shoulders.

I'd been so young when she had died that these flashes were all I had left of her. Her laughter had been infectious. What wouldn't I give to hear that laugh again! I could hardly believe that Fallon had managed to speak to her beyond the grave. Though part of me was well aware that that was the least of what necromancers could do, it still seemed incredible.

And he'd said that she was proud of me. My eyes swam with sudden tears, and the flames in front of me blurred. My mother was proud of me.

I'd waited all my life to hear that.

If only I could hear it in person. I wanted to speak to her, to make up for all those years I'd missed with her. There was so much I wanted to tell her, and even more that I wanted to know about her. I didn't even know where she'd come from, or anything about her family—my family—other than that there were some Maoris in her family tree. Her father? Her grandfather? She must have told me, but I couldn't remember. As a child in the Realms, the human side of my family hadn't seemed important, mainly because of my mother's attitude—she was completely dazzled by the beautiful fae she'd married and the magical world he'd brought her to, and had no interest in the human world she'd left behind. As an adult, I deeply regretted the lost opportunity to connect with my human family.

Could Fallon make it possible for me to speak to my mother? Was this not just an opportunity to have a father again, but also a mother, at least in some capacity? My pulse began to race as I contemplated new possibilities. In my mind, we were a family again, only this time I would be old enough—and experienced enough in the alternative— to appreciate that.

Unless Ash was right and it was all some elaborate con that Fallon was running. He was certainly capable of lying blatantly to my face. Those old tales of the fae not being able to lie were, sadly, only tales, and Fallon had already proved himself well and truly capable of deception.

If so, what was the aim of the con? It had to be the dagger—that was the only thing that fit with the timing of his overtures of friendship, assuming he was lying about having tried to contact me before. It wasn't until I'd become the wielder of the dagger that he had discovered this deep-seated desire to reunite with his long-lost daughter. But what did he want it *for*? Surely he had no ambitions to become an assassin himself.

To a man like him, the sheer power of the dagger could

be a draw—but then, if it was power he was after, why would he give back my own Spring magic? Since I hadn't known he had it, he could have kept it for himself. Instead, he'd chosen to give it back to me. That didn't seem like the action of a man who was bent on amassing power.

I glanced down at the ring in my hand. Only the emerald set into it gave it any real beauty. Apart from that, it was a plain, thick band of gold with a slightly flattened top, such as a man might wear on his little finger. It could hardly have looked more ordinary, and yet I could feel a slight buzzing from it, almost as if it were alive with the magic trapped inside it.

I turned it over, checking for inscriptions, but the interior of the band was as smooth as the outside. The temptation to put it on and experience that power was strong, but I wasn't stupid. However much I yearned to believe Fallon was sincere, I wouldn't be wearing any magical jewellery he gave me. There were far too many tales in fae lore of people being controlled through such gifts to risk it, even with Umarenthe's reassurance that it wasn't boobytrapped.

She had said to smash it to release the power trapped within. That sounded like a less risky option. I tugged on one of the threads in my mind, and a few moments later, one of the grey-clad servants knocked on the door of my study.

"Bring me a large hammer and a block of stone," I said.

He nodded and withdrew as silently as he'd come, closing the door behind him. A few minutes later, he returned and placed a blacksmith's hammer and a flat piece of rock the size of a stepping stone on top of the papers on my desk. A little earth was smeared across the top of the rock, and a few blades of grass clung to one edge. It probably *was* a stepping stone, and it amused me to think of the man going out to the garden and ripping it out of the ground.

Once he'd gone, I picked up the hammer, hefting its weight in my hands. Perfect. I laid the ring on the stone and raised the hammer high. Doubtless I could have done this with my magic, but there was nothing like a little physical destruction to put a girl in a good mood. I swung the hammer, grinning, and the impact shuddered through my arms.

The sound of the blow still rang in my ears as a wave of power hit me, and I staggered, the hammer falling to the carpet with a thud. My whole body flushed with heat, and I threw my head back, a storm surging around me. Unseen winds buffeted me, and my skin tingled. The citrus scent of limes—the scent of my magic, but stronger than I'd ever smelled it before—filled the room as green lightning played over my skin, dancing up and down my arms.

When the storm finally died, I felt energised, as if I'd just woken from the best sleep of my life. My fingers tingled, the new power inside me eager for release. The ring lay in the centre of the stone like a little gold donut, completely flattened, and the emerald had shattered into tiny chips and a smear of green powder.

"Well. That was something," I said aloud.

I crossed to the nearest window with eager steps and threw it open. A tibouchina grew outside, its smooth limbs covered in dark leaves and pale brown buds. I beckoned, feeling a surge of power that was different than the gifts Ni'ishasana had given me. This power felt more familiar, a thundering roar that echoed the whispers of Spring power I had known growing up.

The tree bent toward me, its leaves rustling as a branch reached through the window, like a puppy offering its head to be stroked. I laid my hand on it, and the nearest buds burst into glorious flower. A wave of intense green light flooded from my hand, down the branch, and through the rest of the tree as every bud opened in response to my lime-scented magic.

My magic.

I finally had some that was truly mine, and it came so *easily*. It was crazy. I released the tree, flexing my fingers as the branch withdrew and the tree righted itself again. I stared out at the vibrant purple flowers, living proof of my ability, and felt prouder of those flowers than of anything I'd accomplished with Ni'ishasana's help. Something inside me that had been wound tight all these years finally relaxed.

Finally. I was a true Spring mage at last.

And I had my father to thank for it. Surely no one could have given away this much power—because I could tell that it was a very deep well indeed—without some huge prize to be gained? And really, how could he get Ni'ishasana from me? I glanced at it on its stand and felt a hum of agreement from it. We were inseparable. There was nothing to fear. I'd only managed to steal it from Cele-brach because the dagger itself had willed it that way. It had wanted a change of ownership, and had betrayed

Celebrach and supported me instead in order to arrange one.

So, if Ni'ishasana wasn't the prize, what was? It had to be me. As unlikely as it seemed, Fallon Domani actually wanted to be reunited with his daughter, and had been prepared to give up an enormous amount of power in order to see that happen.

Wonders never ceased.

17

———

Flush with new power, I went in search of Ash just after sunrise, but found Mezzi instead, heading across the green lawn towards the gate with a small, discreet pack over one shoulder.

"You've come to see me off?" he asked, tipping his head quizzically.

In an instant, I made a spontaneous decision. My body buzzed with so much new power that I could have burst into flower myself.

"I thought I might accompany you," I said. "At least part of the way."

How would it feel to enter the Realm of Spring with so much of its magic rising in my veins like fresh, green sap? It had been too long since I'd been there. Unless you counted the ill-fated expedition where I'd been fighting to save Lord Nox's life a few weeks back, and I didn't. That had been far too stressful to be a true homecoming.

But if it was a homecoming I wanted, there was somewhere else besides Lord Thistle's estate that I wanted to visit. All the talk of my mother had given me a craving to see the home I'd shared with her again, and the tulips that grew on her grave in the small green clearing behind it.

"I'm flattered," Mezzi said, giving me a sidelong glance from calculating blue eyes.

"It's nothing personal. It's merely that our paths lie together for a little way."

"Then I won't take it personally, and will simply enjoy the company of our beautiful new Serpent for a time."

"I hope you never flirted with Lord Celebrach like this," I said as we passed through the gate and stepped out onto the streets of London. A bus rumbled past, carrying commuters on their way to work, their blank faces staring unseeing out the windows.

"Lord Celebrach wasn't really my type," Mezzi drawled, leading the way around a corner. There was a park not far away. With London stirring to life all around us, that presented the best options for crossing unseen into the Wilds.

"Neither am I," I said firmly.

"I beg to differ. I've always had a thing for powerful women."

I rolled my eyes at his back. He was hardly subtle. I let our link colour with my displeasure, and he shut up.

It was too cold to be outdoors without a good reason, so the park was the domain of the squirrels scampering up and down the broad tree trunks. One stopped to watch us go past, perhaps wondering if we were tourists who were likely to feed it, but our brisk steps soon left it behind.

Mezzi veered off the path and into an area where the trees grew more closely. The long grass brushed my ankles with dew and left my shoes shining with moisture. When he found a spot where two trees leaned toward each other, their upper branches entwined, he stopped.

"Shall I do the honours?"

"Go ahead."

He said nothing and gave no outward signal, but as he stepped under the arch of the tree branches, a timid mist crept out of nowhere. I followed hard on his heels in case I lost him in the mist, and the tingle of threshold magic shivered over my skin. Around us, trees loomed out of the mist, but these trees were larger and far older than the ones that dotted the safe little London park. Their branches leaned down, eager to catch us up in twiggy fingers and drag us off the path that led away into the foggy distance.

As we left London behind, the mist cleared, revealing the Greenway and thick forest on either side. The Greenway was narrow, a mere dirt trail that twisted unpredictably through the trees. I knew if I glanced behind, I would see no sign of it as the trees closed in on our heels. The paths through the Wilds were treacherous, and it required an effort of will and magic to force them to lead those who walked them to their destination.

Mezzi focused on the task of taming the Greenway, leaving me to enjoy the walk through the greenery. I had no fear of the Wilds; I had power to burn, and nothing here would harm me. The Earth magic in the path vibrated in greeting to the Earth magic within me, and my Spring senses delighted in the feel of the forest life around me. I could sense sap rising in strong, young trunks. I could hear buds unfurling and sense the potential of seeds nestled into the nourishing soil, awaiting their turn to grow and flourish. Every tree, every branch, even the tiniest bush and shoot surged with green life, and I was a part of it, my blood surging in response. I had never felt so alive.

Revitalised by the walk, I was surprised when it ended. It seemed to have only been moments since we left London, but a glance at the sun showed me that two or three hours had passed when Mezzi paused in front of a stone archway twined with flowers.

"This is my destination," he said. "Are you coming with me?"

I sent my senses through the arch and discovered we were a long way from Lord Thistle's estate, near a stream I'd never seen before.

"My path takes me in a different direction," I said.

"Good hunting to you, then," he said, then stepped through the arch and disappeared.

Naturally, he would assume I was on Viper business. In fact, I should probably be heading for Autumn instead, to complete the task that awaited me there. But the sun was warm on my shoulders, and I was too bursting with life to think of death.

Besides, even Serpents ought to get some time off occasionally.

I closed my eyes and pictured my destination, holding it in my mind: every window box bursting with flowers, the long sweep of the entry, the way the morning sun sparkled on the tall windowpanes. To make my mother more at home, my father had built the house in a more traditional human fashion. The facade looked more like an English manor house than the typical Spring architecture of linked, open pavilions.

Holding that image in my head and the feeling of love and comfort it evoked in my heart, I opened my eyes. The archway that Mezzi had disappeared through was gone, and in its place, a path wound off through the trees ahead. I followed the path, my footsteps eager.

Before too long, a new structure appeared. Less of an archway and more of a bower, three white posts rose up on either side of the path, joined by thick supporting cross beams. An ancient wisteria coiled up around each post and spread its leafy limbs, heavy with clusters of blooms, over the beams. Sweet-smelling purple flowers brushed my shoulders as I passed beneath them, smiling. The Greenway had chosen a truly appropriate representation for my exit.

Mist obscured my vision for a moment, and when it cleared, the wisteria-hung bower had disappeared, leaving only the faintest trace of perfume to linger in the air. I stood on the road outside my father's house and drank in the sight of its steep roofs and vine-covered brickwork.

Eagerly, my feet took the cobbled path among beds of flowers bursting with colour. Tall pink hollyhocks stood like joyous spears among a riot of rose bushes, lavender, and bright red poppies. Their scents mingled into a well-remembered aroma that would forever mean home in my heart.

I pushed open the front door and entered the dark entry hall. The curtains in the rooms to either side were closed, throwing the house into gloom.

"Hello?" I called.

No one replied, which didn't really surprise me. The house had that empty, neglected feel.

My footsteps were loud on the dark wooden boards as I crossed the hallway into the dining room. The far wall was a bank of glass doors that could be folded back to let the outside in, leading to the garden. I hurled back the curtains, letting in the sunlight. Dust lay on every surface and danced in the air, little motes sparkling like glitter in the sunshine that streamed in. Clearly, it had been a long time since Fallon had stayed here.

I went out into the hall and entered each room on the ground floor in turn, opening the curtains, letting in the daylight. My last memories of this house were not good, full of darkness and blood, and I needed the light to chase them away.

Fallon had lured Willow and me here for dinner, then proceeded to feed poison to our whole guard. He'd poisoned us, too, though not fatally. Only enough to put us to sleep so that he could sacrifice Willow in one of his dark rituals. Thank the Lady that hadn't worked out for him the way he'd planned.

A shudder of remembered horror ran through me as I entered the kitchen. The guards had waited for us around the big kitchen table that night, and I had found them still there, collapsed over their meals, blood leaking from their mouths and noses.

For a moment, that was all I could see as I stood in the doorway, but this was not why I had come. There were no guards here now, so, straightening my shoulders, I marched to the back door and threw it open, then tore the curtains down from the small windows over the sink. Spreading my arms wide, I conjured faelights, which burst into being like tiny suns, driving the shadows before them.

Squinting my eyes against the glare, I stared at the big kitchen fireplace, forcing myself to recall happier times when I'd curled up beside it with a snack, watching my mother work alongside the cooks. She had never treated her servants with the arrogance I'd seen Lady Feronique show once I'd moved to her estate.

Upstairs were Fallon's study and the bedrooms, which opened off a long gallery hung with family portraits. He was almost as proud of his lineage as Lord Thistle himself and had often told me that only the Lord of Spring and his heirs had more power than the people of his own line. That had always sent a shiver of longing and disappointment through me, and I had sometimes wondered why it had never seemed to occur to him that such boasting wasn't the best thing to do in front of his underpowered daughter.

Of course, now I knew different. He'd been aware all along that my power was no shame to the Domani name. I strode down the corridor to my old bedroom, and found it as unchanged as the rest of the house and just as dusty. The bed was nowhere near as large as the one I had at the Nest, but it was still at least a queen size by human standards.

I remembered feeling very small at times, lost within its bulk. Sometimes when I had cried in the night, my mother had climbed in next to me, comforting me with her presence and her warm arms wrapped tightly around me. I stared out the window at the vista of trees moving like a green sea in the light wind that had sprung up, and sneezed as the ever-present dust tickled my nose.

I left my room and headed for my parents' suite. I had to pass the head of the staircase on my way, and I paused as a tiny sound caught my attention.

Umarenthe appeared from the shadows in the hallway. *Your father is here.*

"Alone?"

No.

She didn't elaborate, but my mouth tightened as I hurried down the stairs. He had brought his revenants *here* —here, to my mother's house, dead things in her home of warmth and joy.

"Fallon! I know you're here," I called. I stopped at the bottom of the dark stairs, looking left and right at all the open doorways.

He stepped out of the brightly lit kitchen, my faelights behind him rendering him as no more than a silhouette until he had moved further into the hallway. "I'm not hiding." He gestured at the multiple faelights bobbing around the ceiling behind him. "I take it this is your work?" There was puzzled amusement in his tone.

I shrugged. "The place needed a little freshening up."

"I would have expected an assassin like yourself to prefer the dark."

A figure lurched out of the kitchen behind him. She was a woman, or had been, though I figured that out more from the clothes she was wearing than any other cues. A lot of her face had rotted away, leaving large patches where the yellowed bone of her skull showed through. Her hair was still long and reasonably thick, if rather tangled and matted with bits of weed and stick, but hair was no indication of gender among the fae. I'd seen plenty of fae men with hair just as long.

"Why have you brought that thing here?" I demanded, unable to keep my outrage from showing in my voice.

Umarenthe circled the creature in apparent fascination, swirling closer to examine her face, then back again.

"My children often accompany me," he said. As he spoke, another appeared in the kitchen doorway, though this one was clearly a male, judging by its height and build. Umarenthe inspected this one, too. "They don't like to be apart from me for too long."

"These are not your children," I spat.

"No offence to you, of course, dear Sage." There was a twinkle in his eye that suggested he was enjoying my discomfort. I supposed necromancers had to get their kicks where they could find them, but it didn't exactly endear him to me. For someone who was trying to make a good impression, he wasn't doing too well.

"But what else would you have me call them?" he continued. "They're not pets. We must remember they were once fae like ourselves. And though they serve me, they are more than mere servants."

"Oh? In what way?"

"Because each of them carries part of my essence." He smiled at my evident surprise and added in a tone of great reasonableness, "How else is one to animate the dead? The life force must come from somewhere."

Interesting. "And I suppose that is what allows you to control them."

He nodded approvingly. "That is correct. In some ways, they are but extensions of myself."

I folded my arms and leaned back against the carved newel of the staircase. "I suppose my question, then, should be what are *you* doing here?" Out of the corner of my eye, I saw Umarenthe approach my father, subjecting him to the same scrutiny as she had the revenants, as if trying to see how they were connected. Fallon wasn't the only one who took strange companions everywhere he went.

He cocked his head to one side. "Why should I not be here? This is my house."

He has followed you here, Umarenthe said, *or else he has wards set to warn him if anyone arrives.*

I glanced impatiently at the shadow woman. That much I had been able to figure out for myself. "Your house is covered in dust," I said to Fallon. "Don't pretend that you still live here. Are you following me?"

He waved a hand airily. "Let us rather say that I saw an opportunity to visit with my daughter and took it. You are a hard person to get hold of, you know. I might just as easily ask what *you* are doing here."

"Taking a little trip down memory lane," I said.

"Ah." An expression of pain crossed his face, so quickly

I couldn't be sure of what I'd seen. "And have you enjoyed your stroll?"

Maybe it was that fleeting glimpse of pain I'd seen, but I discarded what I had been going to say and said simply instead, "I miss Mama."

He gazed at me steadily, and the pain was back, more obvious than before. Silence pooled in the dim hallway while the revenants watched from their empty eye sockets.

"I miss her, too," he said, and there was no denying the truth in his voice or the compassion in his eyes.

I moved closer so I could see him better. "How did you speak to her? Can you do it again?"

Understanding softened his expression. "Would you like to speak to her, Sage?"

I breathed out shakily and nodded. "More than anything."

He gave no command—I supposed he didn't have to if his connection was as strong as he suggested—but the female revenant approached me. It was all I could do to hold steady, having the creature so close. She was not a pretty sight, and I wondered briefly who she had been.

"Silva will assist us," he said. "Are you ready?"

"What— Here? Now? Don't you need some kind of ritual?"

He raised an eyebrow. "Expecting black candles and blood sacrifices, Sage?"

Since that pretty much *had* been what I was expecting, I said nothing.

"We do like to work in darkness, however." He flicked a hand behind him, and all the faelights in the kitchen abruptly went out, plunging the hall into a deeper darkness. His teeth flashed white in the dim light as he grinned. "Rather like assassins."

He began to mutter under his breath. It didn't sound like any language I recognised. Shadows gathered around us, the darkness pressing in, and Umarenthe moved to my side, her eyes fixed on the revenant in front of us.

Do you feel that? she asked, a strange excitement in her voice. *That tugging sensation?*

I felt nothing except a growing unease as the revenant tipped her ruined head back and stared sightlessly at the ceiling two stories above us. The shadows swirled around her like a miniature tornado, and there was a sudden rushing sound, as of a great wind.

Fallon sighed, and the revenant's sightless gaze swivelled toward me again. She rolled her shoulders, as if getting comfortable, and tipped her head to one side. "Is that you, my little whirlwind? You've grown so much I hardly know you."

I sucked in a shocked breath. The voice was unfamiliar, but those words—I'd completely forgotten, but the memory came rushing back. My mother had often called me her little whirlwind, laughingly accusing me of having enough energy for two children.

"Mama?" My voice cracked. I tried again. "Mama, is that you?"

"It is. Oh, my darling, how I've missed you." The creature reached out for my hands, but I tucked them behind me and stepped back abruptly.

Her head drooped. "I see," she said, more quietly. "This

form I wear repulses you." She turned to regard my father. "Couldn't you have found something better than this decaying husk, Fallon? I just want to hold my baby in my arms again."

Hot tears pricked at my eyes. "I'm sorry, Mama. I can't—"

"No, it's all right." The revenant's ruined mouth stretched into a horrible rictus, which was presumably meant as a smile. "It's enough for me to see you. You're so tall! Are you well? Tell me about yourself. I want to know *everything*."

"I'm ..." Where did I begin? "I'm well, Mama. I came into my power at last." I glanced at my father, but found his gaze riveted on the revenant's face, a peculiar expression of longing there.

The revenant clasped her hands at her chest in another suddenly familiar gesture that tore at my heart. "That's wonderful! I was so worried."

Was she? My meagre memories held nothing of that, but I supposed a mother would have hidden such concerns from her child.

"I have more power than I ever dreamed of," I said. "I am—"

The revenant jerked suddenly, and her hands fell to her sides. "Oh, I can't ..." She shivered, and her head lolled. The shadows swirled again. "I love you, Sage," she gasped, before sagging.

"Mama?"

There was no response. The revenant appeared to be asleep on her feet.

"Where did she go?" I demanded of Fallon. "Bring her back!"

He shook his head. "I can't. It takes too much power to hold her here."

Rage rushed through me, burning through every nerve ending. It wasn't enough. After all this time, I needed more than a few moments.

"You're a necromancer. That's what you *do*."

He sighed wearily. "This isn't her body, Sage." He spoke patiently, as if to a fractious child. "That makes it far more difficult to hold her spirit here. If I forced her into her own corpse, I could bind her here forever, but is that what you want? She's been dead for years."

Eighteen, to be exact. I had felt the passing of every one. After eighteen years in the ground, she would be in worse shape than the creature before me. I didn't know if I could bear that.

"So that's it? That's all you can do?" I couldn't keep the frustration from my voice. "What were you doing all those years when you left me behind?"

His eyes were deep pools of sorrow. "Searching for a way to truly bring her back to life—but all the necromancy in the world can't do that. I tried, Sage, but it takes more power than any one person has." He rubbed tiredly at the bridge of his nose, as if a headache gathered there. "It would need the power of many different Realms working together—possibly all of them. And, sadly, we necromancers are not known for our exceptional teamwork. If there was any way at all, you know I would do it—but trust me, it's better to let her go and remember her the way she was."

I stared at him, emotions whirling through me too fast to grasp. Rage, sorrow, despair, regret. And then, last of all, as if my body was some kind of damn Pandora's box, hope.

He needed the power of many Realms working together to restore my mother to true life? Or only the power of the one who wielded Ni'ishasana?

18

———

I told no one where I was going. The Vipers were not my keepers. With the dagger tucked safely into my belt, I slipped out into London's streets.

The air was ... bracing. Strange how you don't realise how good you have it until it's gone. Sydney's temperate climate was much more to my taste than the frigid British weather. My breath billowed in great white clouds in front of my face, and I thought rather longingly of the hot Sydney days. It was summer in the southern hemisphere.

Maybe I should move the entry to the sith back Down Under. Or even somewhere tropical—Hawaii, perhaps, or Fiji. The world was truly my oyster now, and there was no reason to limit myself to what I had known. I could see the world. Sydney held many happy memories for me, but it wasn't the only great city in the world.

I yawned, releasing another cloud of steaming breath into the freezing air. I'd headed straight back to the Nest from Fallon's house and caught a few hours of sleep, though not nearly enough. But I figured my chances of getting in and out of Whitehaven without being caught were probably better in daylight, while most of the palace was asleep. It was worth sacrificing my own rest.

The weak sunshine of late afternoon did absolutely nothing to warm me, and I walked briskly, heading for the nearby park. Only a little longer and I would be in the Realms, where the temperature was more to my liking.

The park was busier than last time I'd been there. The squirrels were out in force, as were the ducks, who watched with interest gleaming in their beady eyes as people walked along the side of the small pond, just in case anyone decided to distribute breadcrumbs. They eyed me hopefully as I passed, but I didn't slow my brisk stride, and the pond was soon behind me.

A weird sense of being watched tickled between my shoulder blades, and I turned suddenly, raking the park with a suspicious gaze. No one appeared to be watching me. A young couple lay on a picnic blanket, far too engrossed in each other to notice anyone else. A mother with a trio of kids in tow headed towards the expectant ducks. And in the distance, a handful of people used the path that crossed from one side of the park to the other, hurrying through on their way to somewhere else.

Maybe I was simply being paranoid. Maybe it was the damn ducks with their gimlet eyes. I shrugged and headed for the same place that Mezzi and I had used previously, where the trees grew closer together.

I cast another glance behind me, still suspicious, before stepping through the natural arch of the trees. No one was behind me, so I put it out of my mind as the threshold magic skittered over my skin and mist billowed around my feet. Even if I had been followed, no one would be able to track me down once I was in the Wilds. I stepped through into the Wilds and stopped, making sure that the gate had closed behind me without anyone else coming through before I proceeded along the Greenway.

I held my destination firmly in mind as I walked—the gleaming white towers of Whitehaven, capital of the Realms and home of King Rothbold. I walked for some time, listening to birdsong in the trees around me punctuated by the occasional rumble of my stomach. Maybe I should have grabbed something to eat before I left the Nest. In a couple of hours, it would be fae breakfast time, and I hadn't eaten for a while. It would be too bad if my gurgling digestive system gave me away in the middle of attempting to break into the palace.

Perhaps an hour had passed, and the shadows were beginning to lengthen, when a tall archway made of white stone reared over the path ahead. The Wilds were a funny place—sometimes it could take all day to reach one's destination, and other times, the journey would be over in a matter of minutes. Usually, the stronger the traveller's magic, the faster the journey, but that wasn't always the case. The Wilds remained capricious, unknowable to anyone but the most powerful earthcrafters, like the king's sister, Yriell, or even Rothbold himself. And they weren't giving away their secrets.

Before I walked under that archway, I used my Day magic to draw a light-weaving around me. I'd been to the palace frequently enough in recent times that I could easily be recognised. Rather than bothering with a Glamour to change my features, I figured I'd skip straight to the good stuff and waltz in completely undetected.

I passed through the archway and into the Realm of Day, where Whitehaven was situated. Even the streets here gleamed, though they weren't made of the same dazzling white stone as the palace itself. They were just clean, with not a speck of dirt or litter anywhere to be seen on the pale marble that lined the streets close to the palace. It was certainly a contrast to grey and dismal London.

There was no one about. I passed large and beautiful homes situated on equally large and beautifully manicured grounds, the city dwellings of fae Lords and other highly placed dignitaries. The servants might well be stirring inside, stoking fires and preparing breakfasts, but no one was on the streets. I strode toward the palace, my rubber-soled shoes making no sound.

The gleaming towers of the king's residence shone brightly in the late afternoon sun, but not as brightly as legend would suggest. Just as well—I had no desire to be blinded by the sight. I was a woman on a mission, and I approached the high stone walls at a brisk pace.

There were a dozen guards lined up outside the main gates of the palace, all standing at stiff attention. That was more than normal, and might have been a problem if I had been planning on walking in through the main entry. Instead, I turned away, keeping the shining white wall on my left, and disappeared around the corner.

The walls towered above my head, twenty feet high or

more. This close to them, I could no longer see the towers inside. The wall enclosed a lot of land, and the bulk of the palace sat about as far as it could get from the wall, on the edge of the cliff overlooking the sea far below.

Calling on my Air magic, I lifted off the ground, and the towers came into view again, their pennants snapping in the sea breeze. I kept rising until I could look down on the entire sprawling palace complex and see all the beautiful gardens and forested areas within. Then, I let myself drift towards them—only to slam against an invisible barrier as solid as the wall far below.

I rebounded, rubbing my face. Damn, that had hurt. Cautiously, I inched forward again, arms outstretched protectively, and found the barrier still as unyielding.

Well, that presented a bit of a problem. I soared higher, trailing my hand along it, and felt it begin to curve. It seemed the king had erected an invisible dome over the whole palace compound.

Smart of him, and probably something I should have expected. Not every intruder would be trying to sneak in through the gates, after all.

Disgruntled, I headed for the ground again. Now that I thought about it, it should have been obvious. I knew the palace had wards to prevent unauthorised entry, but since I hadn't had the ability to fly before, I hadn't considered that these wards would have to extend into the sky over the grounds, too. Live and learn.

I landed in sight of the main gates and their twelve serious guards and contemplated my options, which didn't take much time at all. It seemed my only recourse was to do as I had done in Autumn when I'd stalked Lord Eldric and sneak in on the heels of some more legitimate visitor. I crept closer and settled in to wait.

Perhaps twenty minutes later, people began to appear on the streets, though as yet no one had approached the gates directly. I watched a man in the forest greens of a hunter stride down the road towards my position. There was something about those broad shoulders and the way he carried himself ...

Bloody hell! It was Ash.

He walked straight past the gates and continued on towards where I waited. What the hell was he doing here? He had no assignments at the moment, no reason to be anywhere near the capital. My eyes narrowed for a moment as it occurred to me that he could have some treacherous reason for being here, but then I took a deep breath and told myself not to be a fool.

As he drew closer, I was tempted to stick my foot out and trip him. The only thing that stopped me was the realisation of how suspicious that would look to the gate guards.

I had no desire to bring either Ash or myself to their attention, so I contented myself with whispering his name instead.

His body jolted as if I had slapped him. "Sage? Where are you?"

"Walk around the corner and I'll join you," I said.

Safely around the corner, I checked that no one was in sight, then reached out and touched his arm, willing my light-weaving to flow over him as well. Most Day mages would have had trouble extending a light-weaving beyond their own body, but Ni'ishasana's power made it possible. His posture relaxed as I became visible to him.

"What are you doing here?" I demanded.

"Following you."

My eyebrows rose in surprise. "Following me?" Well, at least I knew why I'd had that itchy feeling that I was being watched back in the park in London. "How is that possible?"

"I trailed you until you disappeared into the Wilds. Then I followed—"

"How could you follow me through the Wilds?" I cut in. "I made sure that the gate was closed behind me."

"I didn't. I had to use trial and error. First, I went to Autumn, but there was no sign of you there, so then I tried Spring."

I frowned at him. This wasn't making any sense. "What do you mean, there was no sign of me? You couldn't possibly have searched an entire Realm in, what, half an hour?"

"No need." His grey eyes glittered strangely as he placed a hand over his heart. "I can feel you here. The tie that binds us ... it is a lot stronger than the one that tied me to my father. Maybe it's because you were my apprentice, or maybe ..."

"Or maybe?" I prompted when he paused, fascinated by the struggle I could see in his eyes.

He looked away, then drew a deep breath and seemed to find his courage. When his eyes met mine again, his gaze was sure. "Maybe the bond between us is something more personal."

I opened my mouth, heat rushing up my neck and bloom in my cheeks, then closed it again. He was distracting me from my purpose—but then, what a very fine distraction he was.

My hand was still on his arm, of course, or else he would have been visible, and I was conscious of his warmth and the hardness of the muscle beneath my fingers. I hardly knew what to do with the intensity of emotions I saw in his eyes—but I noted that he hadn't gone as far as giving those feelings words.

"So you merely had to be *in* a Realm to know whether or not I was there?"

He nodded.

Well, that was some bond. I could probably have done that myself, but I was the Serpent, the one wielding all the powers of Ni'ishasana, the source of all those bonds. It surprised me to discover that anyone on the other end of one of those tethers could use it to trace *me*. Probably he was right, and it was the remains of our Adept-to-apprentice bond that allowed him to do it. For the moment, I couldn't afford to think about his other explanation. This was no time to be distracted.

"And when you didn't find me in Spring, you thought to come here? Why?"

He shrugged. "I could have checked every Realm in turn, and I would have if it had become necessary. But power draws power, and Whitehaven seemed as good a place to look as any."

"But why are you following me?"

"I was afraid you were meeting with your father again. He means you harm, Sage. I'm sure of it. He wants the dagger."

Little did he know that I'd already met with my father and managed to live through the experience just fine. "You worry too much."

"And you don't worry enough. So why are you here?"

I shrugged. "Why else? To kill someone, of course."

He frowned. "But we don't have any current targets in the palace."

"The Vipers may not, but I do."

"Who?"

I gazed up at him, my hand moving almost unconsciously to stroke his arm. His protectiveness towards me, though completely unnecessary, was adorable. He was strong and dependable in a world suddenly turned upside down. At the moment, that strength and the way he stood calmly staring down at me, ready to accept any challenge, was very appealing.

I had planned to do this alone, and perhaps the sensible thing to do would be to send him away—and yet my hand closed over his bicep, and I heard myself say, "Sir Ebos."

To his credit, he didn't flinch. He didn't even blink. "That's quite a major target. Why do you wish him dead?"

And just like that, he was with me, unfazed by the danger or the difficulty of the task. He actually looked a little relieved, as if he was glad to be off the difficult topic of emotions and onto something more familiar.

"Because he stands between me and something I want."

I was here to add the magic of Fire—the only Realm it was missing—to Ni'ishasana's arsenal. Fallon needed the power of many Realms working together to bring back Mama—so I would provide the power of *all* of them.

Most of the Vipers' jobs were performed for that same reason—someone wanted something belonging to someone else. Power, usually, or land. Sometimes even a person. The ones that weren't were usually motivated by revenge. Those who stood between ruthless people and what they wanted tended not to last long. It was Ebos's bad luck that he was the only wielder of Fire I knew.

Ash had killed many people for less. So why was he looking at me with that disappointment in his eyes? My reason wasn't pure enough for him? He had no right to judge me. No right even to question me.

I met his gaze squarely. "Take my hand."

"Why?"

"Because your Serpent gave you an order," I snapped.

Carefully expressionless, he offered me his hand.

"And because it will make it easier for me to keep you within my light-weaving," I added, relenting a little as his warm hand closed around my own.

He cocked his head to one side. "You are still working a light-weaving? But I can see you."

I nodded. "That's the way light-weaving works. The weaver can see themselves, but no one else can. And because I'm touching you, you are also drawn into the weaving."

I tugged him around the corner, towards the guarded gate. I hadn't told him my plan, but it didn't take a genius to figure it out, and Ash was certainly smart enough to put two and two together.

A horse clattered down the marble streets towards the gate, and I quickened my steps. At last—this looked promising. The rider drew the horse up before the gate and leaned down to offer the guard captain his papers. The captain ran his eye over them, then handed them back, nodding to his men. Two of them leaped to open the gate.

"Proceed." The captain waved the rider through.

Hard on his heels, Ash and I followed, walking as close as I dared. The horse smelled of sweat and something even less pleasant, which was only to be expected, considering how close we were to its rear end. When it twitched its tail, I got a face full of horsehair.

Then, we were through the gate, and the horse and rider suddenly disappeared. I flinched in surprise and stopped as the guards pulled the gate closed behind us with a clang. The horse and rider had both blinked out of existence as if they had never been.

"The palace," Ash murmured.

I looked up. The palace itself had gone as well, and the path, which had wound off through the trees toward it, now ended as abruptly as if some giant had sheared off the edge of the world. In its place was only featureless white. I rushed forward to that edge and found a barrier as hard as any wall. I dropped Ash's hand and turned, my heart pounding uncomfortably.

"Your light-weaving," Ash said, a knife appearing in his hand as if he expected to be attacked at any moment.

"Not necessary anymore," I said, "and neither is that knife."

I strode back to the gate and tugged as hard as I could, but, as I had suspected, it refused to budge.

Ash glanced around, assessing the situation with his usual cool calm. "We're in a trap, aren't we?"

"Afraid so." I paced out the dimensions of our strange cell. Fiendishly clever. Somehow, the palaces wards had detected our unauthorised entry. Instead of following the horse and rider up the path toward the palace, we had been shunted sideways. "It's some kind of sith."

"A very small one," Ash agreed, watching me prowl along the edges of it, my hand trailing along the featureless wall that hemmed us in. "Can you get us out?"

That was a damn good question. I was betting our entry had also triggered alarms, and someone would be along sooner or later to see exactly what they had managed to catch in their trap. Probably sooner. And we didn't want to be here when they arrived.

"Piece of cake," I said with forced cheer, not sure if I was reassuring him or myself. "Just give me a minute."

He nodded and leaned back against the wall, folding his arms, as if we had all day for me to figure this out. But minutes might be all we had, and he would have realised that, the same as I had. But I appreciated his confidence in me.

I laid my palms flat against the unyielding gate and closed my eyes, drawing on my power. My advantage was that whoever had set this trap had not expected to ensnare anyone of my strength and versatility. I drew in a deep breath and began to work.

Merely forcing the gate to the sith open would be no use—that would only land us back out on the street outside the palace, in the middle of a dozen angry guards who were no doubt on high alert by now. I needed to move this sith as I had done with the Nest the other day, so that its gate opened in a completely different place, though still within the walls of Whitehaven. Then, Ash and I could escape it unseen and continue on with my mission.

The Nest was thousands of times bigger than this tiny sith, which was why it had taken me several hours to reposition it. Something this size should be child's play by comparison—except that whoever had put it here had not meant it to be easy to escape, whereas the Nest was mine to move as I pleased. This would be more of a challenge.

But my blood was up, now, and I refused to be turned away from my goal by this setback. Ebos's hours were numbered.

Ash cleared his throat. "Does it seem to you that the walls are closing in?"

I threw a startled glance at him over my shoulder. He was no longer leaning nonchalantly against the wall, but regarding it with poorly concealed concern. God dammit.

He was right. Our little prison had shrunk. I moved one hand off the door and felt a steady vibration through the wall beside it.

Perhaps the king never meant to come and check on the flies caught in his ingenious web. Perhaps he meant them to die alone, crushed to death, instead.

Ash met my eyes, his voice steady as he asked, "Is there anything I can do to help?"

I shook my head and turned back to the problem of the gate, attempting to focus despite the dread that gnawed at me.

Umarenthe, I said in my mind. *Help me.*

The shadow woman didn't appear—there weren't enough shadows in our sunlit little deathtrap for that— but I heard her voice. *Relax. This has Rothbold's stench all over it. We are more than a match for him. You know what to do. Do it.*

I closed my eyes, willing the magics in the trap to become visible to me. Lines of shining gold sprang to life all over the gate. Though my eyes were still tightly closed, I could feel them through the skin of my palms, radiating up my arms and through my whole body. As I had with the Nest, I sought to become one with the mesh of golden lines. One had to merge with the magic of a sith to be able to command it.

The golden lines pulsed, as if in anger, at my attempts. The magic of the Nest had welcomed me; I had sunk into it as if it were a warm bath. The magic of this tiny sith vibrated against me in fury, lashing out at me with a thousand stinging cuts. I gritted my teeth and pushed harder, though it was like being attacked by a swarm of stinging hornets, each intent on injecting me with their angry poison.

Ash pressed himself against my back. I hadn't realised until that moment that I was sagging. With his hands on my shoulders, I straightened them and pushed yet more of my power against the royal magic. The king was an Earthcrafter, so I focused on the magics that most opposed Earth: Fire, Air, and Ocean. A triple threat to bring to bear against the power of surely the strongest Earthcrafter in all the Realms.

I pushed harder against the angry, buzzing lines of magic. Slowly, slowly, I gathered first one, then another, into my grasp. Pulling and twisting, I sought to bend them to my will, and gradually, darkness crept over the golden lines, dimming their power. At first, it was only a little, and the strain was immense.

"The sith is shrinking," Ash warned in a tight whisper.

I didn't open my eyes to check. The urgency in his voice told me everything I needed to know. All I could do was renew my attack on the king's power, urging the darkness to grow faster, pushing for even more golden lines to dim and bend to my strength.

Long, agonising moments passed until I had them all contained. Shaking from the effort, I opened my eyes and found that I could have reached out and touched the walls on each side without moving from my spot, if I had so wished. Ash said nothing, but his arms snaked around me, supporting me from behind.

I clenched my fists, the mesh of power that controlled

this sith within my grasp, then jerked hard to one side. The world whirled in a dizzying rush—though, to my eyes, nothing actually moved—then settled again as something seemed to snap into place. Confidently, I rested one hand on Ash's brawny forearm, calling up a light-weaving to cover us both, while I jerked open the gate to the sith with the other.

We almost fell through in our rush to escape the trap. Ash breathed a shuddering sigh of relief that ruffled my hair.

"Hush," I cautioned him, then slid my grip down to take his hand.

We were inside the palace, as I had hoped. I glanced behind me at the half-open door we had just stepped through. On the other side lay a perfectly innocuous sitting room, nothing like our tiny, shrinking prison.

I closed the door noiselessly and took a moment to focus on the sith that was still attached to it. This time, it responded more readily to my commands, and I didn't experience that dizzying rush of dislocation as I sent it back to its previous position at the gate. Perhaps it was because I was no longer inside it.

Let Rothbold make what he would of that when he came to uncork his tiny prison and found it empty. I smiled as I pictured his confusion and led Ash down the hallway.

I wasn't personally familiar with much of the palace. I'd been here a couple of times but had mainly only seen the public areas, like the throne room and the ballroom. However, the Vipers had a very detailed set of maps, and I had studied them before I'd set out on this little expedition. As soon as I got my bearings I would know where I was.

The corridor we were in, like the ones I had seen on previous visits, had a gleaming white marble floor. It wasn't very wide, which suggested it wasn't one of the main hallways, and there was no other decoration, nor were there any guards in evidence.

Up ahead, a larger hall crossed over ours, and I could hear a steady tramp of feet approaching from the right. Ash and I exchanged a wary glance and crept closer to the intersection, pausing in the open doorway to what looked like a music room in case we had to retreat in a hurry.

The sound of booted feet striking solid marble grew louder, and the first of a troop of guards came into view. He crossed straight over our corridor, looking neither left nor right, apparently focused on his destination. Several more followed in a tight cluster, which seemed an odd formation until I realised that Rothbold himself was hidden in their midst. I caught a flash of a golden circlet atop dark hair, the forehead beneath it screwed into a frown, and then he was past, with more guards bunched up behind him.

Once the group had moved on, we crept out into the corridor they had used, which was far grander and stretched straight towards a set of double doors at the end. I knew where we were now—and that Rothbold was headed to the main gates.

The quarters assigned to the king's Chosen knights were on the second floor, not far from the royal family. Ash and I trekked through the vast corridors of the palace, passing animated murals where magical battles played out as if the paintings were TV screens. The tiny figures of armies surged back and forth across the landscape as fireballs erupted above them and whole forests marched among them, dealing death and destruction.

Overhead, in the endless marble corridors, fantastically decorated ceilings dripped with jewels. Further on, the jewels gave way to a kind of living décor, where trees rose up on either side, their branches meeting above us. I could have sworn I was outdoors. Magnificent marble staircases swept upwards to the higher levels of the palace, and enormous arched windows beckoned the passer-by to enjoy the gardens that could be seen beyond.

We moved through courtyards full of exotic birds that trilled in three-part harmony as we slipped by them unseen, and fountains that sang with siren voices. Whitehaven was a place of wonders, so big it was possible to get completely turned around if you weren't particularly careful. The Vipers' maps had even shown places that were deliberately designed to trap the unwary intruder so that they would linger there or circle around in the same route unknowingly until the guards came for them. I was careful to avoid those sections and took Ash by a winding route up through the levels of the palace.

When we gained the royal family's wing, the guards doubled, then tripled. Everywhere you looked, another pair of armoured men, silent as statues, was stationed outside a door, and it took all my willpower to walk past them with confidence, despite the protection of my invisibility. Even Ash must have felt the tension—his hand tightened on mine.

We moved as quietly as the Vipers knew how and eventually, we gained the relative safety of the corridor where the king's Chosen were housed. A pair of guards stood, their pikes at attention, at the entrance to the corridor, but the individual doors opening off it had none. We crept past them, all the way down to the last door on the left, which was Sir Ebos's. I glanced back at the guards, but they were facing away from us, guarding the corridor from intruders, unaware that we had already well and truly intruded.

I turned the door handle with infinite patience and was rewarded with the tiniest click as the latch released. Clearly, Sir Ebos felt no need to lock his door with two guards monitoring the traffic in the corridor.

He was about to learn his mistake.

I eased the door open a fraction of an inch. The room felt empty, but I sent Umarenthe to check it out.

There's no one here, she said after a moment, so I opened the door wide enough for Ash and me to slip inside, then closed it behind us.

It was a massive room, far bigger than I had been expecting, though it stood to reason that the king would honour his Chosen with accommodation befitting their station. One wall was taken up by a long row of tall, arched windows, bigger than those of any human cathedral. The glass in them was crystal clear, offering a view over a spectacular tropical garden. The bright plumage of exotic birds could be seen flitting among tall palms and other jungle species I couldn't name. Opposite the great wall of glass was a fireplace big enough that a dozen men could stand abreast inside it without having to crouch. Did Sir Ebos feel the cold? That would make sense, since dragons were reptiles.

At the opposite end of the room from where we had entered, double doors equally as huge led into what I presumed must be the bedroom, although they were closed at the moment. A shadow slipped out from under them as I watched and formed itself into the shape of Umarenthe, who glided forward unerringly to meet me.

What now? she asked.

"We lie in wait for him here," I said to both her and Ash.

Ash nodded, and the knife appeared in his hand again. "It could be a long wait," he pointed out. "You should try to get some rest—you must be tired after the effort of escaping that trap. I'll keep watch."

I arched an eyebrow. "Sleep? And miss the anticipation of the kill? I don't care how long it takes; I will be waiting right here."

And the second Sir Ebos walked through that door, I would be ready to drive my dagger straight into his heart.

20

*A*sh was right. It was a long wait.

King Rothbold had probably kept his knights busy scouring the palace and its enormous grounds all night for any trace of the little mice who had escaped his clever trap. The hours of the night had dragged past as I kept my long watch, and I had resigned myself to not seeing the room's occupant until he came back after daybreak to go to sleep.

But it was still night when I heard his voice in the corridor outside, greeting the guards, then his footsteps, almost completely muffled by the carpet in the corridor. My whole body tensed at the sound. Ash and I exchanged a quick glance, and I shifted my grip on Ni'ishasana, anticipation flooding me with adrenaline.

The door handle began to move— more slowly than a glacier, it seemed to me in my heightened state of awareness—and then the door opened.

He was finally here. I held my breath as time sped up again.

We let him enter and close the door behind him, since there was no sense in making our job harder by alerting the guards, but this turned out to be a mistake.

He walked past us, one step, two steps, three. Then, Ash and I leapt as one for his back, Ni'ishasana vibrating eagerly in my hand. My eyes were glued to the place on the knight's back where I needed to strike to slide the dagger through his ribs and drive it into his heart.

The man must have had the hearing of a bat, or else he'd sensed a disturbance in the air, because he twisted at the last second, drawing his sword like a bolt of lightning and slashing it out before him.

Ash let go of my hand to avoid being skewered and immediately popped into view. Ebos's eyes narrowed as he stepped in with a killing thrust, but I charged, stabbing at him with Ni'ishasana.

Somehow, he managed to evade that blow, too. Ni'ishasana sliced through his armour like butter, but it only left a long slash across his back.

Ebos whirled, now aware that there was more than one enemy in the room, and sensibly backed up toward the fireplace. With an imperious gesture, he swept the flames from the hearth and out into the room in a lethal strike. Fire boiled up and hurtled towards us, twisting like a tornado.

I blasted it with Air and sent it roaring back in his face. My Air also picked up two chairs, sending them tumbling towards him in the maelstrom.

He ducked one and swatted the other out of the air contemptuously, turning it into so much kindling. Then, he prowled through the flame as if it wasn't there, sword in hand and a feral grin on his face.

"Who are you, little man?" His gaze was fixed on Ash, but his nostrils flared. Was he trying to sniff me out? "Could you think of no easier way to die?"

With his free hand, he hurled another blast of fire at Ash, the only opponent whose position he could be certain of. This one didn't come from the fireplace, but sprang to life in his palm, like a living extension of his body, and hurtled through the air in a well-aimed and deadly ball.

I thrust my arm out at the same time as Ash lifted his, and a wall of ice slammed down between him and the oncoming fiery destruction.

Well, would you look at that? Great minds did think alike. Satisfaction at this rare display of harmony between us warmed me. With the combination of both our powers, the wall of ice was a majestic thing indeed, and rose all the way to the high ceiling above. The large chandelier in the middle of the ceiling rocked, its crystals tinkling, as icicles formed on it.

Ebos's brows rose. "Impressive, but you'll need more than that to save you."

Behind me, the door to the chamber flew open, and the two guards from the corridor appeared, swords drawn.

"Sir Ebos!" the first man through the door cried, rushing into the room. His companion took one look and fled, presumably going for reinforcements. Damn, we would have to hurry this up.

The first guard, in his eagerness to reach the traitor knight's side, charged straight past me, so close he almost brushed against me. Calmly, I reversed my grip on Ni'ishasana and clubbed him in the back of the head with the heavy hilt as he passed. He went down like a sack of potatoes and lay still.

"So that's where you are," Ebos said, his eyes glinting.

Another fireball swept out. I sidestepped it with ease, and an armchair burst into abrupt flame. I frowned. That had seemed too easy—despite how close we were standing, the fire had come nowhere near me. Perhaps he'd been worried about accidentally incinerating the downed guard.

In no more than an instant, the fire had consumed the chair, reducing it to a pile of ash. Ebos gestured with his hand, and the ash rose up. Guided by a baking hot wind, it flew all over my side of the room, plastering everything in a grimy layer of hot ash—including me.

"Clever," I said, focusing on the great stones of the hearth behind him. Now I was visible, if only as an ashy silhouette. "But not clever enough."

I heaved, and the stone wall flowed like water under my will. Stony hands reached out and grasped Sir Ebos in implacable fingers, dragging him back against the wall. He strained against their granite grip, his face reddening with the effort. He managed to rip one of the stony hands free of the wall, but I merely grew another in its place.

At my urging, the stone at his back flowed away so that

he began to sink into the wall. His struggles increased, and I smiled, advancing toward him. Ni'ishasana vibrated with eagerness in my hand.

"I will pulverise your flesh and grind your bones to dust," I promised. "But first, I will take your power for my own."

His eyes widened at the sight of the twisted blade, gleaming dully under a layer of ash.

And then he smiled.

"Don't count your dragons before they're hatched, assassin."

His skin blackened, and his face bulged and flowed like molten glass, forming a new and terrifying shape as he doubled and tripled in size. Black scales rippled over him, appearing from nowhere, and the stones of the wall groaned like some rocky giant in its death throes.

A roar like a thousand thunderstorms filled the room, and suddenly, the wall exploded, shards of rock flying everywhere.

I threw up a hasty ice shield and felt the blows that hammered it as if they fell on my own skin. The ice creaked and groaned, shattering almost as fast as I could reform it under the onslaught. Then, Sir Ebos spread his mighty wings and shook the last of the rock from his body like a dog shaking water from its coat, spraying further destruction through the room.

The long, nightmare face of the dragon turned toward me, and he opened his jaws. They were lined with teeth longer than my arm, but I was more concerned with the molten glow lighting the back of his throat. It was like looking into the heart of a furnace, or maybe a volcano. A volcano that was about to erupt.

I sprinted across the room and dived behind Ash's massive ice shield. The dragon roared, bringing icicles crashing down from the chandelier. Each one landed like a spear, digging a small divot out of the marble floor as it shattered.

That seemed like as good a plan as any. Immediately, I began tearing great, long shafts of wickedly pointed ice from the top of the wall and hurling them at the dragon in a continuous rain of death.

The dragon bellowed, then sprayed fire at the incoming missiles. Only one made it through, though it tore a good-sized hole in one outstretched leathery wing. That was good. Anything that kept the beast earthbound gave me more of a chance.

Somehow, I had to get Ebos back into human form, since I had no chance of taking his life with Ni'ishasana while he wore his dragon one. Ni'ishasana brimmed with mighty magics, but its blade was only the length of my forearm. It could probably pierce that armoured hide, but it seemed highly unlikely that it could reach deep enough to hit one of the dragon's vital organs.

This night was not turning out as I had expected. My first real assassination and everything was going to shit.

Beside me, Ash began hurling vicious shards of ice, too, but the dragon played its fire along the ice wall, and soon, we were ankle-deep in water. I left the maintenance of the wall to Ash and dragged a stone directly from the fireplace to smash against the dragon's head from behind.

Ebos roared and swung his great head to face the new threat. I pelted him with more stones, destroying the fireplace completely to get enough ammunition for the job. He roared in pain as the heavy blocks slammed into him, and tucked his vulnerable wings close to his side. Lashing his ridged tail, he batted stones out of the air. I merely picked them up and hurled them at him again. I could play this game forever.

Seeming to realise this, the dragon snarled and flicked the latest missile straight at the ice wall. It hit directly in front of me, and a massive crack appeared, sending fine lines in a dangerous web across the whole face of our protective wall.

Ash narrowed his eyes and renewed his icy assault on the dragon, whipping up a blizzard to whirl around the creature.

"Good thinking. He's a reptile."

Ash nodded. "If we can get him cooled down fast enough, all the fight will go out of him." But his voice trembled with effort, and I could see the strain that keeping up this barrage of magic was having on him.

I turned back to the battle and renewed my assault with the rocks, but this time, I dropped them from straight above. There would be no more tail flicking.

The dragon roared again, though there was something different about the sound now. Was that pain? I could barely see the creature through the storm of ice and snow that filled the room.

Another blast of fire raked our wall, but it was weaker than the previous one. Ebos was struggling now. It wouldn't take much longer to subdue him. Timing would be crucial. More guards were no doubt on their way, and we had to defeat the dragon before they got here. It was just a matter of who could hold out longest.

Evidently, Ebos realised this, too. Another flash of fire scoured the ice and snow. Black scales rushed past on the other side of our ice wall, appearing suddenly from out of the blizzard. The beast was bleeding from several jagged holes where our ice spears had managed to penetrate his scaly hide. His spiked tail loomed out of the snow, and I threw my strength into the wall, firming the ice in readiness for a mighty impact.

But the tail only struck a glancing blow, almost an afterthought, as Ebos surged past. The ice wall wasn't his target. Instead, glass exploded as he smashed straight through the high, windowed wall to the outside world and spread his massive wings.

"He's getting away!" I yelled, launching myself into the air, the winds of my Air magic holding me aloft. Ash ran after me, his boots crunching across broken glass and pieces of shattered ice.

The dragon laboured to gain height, its massive leathery wings pumping, apparently unhindered by the single tear our ice spears had managed to inflict on that enormous wingspan. I arrowed through the sky toward him, determined not to lose him now.

But it seemed that Ebos had no intention of running. The dragon banked into a tight curve and came roaring back toward us, its massive jaws agape. Shouts rose from the palace, and I risked a glance behind. Guards were pouring out of the ruin of Ebos's chamber and fanning out into the jungle gardens.

My heart clenched with sudden fear. Ash was down there, earthbound. Alone. They would find him, and they would show no mercy. I scanned the gardens for a glimpse of him, but he was too good at his job; I found no sign of him.

I spun in mid-air and hurled an enormous blast of Air at the dragon, hoping to smash him from the sky, but it barely troubled Ebos's flight as he arrowed down out of the dark.

He opened his mouth as he levelled out above the trees and took a long strafing run across the garden, blasting it with flame. The guards yelled and stopped their headlong run into the trees, falling back against the building.

Ebos meant to burn Ash out. Perhaps he sensed that this would be the only way to distract me from my target. I swooped down, the wind rushing against my face as I sped above the trees on a course to intercept the dragon. With my Spring magic, I urged those trees to reach up and entangle the great beast.

Vines shot into the sky, and tree branches whipped about, doubling in length in seconds. They all reached for the dragon as he soared overhead. Several strong vines lashed around one enormous clawed foot, but the dragon's speed was too great. The vines simply ripped in half as the monstrous beast continued on.

I hurled ice after him, but he was harder to hit in the open sky. Shouts rose from the garden below me, and two armoured figures lifted into the air, powered by their own streams of Air magic. They hurtled towards me.

Where was Ash? I darted lower, sending a sheet of ice toward the two Air mages as I searched frantically for any sign of him. One of the guards managed to duck, but the other fell screaming from the sky, like a frozen comet, and crashed into the trees below. The dragon banked again and surged back toward me, roaring defiance.

There! Was that a flash of a black-clad figure at the edge of the flaming trees?

Yes! A hail of ice spears launched into the sky as the dragon passed overhead, ripping three new holes in one leathery wing.

Ebos screamed and pivoted almost on a wingtip. I would never have believed that such a vast beast could manoeuvre so tightly, but already he was almost on top of Ash's position. Desperately, I called on every ounce of Air magic available to me and hurtled through the night sky. The dragon's mouth opened, ready to incinerate Ash and every living thing below.

I screamed, though the rush of my passage whipped the sound away, and hurled more ice at the beast. If I could get a few ice spears down its molten gullet, perhaps there would be no more flame.

The dragon's vast, reptilian head turned, tracking me through the sky. In the confusion of the fight, I must have lost my grip on my shadow-weaving. No time to fix that now. Ebos drew in a deep breath, and I threw out ice as fast as I could make it, diverting some of my Air magic to hold it in place in the sky. I needed a shield and I needed it fast.

The dragon breathed out in a long, deafening roar, but there was no flame. Instead, great gouts of liquid spattered against my ice shield.

Spit? Was Ebos *spitting* at me?

It happened so quickly I didn't realise the truth until it was too late—until the acid had eaten through my wall of ice as if it didn't exist and pelted onto my unprotected skin.

I screamed in agony and dropped from the sky.

21

Twisting and contorting in terrible pain, I fell to earth, crashing through the treetops, barely holding onto consciousness. I had enough Air left to cushion my fall so that I slammed to earth without breaking any bones. Though, in truth, I'm not sure I would have noticed a broken bone over the bright agony of the acid burns.

Ash rushed to my side. With great presence of mind, he buried me in a mountain of snow, bringing immediate relief. With his help, I struggled free of the snow, its chill easing my burned skin even as it washed the acid away. Above us, the dragon trumpeted in triumph.

"Quickly," Ash said, drawing me staggering after him into the unburned sections of the garden. "Ebos will strike again at any moment. He knows he has us cornered."

"Does he?" We'd see about *that*.

I reached out for Ash's hand and nearly shrieked in agony as his fingers closed on my burned skin. I took a moment, trembling and trying to force the pain away by sheer willpower, sucking in laboured breaths.

"Don't let go," I warned him, though I had to force the words out through gritted teeth.

Calling on my Earth magic, I softened the ground beneath our feet, and Ash and I simply sank into the growing hole in the soil. Once we were deep enough, I closed the pit over the top of us, retaining only a small pocket of air around us so that we could breathe. Then, I forced the pocket out ahead of us, forming a horizontal shaft that burrowed out in the direction of our travel and closed up again behind us as we passed.

Ash called a faelight so that we could see—not that there was much to see except the dark earth, dripping with worms and small, skittery creatures. Tree roots criss-crossed over our heads, occasionally reaching down the walls of my temporary tunnel. I had to use Spring magic to gently encourage them out of the way.

Holding his hand, I headed off down the passage. My Earth and Spring senses told me roughly where we were within the grounds of Whitehaven, and I headed for one of the smaller side gates in as straight a line as I could manage. No doubt the wards would stop me burrowing directly underneath the walls, so we would have to come up and fight our way through.

But that was a problem for future me. Present me was doing all she could just to hold the Earthcrafting in place while still managing to put one foot in front of the other.

The longer we travelled through our eerie tunnel, the more I staggered. Every brush against the dirt walls caused more pain to my burned body. My clothes had protected me somewhat, but some of the acid had eaten straight through before Ash's snow had washed it off, and my shirt hung in rags around me, showing glimpses of raw, seeping skin beneath.

The journey passed in a haze of suffering. Fae bodies had immense healing abilities, but mine was only half fae, and not all of Ni'ishasana's might could help me in this. Given a few days' rest, I would probably be fine—but rest was still a long way away. First, I had to survive.

The earth around us trembled, and our tunnel abruptly constricted as a massive wave of Earth magic crashed against mine.

"What's happening?" Ash cried as the floor of our tunnel bucked.

He caught me before I fell, but I whimpered in pain. "It's the king."

It had to be—I felt like a swimmer being circled by a great white shark as his power butted against mine again. It was immense. Monstrous. Deadly. There was no way I could fight back in my current condition. Ni'ishasana might contain unimaginable power, but it still needed a wielder, and there was only so much my body could cope with.

"We've got to get out." I angled our tunnel towards the surface, knowing that it could soon become our grave if I couldn't escape the king's power. The earth parted abruptly, vomiting us out in a strange eruption. We must have looked like zombies crawling from the grave, both drenched from our efforts with ice and snow, with dirt plastering our damp skin.

Ash's hand was still in mine, and I spread a light-weaving over the two of us. We had come up in the middle of a large rose garden and the area was too well-lit for shadow-weaving. I hastily closed the hole behind us and righted a couple of rose bushes that had not enjoyed the experience.

"Quick," I said, spreading ice all over the ground in an effort to disguise our location from the king. "There's a small gate over there."

Ebos's shattering roars sounded in the distance behind us, and the whole palace was lit up like a beacon. Figures of winged fae soared around its towers and spires like moths against the light, and I knew that more guards would be spreading out through the grounds, searching for us.

Pain and exhaustion were eating into my reserves. I didn't know how many more enemies I could take on. My heart was hammering from the effort of resisting the king's magic, and I certainly didn't want to have to face the damned dragon again. They were a lot harder to kill than I had been expecting.

The side gate, though smaller than the main gate, was still large enough to admit a carriage or several horsemen riding side-by-side. Through its gilded bars, I could see half a dozen guards standing stiffly at attention in the street outside. Green lawns covered in ice rolled unbroken between us and the gate.

"Let's go," I muttered, "before I pass out."

Ash ran an assessing glance over me, then lifted me into his arms like a child. I couldn't help a gasp of pain as his arms pressed against my tender flesh, and I cast a hasty glance at the distant guards in case they had heard. Being invisible didn't make us soundproof. But no one turned in our direction.

Ash hurried across the icy lawn. "Where is the king? Can you tell?"

A strange rumble sounded behind us. Over Ash's shoulder, I saw the whole rose garden sink into the ground, and then the cave-in began to spread, lawn crumbling away and falling into the growing hole.

"Run," I whispered as the hole reached out for us, lapping almost at Ash's heels.

Ash exploded into motion, running as hard as he could for the gate. With a grunt of effort, I slammed the gate open with a vast gust of Air.

The fury of my Air hurled the guardsmen aside like toy soldiers even as it covered the sound of Ash's rapid approach. Still, the guards were professionals, and they were swiftly on their feet again, swords drawn and magics at the ready. Our advantage was that they didn't know exactly what they were guarding against, so they watched the moving sinkhole, expecting an enemy to leap out of it, not realising that the enemy was already upon them.

I pulled a tight bubble of Air around us to muffle Ash's footsteps as he hurtled past the guards. He ran at top speed, as if I was no burden to him at all, and I couldn't help admiring his strength even as my own faded. He needed to hurry, before I lost my grasp on Air, light-weaving, and consciousness all at once. I sagged in his arms, the jolting motion of his run sending searing stabs of agony through my body with every step.

My head spun and the world turned fuzzy and indistinct around me as Ash gained the opening of a wide boulevard that led away from the palace. My light-weaving wavered and I strained to hold onto it as I heard a shout from the guards behind us. Ash powered on, leaping the low stone wall of some public building featuring a gleaming colonnade of arches at the top of a long flight of wide steps.

Finally, the effort of his headlong flight was beginning to show. Ash panted beside my ear, stirring my damp hair, as he laboured up the steps. His goal was clear—any one of those archways would form a perfect gateway into the Wilds.

Glancing over his shoulder, I saw the closest guard stop in the middle of the street to draw a bow. A bow. Where had that come from?

Not important, I told myself sternly. *Focus on the fact that he can see you.* Clearly, I had lost my grip on the light-weaving. Hastily, I sent another blast of Air to disrupt the arrow's flight and managed to knock the man from his feet into the bargain.

My vision swam, and darkness beckoned, mist boiling around us. Unconsciousness claimed me as Ash leaped through the arch. The last thing I remembered was the tingle of threshold magic over my burnt skin.

22

We weren't in the Wilds when I opened my eyes, so I must have been out for a while. A sky filled with the clear, pale light of early morning greeted me.

The air was frigid, and I shivered in my damp clothes, but I was lying on something hard and surprisingly warm, which turned out to be rock, black and smooth. Glancing around, I saw clumps of snow on damp ground amid small, bare trees, and black rock walls rearing in an almost complete circle around me.

"Where are we?" I looked around, but Ash was nowhere in sight. I lay next to a pool that gave off a smell like rotten eggs, and I wrinkled my nose as I gazed out across the still water, noting little tendrils of steam rising from it. The air was sharp and cold in my lungs, and somehow thinner than I was used to. Were we in Winter? What was this place?

I groped for the reassurance of the dagger and was

speared with a lance of sheer terror when I didn't find it thrust through my belt. After a moment, however, I located it on the rock beside me.

"Ash?" I called, a little louder this time.

Nothing stirred. Icy dread had begun to creep along my shivering limbs when he appeared from a break in the encircling walls that I hadn't noticed. In fact, unless you had been staring straight at it, it would have been very difficult to see at all, though the camouflage seemed a natural formation and not something made of magic.

Ash had an armful of some kind of weed or herb. He crossed the slushy ground toward me with quick steps, and a rare smile bloomed on his hard face. "You're awake. How do you feel?"

"Like absolute shit," I replied. "As if I've been chewed up and spat out by something particularly large and toothy. Although the fact that I'm not dead yet suggests that our situation has improved at least a little. Where are we?"

"Not far from Kelvarus, the town where ... where I used to live."

I had the impression he'd been about to say something different, but I lost my train of thought as he crossed to the small fire he'd built up nearby and added the weeds to a pot that was boiling merrily there.

I eyed the pot in confusion. "Where did you get that?"

He flashed his teeth at me in another tight grin. "From Kelvarus. This shanovar will form a paste that you will find very soothing, once I've reduced it down." He poked the weeds with a stick, pushing them more fully under the boiling water.

I wasn't familiar with shanovar—my apprentice studies had been cut short, after all—but I had every faith in him. The man knew his stuff. For a moment, I let myself relax into the sensation of being taken care of by someone else.

The boiling greenery had a sharp, pungent smell that cut across the rotten-egg scent of the thermal pool permeating the area. I closed my eyes and listened to the snap and crackle of small branches as Ash fed them to the flames of his little cookfire.

"Why are we here?" I asked. I was shivering, despite my best efforts to control my own body temperature. The fight with Ebos, and then with the king, had taken so much out of me that it was taking a concentrated effort when normally it was an unconscious process. "My bed at the Nest would have been a lot more comfortable than this rock."

"Did you really want the Vipers to see you like this, weak and vulnerable?"

His voice came from right next to me, though I hadn't heard him move. My eyes flew open as his fingers began unbuttoning my shirt.

"What are you doing? Ouch!"

He ignored both my protest and my squirming. Carefully, he eased the shirt down my burnt arms and threw it aside. "You're going into shock. Regulating your own temperature is clearly beyond you right now. You need to warm up."

"And taking off my clothes is the way to do that?" I'd

dreamed of him undressing me, but not like this. I was burnt and dirty; my right bicep was seeping clear fluid from a painful cluster of acid spatters, and I stank of sweat and smoke.

"Getting you into the water is the way to do that." He hoisted me into his arms and stepped into the pool, fully clothed, wading out until he was chest-deep and I was floating, supported by his strength.

I sucked in a pained breath as the warm water heated my skin. Parts of me were frozen almost solid, and the water felt boiling against those. Other parts were already burned, and those parts were convinced I'd been dipped in molten lava. Both parts agreed that Ash was trying to kill them.

"I thought cold water was better for burns? You're going to cook me." I could hardly keep still, writhing in his arms as my numbed skin came tingling back to life. It felt as though I was on fire.

"Stop complaining and take off your pants."

He let my feet drop, and I stood up, glaring at him. "What for?" I already felt oddly vulnerable, with him fully dressed and me in a lacy black bra. Thank goodness I hadn't worn an old one with sagging elastic. That would have made my humiliation complete.

He made an impatient sound and strode out of the water. His wet shirt clung to every muscle as he bent and removed the pot of shanovar from the fire, then carefully tipped the sodden mass out onto the warm stone around the pool and spread it to cool with a stick. "The acid burnt through your pants in at least three places. We'll need to treat your legs, too."

I struggled with the button on my jeans, my cold fingers and the wet fabric making everything stiff. But I didn't want to be stripped like a child. I was the Serpent of the Vipers, and I could damn well undress myself.

Even if I nearly fell over and inhaled a lungful of water in the process. Fortunately, Ash was too focused on whatever he was doing with the shanovar to notice. Cooling it faster with Winter magic, by the looks of it. He'd worked it into a thick lump of a clay-like consistency by the time I had my jeans off, and I lobbed them to splash in a sodden lump at his feet.

He stepped into the pool again, coils of steam swirling about his legs, but stopped when he was knee-deep. "Come here."

I eyed the green muck in his hands as I approached. Anything was better than looking into his face, watching him watch me. Though his expression was as businesslike as any doctor's, I felt horribly exposed as I rose from the water, revealed in all my half-naked, burnt and scabbed mess. I had never felt less attractive in my life.

"Is this going to hurt?" I asked suspiciously.

"It will cause more pain than you ever imagined you could feel and still live," he said, his tone grave.

"Really?" My gaze shot to his face in horror and saw another smile bloom there.

"Of course not. It would hardly be much use as a healing salve in that case. Show me that arm." He slathered green goop on my right bicep, where the burns were worst, his fingers spreading it with calm competence. "Don't be such a baby. You'll feel better in a moment."

I opened my mouth to retort that he was *hurting* me, despite his obvious care, when the pain of even his light touch suddenly faded, replaced by the most divine numbness. My knees almost buckled with relief at the sudden cessation of pain, and I moaned like a porn star. "Oh, my God. That feels so *good*."

He started on the other arm, and I let my head tip back, eyes half-closed in ecstasy. His fingers trailed down my arm, leaving bliss in their wake.

"Yessss. Give it to me."

I swayed on my feet, and then he started on my chest. His fingers on my skin there, so close to my breasts, produced a tingling of a different kind, and I peeked up at him through strands of wet hair. His face held an expression of fierce concentration, but there was something else in those grey eyes ...

I closed my hand around his wrist, holding his fingers splayed against my chest. "What about you?" My voice was husky. "You have some holes in your shirt, too. Let me look at you."

"I'll be fine," he said, not moving.

I stared up at him, no longer cold in the slightest. Heat bloomed within me as I backed away, drawing him with me into deeper water. Then, I let go of his wrist and began to undo the buttons of his ruined shirt.

He watched me with wary stillness. "What are you doing? I said I'm fine."

Slowly, I slid the shirt from his shoulders, my hands

caressing their way across his warm skin, then sliding down over taut biceps. I trailed my fingers down each arm, and the shirt fell into the water behind him.

"Clearly, that was a lie. Look at this." The hard planes of his chest were pocked with holes where the acid had eaten into his flesh. "You look like an extra from a zombie movie. Give me some of that stuff."

Wordlessly, he held out the salve, and I scooped a generous amount and dabbed it carefully on each burn, my fingers lingering on his skin. It was so soft, and yet there was such strength beneath the surface. I stroked idle circles across his chest, the water swirling around me as I moved closer.

We were almost touching, but it wasn't close enough. My hunger for him was enormous. I wanted to be *in* his skin, curled up inside him, knowing every curve and angle of his body. Knowing every thought that flitted behind those inscrutable grey eyes.

But at the same time, I wanted the touch of his hands on *my* body, wanted to be crushed by his weight and feel his mouth possess mine. I wanted to give myself over to him—and for the first time in a while, I felt the dagger stir. It didn't like not being in control. I could feel it, in the dim recesses of my mind, recoiling at the thought of ceding such power to someone else.

How strange that it had been so quiet and I hadn't noticed—how long had it been since Umarenthe had chimed in with her opinion on what I was doing? I cast my mind back, even as my hands busied themselves. She had answered when we had first entered Sir Ebos's rooms, but the last time she had spoken before that was at my father's house. A whole night of silence—silence and a sense of calm. That ever-present anger had disappeared, too.

I pressed my lips to Ash's skin. His arms crept around me, almost as if he wasn't aware of what he was doing, and pulled me against him, closing the distance between us. Fitting myself against his body felt like coming home, and I pressed against his warmth, forgetting the conundrum of the dagger. My arms slid around his waist as I kissed another spot over his heart. My lips lingered there, tasting his skin, and his heart hammered against my mouth.

"Does that feel better?" I asked between kisses, my mouth working its way up towards his throat.

"Sage," he groaned as my teeth nipped at the tendon in his neck.

Then, one hand tipped my face up to his, and his lips claimed mine in a passionate kiss. His tongue plundered my mouth, and a thrill of lust surged through me. This was no gentle expression of love, but a cry from his soul, and the desperation of it awoke an answering urgency in me. My tongue explored his mouth as my nails raked across his naked back, but it still wasn't enough. I wanted more. *Needed* more.

Without breaking that toe-curling kiss, I worked my hands between our bodies and started tugging at the button of his pants. I almost had it undone when his mouth swooped on my neck, and I lost all focus for a moment. God, that felt good. My nipples tingled with desire, and it took me long seconds to remember what I was doing.

The button came undone at last, and I fumbled at his zipper. A fire raged inside me. I needed him to quench it *now*. I hooked my thumbs in his waistband and tugged, but the wet fabric clung stubbornly to his hips.

"Take off your pants." My heart was pounding so hard I could barely speak, and my voice came out in a breathless gasp.

The effect was immediate. He froze, then lifted his head, pulling away from me. His lips were swollen, his eyes drugged with desire, but his voice was cold. "Is that an order?"

I stared up at him, desire and sudden rage warring within me as the dagger sprang to life.

He thinks he's too good to follow orders, it whispered.

Ni'ishasana was right. The minute I gave him anything that sounded even remotely like an order, all his fire became ice, leaving me hanging.

You need a better man, the dagger said. *A different man, who will delight in serving you.*

But I wanted *this* one. My need for him was overpowering, a physical ache that throbbed at my core.

He thinks he is too much of a man to take orders from a woman.

I swallowed, fighting for control. His eyes had hardened—how could he cool down so fast? I opened my mouth. All I had to do was tell him it was no order, that there was no such thing as orders between us, because what we had was special. But the words wouldn't come. Rage flooded through me, making me shiver with its intensity. I was the Serpent. I didn't have to explain myself to anyone.

That's right. He has too much pride. Cast him down.

"Why is it always about orders, Ash?"

"Because I am bound to obey every order from the Serpent." His eyes bored into mine. "Just as you are bound to the dagger. But it doesn't have to be like that." His voice was unsteady. He wasn't as cool as he appeared.

"It doesn't?"

"We could destroy the dagger, Sage. And then we'd both be free."

Kill him! the dagger raged, and I staggered as its fury hit me like a blow. *End this madness now!*

The dagger lay on the rock next to the pool, only a few short steps away. All I had to do was pick it up and drive it into his heart.

"No!" I cried, feeling the power build within me as the red mist began to coat my vision.

Ash thought I was talking to him. "I'll help you. We can do this. We *have* to do this."

He was so beautiful. So earnest. Droplets of water stood on his sculpted pecs and lingered on his bruised lips. The man had the body of a god—a pissed-off god, at the moment, but still a god. He didn't know how close he was to death. How hard I fought for his life.

Yes, the dagger insisted. *Kill him now. It's the only way.*

"It's the only way, Sage," Ash said.

I didn't have much time left. Another minute and I'd lose control. So, I reached for the magic that bound me to Ash. It appeared to me as a line of blue light stretching between us. I could feel his anger on the other end of that tether, mixed with a black despair. Desperately, I tore at the light, ripping it to pieces.

I felt it in my soul when the bond was severed. My consciousness of Ash's inner life disappeared, snuffed out in an instant.

He felt it, too—his eyes widened in shock. "What have you done?"

"Given you what you've always wanted." I shoved him away. "You're no longer a Viper, Ash. You're free to go. Get out of here."

23

$\mathcal{I}$ stormed out of there still shaking with fury, my damp clothes clutched in one fist, the dagger in the other. Ash called my name as I opened a gate to the Wilds, but I ignored him and stepped through, letting it snap shut before he could follow.

Only then did I let my iron grip on my power relax. Bent over with my hands on my knees, I drew in deep, ragged breaths until the killing fury subsided.

Lady save me, I had almost killed Ash. *Ash*. That was so many kinds of wrong I could hardly believe it, but part of me had really wanted to do it. What was *wrong* with me?

I stared at the dagger in my hand, but it was quiet now. Satisfied, perhaps. After all, it had got what it wanted— Ash might still be alive, but he was out of my life. I would probably never see him again.

A chill pierced me at the thought, and I rubbed my cold arms, dislodging a chunk of Ash's healing salve. What now? Ash had been the best thing about living among the

Vipers. The one person I had looked forward to seeing when I woke up every night. The one person who had cared for me.

I scrubbed at another remnant of shanovar paste—the most recent evidence of his care. His love. *Call it what it is.* He may never have said the words, but his actions showed it, time and again. And now he was gone, freed because it was the only way I could think to save him.

And I was cold, and it was time to stop standing around, half-naked, feeling sorry for myself. I dried the remnants of my clothes with a blast of Summer magic. The pants were in pretty good shape, apart from a few acid holes, but the shirt was more hole than shirt, and it flapped around me as I moved through the Wilds.

I wasn't ready to return to the Nest. The thought of going back there without Ash held exactly zero appeal at the moment. It would take me a little while to get used to the idea, to stop feeling like there was a gaping, Ash-sized hole in the world. In the meantime, I bent the magic of the Greenways towards taking me somewhere that felt more homelike.

It wasn't until I stepped into an alley not far from The Drunken Irishman, all ready to drink myself into a stupor, that the problem of my shredded shirt occurred to me.

Gah. I was thinking like a person with no magic. I could Glamour myself a new one. Or use a light-weaving. I had options now.

Still, I hesitated at the mouth of the alley. To my right, a couple of minutes' walk away, was The Drunken Irishman, my former home away from home—scene of many a late night with friends, drinking and laughing, playing in the band, or just playing pool. To my left, a much longer walk —but still within walking distance—was my actual former home. And suddenly, my heart ached for home. For the comfort of a familiar place where no one was judging me or plotting against me, where the absence of a certain sombre assassin might not hurt as much.

Plus, I had a wardrobe full of unshredded shirts there.

My mind made up, I headed for Willow's sith, walking the quiet morning streets alone. The Drunken Irishman would have been shut at this hour anyway. I wrapped a light-weaving around me to be safe—it was easier than having to fob off concerned citizens if anyone saw me.

My shirt hung in tatters around me, revealing swathes of angry red skin and grungy clumps of healing salve that clung on tenaciously. I looked as though I'd just emerged from a swamp somewhere, though thankfully I didn't smell quite that bad. Only a faint aroma of rotten eggs still clung to me from my dip in the Winter pool. First thing I was doing when I got back to the Nest was taking a nice, long bath.

And maybe putting Ni'ishasana in a timeout on its stand in my office. The excitement of wielding my powers had faded, replaced with an uneasy awareness that something wasn't right. Almost killing Ash had shaken me to the core. I was the wielder of Ni'ishasana, wasn't I? So why did I feel as though sometimes the dagger was the one in charge?

I had never felt so alone as I stalked the streets. The Vipers feared me or hated me. Sometimes both at once.

They wanted me dead or they wanted my favour and were prepared to offer me smiles to get it, whatever their true feelings. My former friends—well, we hardly moved in the same circles, now, did we? The leader of a bunch of deadly assassins couldn't just drop in for a friendly pint with the leader of a soft rock band. One of these things was not like the other.

And then there was Ash. He'd been my greatest supporter, the rock that I'd leaned on, and he was gone. The chances of my ever seeing him again now that he'd finally gained his long-sought freedom were so vanishingly small they weren't worth considering. And yet, I did consider them, all the way down Victoria Road, while people whizzed past in their cars, unaware there was anyone on the footpath.

I missed his strong, steady presence already. I missed knowing he had my back. And I missed the way those cool grey eyes warmed a little when I entered a room, then lingered on me as if he couldn't quite bring himself to look away.

All of which is stupid, I told myself, trying for a firm tone. *You can't go through the rest of your life pining for him.* I needed a serious pep talk. Why should the loss of one man make me feel so alone? I had to stop thinking about him.

You have us, Umarenthe said, coalescing from the shadows under the neatly trimmed hedge I was passing. Celebrach appeared on my other side.

Just what I needed—another reminder of his missing son.

He was becoming a liability, the former Lord Serpent said. *Better to be rid of him.*

Funny how he'd never seemed to feel that way when he was alive. Celebrach had held onto his son despite every act of defiance, every moment of rebellion. Did Ni'ishasana steal its former owners' personalities as well as their souls? Was this really Celebrach I was talking to, or only the dagger itself manifesting under a different guise? My own future as a shadowy inhabitant of the dagger was looking less and less appealing as time went on.

"He was never a liability," I said, stung. Celebrach had never been one of my favourite people, and, as a representative of the dagger, I was even less impressed with him this morning. I wasn't sure I wanted to talk to any of Ni'ishasana's captive souls. "He was more than either you or I deserved."

His feelings for you made him unreliable, Umarenthe said firmly, as if that settled the matter.

I had a strong urge to ask her what the hell she knew about feelings, but I didn't want to prolong the conversation. I was *not* happy with Ni'ishasana and its souls.

You forget, you are not alone, Celebrach said. *Your father loves you.*

Another urge, stronger than the previous one, almost overwhelmed me—this time, to roll my eyes. Celebrach, of all people, was going to talk to me about fatherly love? The irony was almost too much.

"Maybe," was all I said.

Sure, Fallon was making all the right noises at the moment, and I had to admit, I *wanted* to believe he was sincere. Wanted to believe Fallon loved me and wished nothing but the best for me, like a real father should—wanted it so much it was a physical ache in my chest. But could I trust him?

I was starting to feel as if there was no one left I could trust, now that Ash was gone.

And goddammit, I was thinking about him *again*. My thoughts kept circling back to my serious assassin, like probing at a sore tooth with my tongue. I couldn't leave it alone, even though it hurt.

You still doubt Fallon after he brought your mother back for you? Umarenthe asked.

My mother loved me. That was a truth I could rely on, even if I trusted nothing else. And I had failed to acquire Ebos's power for her.

But maybe the dagger would be enough to bring her back without it. Fallon hadn't said it would take *all* the powers of the Realms working together. Only most of them. Did he actually know, or was he guessing? We needed to discuss this.

"I should talk to him," I said.

Good idea. We should go see him now.

I shook my head. "It's only two more blocks to Willow's place. He can wait."

My poor mother had been dead eighteen years. Another few hours weren't going to make any difference, and I had a powerful urge to see Willow again. The company of Ni'ishasana's wraiths was no substitute for that of real flesh and blood friends. I hadn't felt so alone since I'd been locked in the storeroom at the Nest, waiting to find out if Ash meant to kill me or apprentice me.

And there I went, thinking about Ash again. Dammit. I needed a distraction.

You're wasting your time with her," Umarenthe said. *She's no friend of yours.*

I gritted my teeth. The dagger had hated Ash—now it hated Willow, too? "Nevertheless, that's where I'm going."

I walked faster as I turned in to Willow's street. Was it weird to be delighted at the sight of the familiar cracked and uneven pavement, lifted by the roots of street trees that had grown much larger than the council had envisaged when they planted them? I even felt a fondness for the ugly block of red-brick units on the corner that I had never experienced when I actually lived here.

They did say that absence made the heart grow fonder, but this was ridiculous. Even the yapping of the annoying rat-sized dog that lived three houses down from Willow's sith didn't bother me the way it used to. Instead, I waved as I passed, and grinned as the creature went into a predictable frenzy, promising that he would rip me limb from limb if only the fence wasn't separating us.

The only thing that dented my pleasure was drawing level with the next-door neighbour's house. I'd found Nevith collapsed under those bushes right there, his throat slit from ear to ear, his blood soaking into the soft grass.

The Vipers had done that.

Old fury surged through me, surprising me with its intensity. Thinking of the Vipers usually gave me such satisfaction. But as I stared at the place where his body had lain, it was hard to feel anything but hatred.

Ridiculous. I shook my head, as if doing so could dislodge this strange emotion. *I* was a Viper now, though my only kills so far were members of the team that had infiltrated Willow's sith that night and my predecessor. I could hardly hate myself, could I?

I paused outside Willow's place, regarding the tiny house with affection. The top corner of the fly screen on the screen door had come adrift from the door frame and sagged as if exhausted by the struggle to remain vertical. The front yard was overgrown with weeds and grass that waved knee-high, and the paint on the window frames peeled and flaked. The whole effect was particularly uninviting, but this unprepossessing exterior hid the lush gardens and comfortable pavilions of a sith, a tiny bubble of the Spring Realm broken off and anchored here as a refuge for the nobility of Spring.

Willow and I had made it our home when we'd left Spring after her father had exiled me. She had said if I wasn't welcome in Spring, then she didn't want to be there either, and had refused to return until Lord Thistle had changed his mind.

For the first time, it occurred to me to wonder if I was still welcome *here*. Willow might have changed the wards so that when I walked through the sagging gate I would find myself in the unkempt front yard in front of the dilapidated little house instead of treading the soft grasses of Faerie. It only made sense, in a way. I was an assassin now. Who left their home open to an assassin?

Only one way to find out. I set my hand to the gate, which squeaked a protest as I swung it open. The tingle of threshold magic, like the feet of hundreds of tiny insects tickling over my skin, was more welcome than it had ever been before as I stepped through and saw the towering trees and sweet-smelling flowers of Willow's Spring garden.

I stopped there for a moment and took a deep breath of that floral air, letting my light-weaving disintegrate. Roses, frangipani, jasmine, and others I couldn't pick combined with the sharper scents of lemon-scented gums and pine trees to produce a delicious whole that smelled like home. Everywhere I looked was greenery, shadowed and mysterious even in the morning sun. Through breaks in the trees, I caught tantalising glimpses of the white pavilions nestled in the heart of the garden. The path at my feet wound off into that green haven, inviting me in.

I set off down the path. Colourful birds chattered and swooped through the treetops, and somewhere in the distance, a raven cawed, but there were no signs of people as I neared the open pavilions. It was midmorning, so perhaps they were already in bed for the day—Willow kept to the same nocturnal schedule in the human world that she'd followed in the Realms, so her staff did, too.

Inside my old bedroom, everything was exactly as I'd left it. Though I'd expected that, it still gave me a jolt, as if the Sage who'd lived here might walk back in at any moment. I knew full well that Sage was gone. Still, I went into the walk-in wardrobe and snagged a T-shirt out of a drawer, hastily shrugging into it. My old jeans hung in a neat row, and I eyed them for a minute. Why not? The ones I was wearing were pretty trashed.

When I came back out of the wardrobe, a movement in the bushes outside my room caught my attention. In true Spring style, the whole side of the room opposite me was completely open to the garden outside, and one of the flowering shrubs that stood behind an ornamental pool was quivering in an unnatural way. Someone else might not have noticed the movement, but Ash had trained me well.

Dammit. Stop thinking about him!

While I was still berating myself, a ginger cat emerged from the bushes and paced toward me, his tail waving like a flag above him. I let go of Ni'ishasana and relaxed. It was only Kel, the cat that Allegra had insisted on bringing home after his owner died, though neither she nor Willow were particularly fond of cats.

"Hey, buddy," I said, expecting him to ignore me with his usual feline disdain. "How's it hanging?"

To my surprise, he slunk over and started twining himself around my legs. Even for a cat, Kel was usually pretty stand-offish.

"Are you hungry?"

That seemed unlikely. Zinnia would have fed him before she went to bed, which could only have been a couple of hours ago at most. Her love of providing food to all and sundry extended to animals as much as people.

Kel meowed and rubbed his face against my jeans. I bent down and stroked his soft fur, which he accepted as his due. Maybe he was craving affection. Willow certainly wouldn't have shown him any. She thought he was an arse-hole, since he kept leaving little broken surprises in her bedroom. On one memorable occasion, he'd left a dead rat in the middle of her bed. The swearing that had followed had been particularly creative.

The liquid notes of a harp drifted through the air as I straightened up. Someone was awake.

I followed the sound to a part of the garden where Willow, Allegra, and I had often sat, enjoying the open space where birds sang and wildflowers peeked out of the grass. A large oak spread its mighty branches in the centre of the meadow, and a swing seat hung from one of its boughs. Three comfortable chairs stood beside a fountain artfully designed to look natural. Water bubbled up and over a dozen rocks pleasantly arranged in the middle of a small pool, adding a burbling counterpoint to the notes of the harp.

Willow sat in the grass at the feet of the harpist. His head was bent toward his strings, and I didn't recognise him until he murmured something that made her laugh. I knew that voice. When he lifted his head, I was sure—it was the changeling guy that had been with her in the pub.

Willow began to sing, and I stopped where I was, hidden from them by the trees at the edge of the meadow. A pang of loss pierced me at the easy way they made music together. I missed that. I missed playing in the band, expe-riencing the joy of hearing my instrument blend with everyone else's to form something bigger than all of us. Music had given me more of a sense of belonging even than being a Viper did. There was something so special about being part of creating something from nothing, relying on your bandmates to do their part, and feeling how effortlessly you all worked together and understood each other.

Nothing in my life now felt effortless except the magic. And looking at the way the changeling leaned towards her as he coaxed a liquid flow of music from the harp, and the way she smiled at him as she sang, the magic didn't quite make up for what I'd lost here. In that moment, I would have traded the dagger to be part of that again.

Willow tucked an errant curl behind her ear, the sunlight catching her red hair and setting it ablaze. I'd seen that gesture a thousand times. She was my oldest friend, and here she was, at ease with a person I didn't even know. I'd *always* known the people in Willow's life.

This was a new and unwelcome sensation. Clearly, she didn't miss me.

Of course she doesn't miss you, Umarenthe purred in my ear. The shadow woman didn't take physical form, but I could hear her as well as if she had. *She's no true friend, remember? Your father kept trying to make contact with you, and she blocked him. She only wants what's best for her, not for you. She's not like us. No one will ever care for you the way we do.*

That was right. My thoughts felt like treacle, sticky and slow. I'd almost forgotten. Was I really so gullible that seeing her again was enough to make me pine like a little kid? Sure, her friendship had been the best thing in my life for many years—but that was before I had found Ni'ishasana. Reassuring warmth filled me as the dagger's power thrummed through me. How could I have thought, even for a moment, that anything in my old life was better than that?

Caressing the dagger's hilt in apology, I stepped forward into the meadow. The harpist saw me and broke off in surprise, and Willow turned to see what he was looking at.

"Sage!" She smiled in pure delight and leapt to her feet. "You're back!"

She rushed forward, arms spread wide, but something in my face stopped her before she could hug me. The light faded from her eyes as she slowed.

"I've seen my father," I said. "He says he tried many times to contact me over the years, but you always prevented him."

The changeling came to stand beside her, a determined look on his face. Did he actually mean to protect her from me? I almost laughed. Because, for one thing, Willow's power could crush him like a bug. She didn't need any white knights to come charging to her rescue. And for another, neither of them could stop me doing a damn thing I wanted to. It was kind of cute that he thought he was a match for either of us.

"And you believed him?" Willow asked.

"Is it true?"

Her face shut down. "Of course it's not true. I haven't seen him or heard from him since the night he tried to kill me."

She lies, Umarenthe said, and the pressure in my head increased.

Did I believe her? Willow *looked* sincere, but she had no problem bending the truth when it suited her. "And you like it that way."

"Of course I do! Your father is a monster." Her gaze travelled down from my face and snagged on Ni'ishasana. Her expression hardened. "You used to agree with me. Why are you hanging around with him now?"

"None of your business," I said sharply.

See how she tries to deflect your attention away from her lies, Umarenthe whispered.

"Are you going to let her talk to you like that?" the changeling asked Willow, lifting his chin in a show of belligerence that would have been annoying if it wasn't so pathetic. What was his name? Christopher? No, Christian. What a ridiculous name for a changeling.

"Shut up," Willow and I said in unison.

Well, in some things, at least, we were still on the same page.

"Is that all you wanted?" Willow asked. "To accuse me of keeping you apart from your psycho killer father? Because if it is, you can take yourself off again. You're not welcome here while you wear that dagger."

"How did she even get in here?" the changeling muttered. Seriously, how could Willow stand him? He was so dense.

"An oversight," Willow said, her gaze holding mine in challenge. "I forgot to change the wards to exclude her. An oversight that I will remedy now."

I shrugged. "Fine by me."

What need did I have of her tiny little sith? My own

was a hundred times larger. I headed back into the trees. And if she preferred the company of that stupid changeling and his pathetic beard to mine, she was no loss.

Plus, I was more than half convinced she was lying about Fallon. Something had flickered in her eyes when I'd first asked the question—and if she'd kept me from him for her own purposes, that was it. We were done.

I strode down the path towards the gate, as eager to leave as she probably was to have me gone. The arrogance of her! To tell me that I must choose between her and the dagger. That was no choice at all. What did she offer that could compare with the power Ni'ishasana had given me? Umarenthe was right—Willow was no friend to me.

Your father cares, Umarenthe said, her shape forming amongst the shadows beneath the trees. *Family are the only people you can truly rely on. You should go to him.*

I laughed; a short, bitter sound. "He is, hands-down, the most unreliable person in my life."

A man is allowed a few mistakes. He wants to make it up to you now.

"Why do you care?"

We only want what's best for you. We want you to be happy. And we could help you bring your mother back—imagine what that would be like. You'd be a real family again.

I entered the sunlit meadow near the gate, and Umarenthe's form faded as she lost the shadows, but her words resounded in my head. *Imagine. A real family again.* Yeah, I was imagining all right. I was hanging on to that thought like a lifeline in a sea of loneliness. It was the only thing keeping me afloat.

Soon, Mama. Soon, I promise.

Kel sat by the gate, as if he'd been waiting for me. He stood up and meowed as I came into view.

"Move, cat."

I nudged him gently out of the way with my foot, so I could get the gate open, but as soon as I had opened it more than a crack, he darted through onto the street. I followed him out, slamming the gate behind me.

But instead of wandering off to do whatever cats do, he sat down again and gazed up at me almost expectantly.

"What's wrong, furball? Were you feeling underappreciated in there?"

Allegra had only brought him home out of a sense of obligation, but I noted that obligation hadn't extended to actually taking him with her when she'd moved to Illusion. And Willow barely tolerated him. I was sure Zinnia would have fed him, but there was no one who really gave a crap about the stupid animal now that I'd moved out.

I picked him up. Surprisingly, he settled quite happily in my arms. Even an aloof cat like Kel needed a little love occasionally.

I rubbed my face against his and felt a rumbling purr start up against my chest.

"Welcome to the Vipers, buddy."

24

By the time I'd carried the furball through the Wilds, I was more than halfway to regretting my decision. He didn't weigh a lot, but even a small weight becomes heavy after the first hour. I'd tried floating him on a cushion of Air, but he'd twisted and yowled so much I'd had to give it up and carry him the regular way. So much for my all-powerful magic.

Finally back in London, I was relieved to see the blue police box that housed the entry to the sith. A familiar figure waited beside it, leaning against the brick wall of the station building with his arms folded, and my heart did a little backflip of delight.

"What are you doing here, Ash?" I tried to sound stern, with absolutely no success—the grin stretching from ear to ear was a dead giveaway. How could I have thought I could go through the rest of my life without seeing him? My soul was singing with relief at having him back.

Ash pushed away from the wall, all long limbs and lazy

strength, an answering smile lighting his face. "I live here. But since someone took away my link to the Vipers, the wards don't recognise me. I've been waiting for someone to come by who can let me in."

Confusion tinged my rush of happiness. "What do you mean, you live here?"

He shrugged. "Where else would I go?"

"Anywhere you like. That's why I gave you your damn freedom. Being able to go wherever you want is kind of the definition of freedom."

The cat chose that moment to decide he didn't want to be carried anymore, and I struggled to hold onto the squirming bundle.

"I can't leave you alone. The Lady only knows what you'd do. Look at this—you disappear for a few hours and come back with a cat. Where did you get it?"

"It was Allegra's."

"You've been to Illusion?"

"No. It was living with Willow." And because I didn't want to discuss my visit to Willow's sith, I shoved the cat at him. "Here, hold it. If you're staying, I'll have to adjust the wards so you can pass."

He took the cat calmly, and the pair of them sized each other up. Evidently, Kel deemed Ash acceptable, as he settled down happily in his arms.

Shaking my head, and still smiling, I turned my attention to the wards and soon had Ash's problem fixed. The gate had been set up to only open for Vipers and their servants and families—basically all those who were connected to the dagger. It was relatively simple to make an exception for Ash, though I was careful not to reforge any connection between him and Ni'ishasana. He might not want to exercise it yet, but I wouldn't trample on his newfound freedom. And I was more than a little wary of giving the dagger any power over him after our last clash.

"Try it now."

He opened the gate and we could see the sith on the other side. Hastily, we stepped through before we caught the attention of anyone passing. Usually, our comings and goings were conducted at night. It was early afternoon, and there were a lot more people on the street than we were used to.

Once we were through, and the noises of London traffic were cut off, I realised the cat was purring.

"He likes you." That made two of us.

"What's his name?"

Funny, I would never have picked Ash as a cat person. Or an any-kind-of-pet person, for that matter. Pets required displays of affection, and Ash wasn't big on those. But he was actually smiling as he stroked the cat's soft fur, its delicate head almost disappearing under his big hand.

"Kel. Short for Kellith. He was named after the ex-Lord of Summer."

"Let's hope he doesn't meet a similar fate."

"He should be fine. I suspect he's not actually an Illusionist masquerading as a cat."

We strode down the path towards the imposing main building. With its turrets and towers, it had reminded me of Hogwarts when I'd first seen it, though its cold grey stone wasn't as inviting as that fictional place. And there were no friendly faces waving from paintings on the walls once we got inside. Instead, the décor was focused on violent death—blood-red walls and a carpet that was patterned with severed body parts.

We'd barely started down the main hallway when Sharis appeared.

"Ah, Serpent," the fair-haired Adept said. "A moment of your time?"

"Shall I take Kel to your suite?" Ash asked.

I nodded, and he headed for the stairs.

"Something wrong?" I asked Sharis.

"Possibly. That apprentice of Nuah's has disappeared again."

I raised an eyebrow. What business was it of his? "Atinna is Nuah's responsibility. Why are you keeping tabs on her apprentice?"

"Should it not concern me when apprentices disappear for days on end?"

I cast my mind over the current jobs. Surely Nuah had one? "She's probably doing surveillance for a job."

"They finished their last one two days ago, right after you met with the Adepts."

I sighed. It had been a long night, and all I wanted was a shower and sleep. "So did you ask *Nuah* where she is?"

"She made some noises about 'personal leave'. Since when have Vipers felt the need for personal leave?"

"Vipers are not prisoners, Sharis."

It was unusual for them to be away from the Nest when they weren't working, but not forbidden. I reached for the tie that bound me to Atinna. She was asleep, which made it unlikely she was in any danger. I could tell she was in the Realms, though not where, exactly, without going deeper.

But she was incapable of breaking her bonds of loyalty to me and the dagger now—I'd made damn sure of that when I bound her to Nuah—so I wasn't concerned by her absence. Probably some fae had caught her eye and she was off indulging herself. It happened. I made a mental note to check with Nuah later. I had more important priorities now.

"She's quite safe. Surely you have better things to do than spy on your fellow Vipers. Do I need to assign you more work?"

"I was merely concerned, Serpent. I'm glad to hear she is well." He gave a shallow bow and headed off down the corridor.

I turned my own steps towards the stairs. The acid burns on my right arm were throbbing something fierce. Fae healing was good, but it worked better if the injured person actually got some sleep. It felt as though I'd been awake for days—so much had happened—and I'd been running on fumes for some time now.

The three flights of stairs seemed more of a climb than Everest, and my steps slowed as I dragged myself up the last of them. I trudged down the corridor towards my suite, wondering if Ash was still there. At another time, the thought of Ash so close to my bed might have filled me with anticipation. But right now, I was so tired that he could have danced naked right in front of me without awaking a shred of desire.

Oh. A flicker of interest stirred at the image my imagination had conjured up. Maybe that was a lie. But it would have to be a *very* good dance.

An urge to giggle nearly overwhelmed me. Man, I was more tired than I'd thought. Practically punch-drunk.

I eased the door to my suite open. Only a few more steps to the bed. The relief was overwhelming.

Ash was seated in one of the armchairs in the main lounge area, bent forward, one hand trailing on the floor. He didn't look up, and I paused in the doorway, trying to figure out what he was so absorbed in.

A ginger paw emerged suddenly from under the chair, swiping at something that Ash jerked out of the cat's reach. He flicked it tantalisingly toward the lurker under the chair, wiggling it like a worm on a hook. Was that a ribbon? He must have magicked it from somewhere—I certainly didn't have any in my rooms. My hair was too short for ribbons, even if I'd been the ribbon-wearing sort.

I could practically feel the cat's frustration as the ribbon flicked back and forth, almost within reach. So tempting. The paw lashed out again, and again Ash was too fast.

It was too much for Kel. He leapt out from under the chair and fell upon the ribbon, wrenching it from Ash's hand. Ash laughed as the cat scuttled under another chair with his prize, far enough away that Ash couldn't retake it.

I shut the door behind me. Ash had a great laugh, but I'd rarely heard it before. Happiness bloomed inside me as he looked up, still smiling.

"He sure showed you," I said.

"He certainly did."

I pulled the dagger from my belt and dropped it on a small circular table, then fell into the chair opposite Ash. Seeing him delight in such a simple pleasure as playing with a cat was the high point of my day. I felt a little guilty —I should be pushing him to take his freedom and run— but I was too tired. Too pleased to have him back. And too damn exhausted to keep my eyes open another minute.

I sat back in the chair and let my eyelids sag closed.

"You look worn out," Ash said. "You should go to bed."

I was too tired even to respond with sexual innuendo. "I will in a minute. I'm just working up the strength to get from here to the bedroom."

Maybe I'd fall asleep right here instead. That was becoming a more attractive option by the minute. The bed was so far away.

What is that beast doing? Umarenthe asked. She sounded offended, bordering on outrage.

It was a struggle, but I cracked my eyelids open to see what she was complaining about. The beast in question had abandoned his ribbon—it must have lost its appeal since no one was flicking it about—and was crouched on the table where I'd left the dagger, eyeing it intently. A ginger paw reached out again, but this time there were no claws extended to snatch at an errant ribbon.

For a minute, I thought Kel was going to knock Ni'ishasana off the table, in a typical cat dick move. Instead, he very gently patted at the great ruby in the hilt, as if he was investigating it.

He touched Ni'ishasana! Umarenthe appeared suddenly beside the table, her shape billowing a little as if she couldn't quite keep her anger in check enough to focus on maintaining her shadowy form.

Kel looked up, and I could have sworn he stared straight at her.

Umarenthe, I said in my mind, *move over by the window? Whatever for?*

But she did as I asked, and Kel's unblinking stare followed her, his green eyes round. Interesting. Why could the cat see her when no one else could except me? Could all cats see her, or only this one?

But there was nothing special about Kel, other than that he'd once been owned by a changeling and had spent some time inside a sith. Neither of those things would have given him any special abilities. Yet there was no doubt in my mind that he *could* see her.

When she made no further moves, his attention returned to the dagger—or, more specifically, to the ruby in the dagger's hilt. Perhaps it was only the way it caught the afternoon sun, making it glow with an inner fire, that caught his attention. He poked at it again in that delicate way, equal parts caution and curiosity.

He'd better be careful. They said that curiosity killed the cat, and it sounded as though Umarenthe, at least, would be happy to deliver the killing stroke. I couldn't find it in me to work up the same outrage as Kel leaned over and cautiously sniffed at the ruby. And I didn't think that was just because I was exhausted.

Sure, the dagger had given me a lot, but I was beginning to see that its gifts came with a cost—and not only the prospect of being trapped inside it for eternity after my death. Willow's words kept echoing in my head: *you're not welcome here while you wear that dagger.* Bravado and outrage had kept the pain away at first, but now it was sinking in. My oldest friend had rejected me.

It was almost as bad as being abandoned by my father when I was seven. At least he was back in my life now. It was as if I was only allowed one person who cared about me at a time. My father had handed the baton to Willow, who'd passed it on to Ash, and now it looked like Fallon's turn again.

But Ash cared, didn't he, despite his hatred of the dagger? Why else would he have come back to the Nest and his life as a Viper? He hated being an assassin. But he'd only given me a flippant answer before, and I was too tired to try digging through all his layers right now—he had more than an onion, and peeling them off to get at the truth was exhausting.

Kel lost interest in the ruby and leapt down from the table. He stalked across the carpet and rubbed himself against Ash's leg before jumping up into his lap. Pleasure curved Ash's lips into a smile as he stroked the cat's ginger fur. Kel took that as his due, only kneading Ash's legs a couple of times before settling down.

"He seems to like you."

"Clearly, he has impeccable taste."

"You should take him and get out of this place," I said, trying the direct approach.

Equally direct, he looked straight at me and said simply, "I won't leave without you."

Pleasure flushed through me. Maybe Fallon wasn't the only one left who still cared for me.

"I missed you," I said. "Is that stupid? You weren't gone that long."

"If it's stupid, then I'm stupid, too."

I smiled and closed my eyes again. The pain of Willow's rejection eased, just a little. And if Fallon could restore my mother, that would be one more person whose love I would never have to doubt. Whose loyalty I would never be forced to question.

Living among the Vipers was exhausting in that regard. I was fast losing interest in them—in fact, I couldn't quite understand why I'd ever cared so much about them. I could remember the intensity of my initial bond with them, when I'd first taken up the dagger, but that had faded so much, now, that it felt more like a dream than something that had really happened.

Why did I feel so disconnected from the Vipers now? Why did I care so much that Willow had thrown me out? Not so long ago, I'd hurt her simply for daring to touch me —but I couldn't imagine doing that now. It was as if a veil had been lifted from my eyes. Right now, the best use I could see for the dagger was restoring my mother, and I was determined to get to that immediately.

Well, almost immediately. Tonight would be soon enough. First, I had to get some sleep.

25

———

"**C**ome with me."

Night had fallen. I'd eaten a quick breakfast, though excitement at what was to come had played hell with my appetite, and gone to find Ash.

"Where are we going?"

Predictably, he'd been at the training grounds, sparring with Sharis. Did he mean to continue as an assassin, then, even though I'd released him? Or was he only going through the motions so no one would suspect he was no longer a Viper?

It would be pretty damn obvious, though, once the other Adepts realised I was no longer sending him on jobs.

"You don't need to know," I snapped, for the sake of appearances. For once, there wasn't a trace of anger in my heart. I felt like my old self. "You only need to obey."

Sharis smirked as Ash bowed his head and went to put away his training sword. I ignored him—I had no intention of shouting my personal business in front of the fair-haired Adept. Would he still be smirking if he realised Ash was the only person here who didn't *have* to obey me anymore?

We didn't speak again until we were out on the street in London. A double-decker bus belched a cloud of foul-smelling exhaust as it went past, and I hastened my steps towards the nearest quiet place where we could gate into the Wilds.

"We're going to my father's house," I said, butterflies of excitement fluttering in my stomach at the thought.

He frowned. "You have another meeting with him? The first one didn't go so smoothly."

I hadn't told him about visiting my old home in Spring and how Fallon had brought my mother's spirit to talk with me for those brief, tantalising moments. Nor had I told him of my thinking since, of how I meant to use the powers of Ni'ishasana to aid my father in bringing my mother back to life. The telling of it took some time, and we were through the Wilds and standing on the road outside Fallon's house by the time the story was done.

The house looked as dark and abandoned as last time I'd been here. I drew a deep breath to calm my racing heart.

"Let's go in. The wards will tell him I'm here."

Ash followed me up the path to the door. "He's not living here, then?"

"Not so close to Lord Thistle's estate. He's not welcome in Spring."

I had the feeling that Willow's dad would do his best to kill mine if he knew he was within reach. I was less sure whether he would succeed. Lord Thistle was a powerful Spring mage, widely considered the most powerful within the Realm. But Fallon Domani had other powers, now, that could make him not only his former friend's equal but his superior. The only thing I was sure of was that any battle between them would be monumental.

I led Ash through the house. The curtains I'd opened last time had all been closed again, and the interior had a dark, foreboding feel to it. Only our fae vision allowed us to see where we were going in the Stygian blackness. I didn't linger; I didn't even want to go near the kitchen. Too much history there. Instead, I led him to a side door and out into the garden.

It was sadly overgrown now, but still pretty in a wild way, bathed in soft moonlight. The climbing roses had gotten very leggy, and the mint was absolutely rampaging through the herb garden, choking out less hardy species. But it was green, and the air was still warm from the day and scented with gardenias.

At the far end of the garden, a path ambled off through the trees, and I led Ash along it, between jacarandas bursting with new spring growth. After a short walk, the path opened into a small, grassy clearing where pink and white tulips bloomed year-round in a certain patch. Apart from that rectangular planting, the grass was well-kept and studded with tiny blue flowers.

Ash frowned as he looked around, and I knew his keen eyes and assassin's instincts had noted the same difference I had between the clearing and the overgrown gardens we'd passed on the way.

"There is a preserving spell here that isn't in use anywhere else. Why?"

"My mother is buried here."

His gaze turned to the tulips, corralled into a precise grave shape, and he nodded in understanding.

After only a few minutes, we heard footsteps approaching down the jacaranda-lined path. Fallon appeared, this time mercifully without any of his servants.

"Back so soon?" His gaze travelled to Ash. "And who is this?"

"A fellow Viper," I said.

"A friend," Ash said firmly at the same time.

"Any friend of Sage's is a friend of mine," Fallon said gravely.

Funny, he hadn't felt that way about Willow when he'd tried to kill her, but I bit my tongue and kept the thought to myself. I was here to give him—to give *us*—a second chance, not to throw old wounds in his face. People who had reformed should be given a clean slate and the chance to prove themselves.

He loves you, Sage, Umarenthe whispered as her form took shape in the deep shadows under the jacarandas.

Ash said nothing, but distrust was evident in the stiff lines of his body and the granite expression on his face. I didn't need a Serpent's bond to be able to read that. Well, perhaps what happened here today would prove to him that Fallon's reform was genuine and he didn't need to stand ready to defend me from my own father.

"You told me last time that it would take the powers of

many Realms to bring my mother's body back to true life," I said.

Fallon nodded gravely. "Sadly, yes. That's true."

"I have an idea how we could achieve that."

He gave me an indulgent smile, as if I was a little kid wanting him to admire my dodgy drawing skills. "I'm all ears, but I doubt there are that many necromancers alive, much less enough who would work together so selflessly."

"That may be true, but what if it could be done with only one necromancer, and the powers of Ni'ishasana?"

He glanced at the dagger on my hip. "I've heard many things of the fabled dagger of the Vipers, but never that it had necromantic powers."

"It doesn't," I said. Well, not exactly. "But *you* have, and if I lend you the magics of the other Realms, through Ni'ishasana, then *you* will be strong enough all on your own to accomplish it."

For an instant, his eyes lit with hope—then he shook his head. "It's too risky. We could end up destroying the dagger and still not achieve our goal."

"I don't care," I said flatly, and in that moment, it was true. If I had to sacrifice Ni'ishasana to get my mother back, I would consider it a fair trade.

Is it true? I asked the dagger in my mind. *Does this endanger you?*

No ritual could destroy us, Umarenthe said, gliding closer across the moonlit grass. *We have only one weakness, and it is not that.*

What is it? I asked, momentarily diverted. The all-powerful dagger actually had a weakness? I'd never heard even a whisper of that before.

Let's talk about it later, she said. *You have more important things to focus on now.*

"Are you sure?" Fallon asked.

"Absolutely."

"Very well, then," he said, "I'll prepare the ritual."

He clapped his hands. For a long moment, nothing happened. Then, something stirred in the blackness under the jacarandas where Umarenthe had so lately stood.

I grimaced in distaste as a revenant stepped forward. It wasn't the one I'd seen last time; this one was comparatively fresh, her skin mostly intact, if pale and waxy-looking. She didn't move any faster, though, as she shuffled forward bearing an armload of black candles, which my father took and arranged at the head and foot of the grave.

He slanted a smile in my direction as he did, and I recalled how he'd mocked my expectations of black candles when he had summoned my mother's spirit. "You see? Some purposes require all the trappings."

Another revenant joined the first, this one a big male who was rapidly disintegrating. He presented Fallon with a wickedly curved dagger, its blade as black as the night and its hilt inscribed with silver symbols that meant nothing to me.

Ash drew closer, until his shoulder rubbed against mine, as a third revenant appeared, carrying a simple skin drum the size of a large cooking pot. "You seem well prepared for something you could have had no idea was about to happen," he said, suspicion clear on his face as he watched the revenants lurch around the clearing.

Fallon smiled as he lit the candles with a wave of his hand. Huge blue flames shot skyward, casting an eerie glow on the scene. "I always keep some equipment here. It is my house, after all, and you never know when something might come in handy."

The revenants stood back as he began circling the grave, chanting in a low voice. I didn't recognise the language, but he seemed to be repeating the same few syllables over and over again. This went on for at least ten minutes before he stopped at the head of the grave, pulled up his sleeve, and sliced across his wrist with the wicked-looking blade. In the blue light of the candles, his blood appeared black as it dripped down, and his skin was as pale and ashen as if he were a corpse himself.

Wherever his blood fell on the tulips, they hissed as if burned, then shrivelled, their dried heads bending to the ground on weakened stalks. He repeated the process at the foot of the grave, shaking his arm to scatter the blood across the flowers. One of the black candles spat as a drop of blood landed on it, and its blue flame shot up, momentarily doubling in size. Then, he sat on the grass at the foot of the grave, put the knife aside, and pulled the drum onto his lap.

He used the hand of his injured arm to beat the drum, and little drops of blood fell onto the smooth drumskin. He continued to tap the drum, smearing the blood everywhere.

Though he beat the drum, it made no sound. I glanced

at Ash uneasily. This seemed the most ominous part to me, even more so than the weird blue flames or the revenants themselves. If we couldn't hear the drumbeat, who could?

We stood there a long time, watching him beat the silent drum, long enough for the last of the day's heat to fade from the night air and the shadows to creep closer, blocking out the light of the moon and enclosing us in a blue-lit bubble. Umarenthe had drawn closer, like a moth to a flame, and I wondered if she could hear the drum. Celebrach wasn't far behind her, and many more of Ni'ishasana's shadows pressed in around us. I reached out for Ash's hand.

"Bring the dagger," Fallon said at last, without pausing in his rhythm.

Reluctantly, I let go of Ash's hand and stepped up beside my father, pulling Ni'ishasana from my belt. "What do I have to do?"

"Nothing." His eyes were black pits with blue flames dancing in their depths, his face corpse-grey. "Just give it to me. I am the necromancer; I must be the one to wield its powers."

"You can't wield it; only I can."

"This is the price that must be paid. For this to work, I must be the wielder. Are you prepared to give it up?"

"Get away from him," Ash urged, fear in his voice. "He's going to kill you and take the dagger for himself."

"No, he's not." But I stared down at Fallon, my heart shrivelling at this betrayal. He must have known this all along, but he'd conveniently neglected to mention it until now. He had to actually *be* the wielder of Ni'ishasana? I couldn't funnel its power to him somehow? "Just so we're all clear, you're not talking about being the person holding the dagger, are you? You mean you need to take my place as its wielder."

"That's right. You would lose all the powers Ni'ishasana has gifted you, and I would become its new wielder."

"And the leader of the Vipers?" Ash asked, horror in his voice.

Indeed, it was a sobering thought: a man with Fallon's powers and reputation as the leader of the assassins. Some would say it was a match made in heaven.

Or hell, depending on your viewpoint.

Think of your mother, Umarenthe said. *Her return is surely a prize worthy of a little risk. And how much risk could it really be? What are you afraid of?*

I don't know exactly. A nebulous anxiety filled me at the thought of Fallon wielding the dagger's powers. *But Fallon's a dangerous man.*

So are all those who become Serpent. You are jumping at shadows. Besides, your mother's influence will change everything.

Something about that didn't seem quite right, but I couldn't put my finger on it. My thoughts were tangled— the inside of my head felt full of fog. The dagger's insistence pushed at my mind. Ni'ishasana was right, wasn't it?

Of course it was. I looked across at Ash. "The Vipers don't concern us anymore." For the first time in weeks, I had my priorities in order. All of a sudden, the dagger held no more allure for me than the night I had picked it up. I would give it to my father. That was the right thing to do. The only option. "I'm here for my mother. For my family."

He held my gaze, then nodded tensely. "I don't care who wields the dagger, as long as you are free."

Fallon's smile was ghastly in the blue light, but I smiled tentatively back, a tiny seed of hope sprouting in my heart. We probably all looked like ghouls in the eerie radiance of the black candles.

Umarenthe drifted closer, hovering just outside their fierce blue glow. Her shadowy mouth curved into a smile, too, which was somehow even more disturbing than Fallon's.

No, everything was as it should be. It was only the bizarre situation that was getting to me. I'd never seen a necromantic ritual before, so it was natural to feel uneasy, though the feeling was distant, as if it were happening to someone else. An itch at the back of my neck was screaming *danger!* My body wanted to run, but my mind held firm. I had nothing to fear here.

That's right, Umarenthe said, her voice sending soothing waves of reassurance rolling through my mind. *This is what you want.*

"This isn't some plot of Fallon's," I said, holding Ash's wary gaze with my own. "Remember, this was all my idea. He doesn't have to kill me to take the dagger's powers if I willingly give them up."

At least, that felt right. I glanced at Umarenthe, who nodded.

It's never been done before, she said. That was hardly

surprising, given the hunger for power among the Vipers. *But it is possible.*

And you have no objection?

She shrugged. *The decision is yours.*

What had I expected? That she'd fall to her knees and beg me not to leave her? That my soul was so special that the prospect of losing its company for the rest of her unnatural existence would bring her to tears?

I felt the slightest twinge of hurt at her lack of concern, before I realised how stupid that was. I'd never wanted the dagger in the first place—why should I care if I gave it away? Of course I should give it to my father.

In fact, I'd be better off without it. I recalled how light I'd felt the night I'd gone to the Tower of London—that was one of the few times I'd been without the dagger's terrible presence. And when I'd returned to the Nest and fallen under its spell again, that constant, baseless anger had slammed into me once more.

That anger had controlled me—it had almost made me kill Ash. But now, for the first time in weeks, I was happy. Giving up the dagger was no sacrifice at all. After all this time of being used as a weapon of fear, Ni'ishasana would finally become a tool for good.

It would give me a greater gift than all the power in the world.

26

———

The transfer involved blood, of course, as I should have known it would, but only a little. I sliced my arm with Ni'ishasana's strange, zigzag blade and watched the blood soak into the fae steel like water into sand. Then, I passed it to Fallon so he could do the same.

The blade flashed in the sickly blue light of the candles as he jerked it from my grip, and I stiffened. There was a gleam in his eye that made me want to lunge after it, but I forced myself to relax. My mother needed this. *We* needed this. He was probably feeling the siren call of Ni'ishasana already, and I could hardly blame him for that.

I sat on the flower-studded grass at the head of the grave, so close that the heat of the blue flames warmed my face. Fallon resumed his place at the foot, the dagger clenched tightly in his right hand, and resettled the drum in his lap.

Ash stood to the side, partway between us, watching

Fallon with deep distrust. Did he think my father would *throw* the dagger at me? Its odd, twisting blade was hardly designed for throwing, but he couldn't seem to let go of the idea that Fallon meant to kill me, though I'd explained that my death wasn't necessary to transfer the dagger's powers. I may as well have saved my breath, because he kept watch anyway, determined to protect me. Paranoia came easily to assassins.

According to Umarenthe, I would need to funnel my borrowed powers back into the dagger, where Ni'ishasana could then pass them on to my father.

You'll need to push the flow at first, she said to me as Fallon started up his soundless tapping on the drum again, *but as it speeds up, the momentum will take over and all you will have to do is relax and let it leave you. When the transfer is complete, we can close the connection.*

And then Fallon will be the wielder?

Yes. She hovered behind Ash, just outside the candles' blue glow. There was something odd in her face, but it was hard to read the expression of a being made of shadows. Excitement? Avarice? I closed my eyes so I could concentrate. It was too late for cold feet.

Fallon started up his droning chant again.

Begin, Umarenthe said.

I took a deep breath and pictured a blue thread, like the ones that connected me to the Vipers, stretching from me to the dagger in Fallon's hand. I fed power into it, growing it from a thread to a cable that pulsed with energy. A tug started right behind my sternum.

Ignore that, I told myself firmly. *Focus on the job.*

Fallon cast the drum aside and stood, the dagger held out before him like a light in the darkness. He stared at it the way a man stares at his lover, or a mother her baby, with intense, adoring focus. I stood up, too, anticipation growing inside me.

The flow between me and the dagger faltered, and I refocused my attention on pushing power towards it. I felt strangely light, as if the power leaving me wasn't a drain at all but a release of weight, as if I was shedding shackles I hadn't known were there. I pushed harder, fighting the reflex that urged me to hold onto power at all costs. That reflex was a liar, and I refused to listen.

The tulips covering the grave twitched, though there was no wind. The candles burned straight and true, their blue flames unwavering. I swallowed, excitement gathering in a hard knot in the depths of my belly, and focused on the flowers, watching for another movement.

It came again, more noticeable than the first time. Something was moving beneath the earth. A clump of pink tulips rose higher than their fellows, then toppled aside, leaving a dark hole among the green stems. I leaned closer, straining to see in the dim light.

A patch of earth had been laid bare. It churned, little bits of soil falling among the flowers like rain, then a hand shot up out of the ground. The suddenness made me flinch, and Ash took a step towards me.

"Are you all right? You look pale."

"I'm fine." I brushed his concern aside impatiently, my chest bursting with hope and excitement. Yes, I felt a little faint, but that was only the effort of pushing the dagger's power back towards it.

The cascade of power between us filled my vision when I glanced that way, a bright stream of light, so bright I could hardly believe no one else could see it. The blade gleamed in the eerie blue light of the candles, bursting with the power I was feeding it, ripe and plump.

Perhaps Fallon could see the power arcing through the air—although he was ignoring it, if so. His attention was on the hand scrabbling at the earth. It was covered in dirt, but as more emerged, it became clear that it was mainly bones, with a few scraps of dried flesh clinging on.

I frowned as another hand appeared. More tulips fell, forced aside by the body rising from the ground. The crown of a head appeared between the grasping hands, then popped out as the fingers found purchase. Shoulders rose from the grave as the creature heaved itself from its resting place. Hair hung about them in long, dirty strings.

Why was she still so decayed? I glanced again at Fallon as the revenant climbed fully from the earth and stood waiting among the fallen tulips. She wore a long, white gown that covered most of her body, but it was clear that this was no more than a corpse which had long ago rotted away. Was there some further part of the ritual that had to be done to restore her to herself?

The dagger hummed with power, a note of rejoicing in its song. Umarenthe turned to me, exultation in her shadowy face, and doubt pierced me. Had I been such a terrible wielder that she was *that* glad to see the back of me? Why did she look like the cat that had got the cream?

I had a sudden terrible certainty that there was more going on here than I had thought. I started to struggle, trying to catch the fleeing power as it rushed away from me.

Now, now, Sage, Umarenthe said. *Don't be greedy.*

"Why isn't it working?" I demanded. "Why is she still a corpse?"

Is that any way to talk about your mother? Umarenthe said, a mocking smile curling around her mouth.

"I need it all, Sage," Fallon said. "I can't transform her without all of it. Give it to me."

I staggered, and Ash leapt to my side. "Stop this, Sage! Enough!"

Though Fallon didn't move, I felt an insistent, deep tugging, as if we were playing tug-of-war and he had more kids on his side than I did. He had the look of the team that knew it was winning, too—smug satisfaction was written all over his face.

No, it was more than tug-of-war. This felt like an attack. Like he was reaching deep inside me and wrenching my essence away. I struggled harder, fighting to claw back some of the power I'd given so freely. Fallon had tricked me—and the dagger had helped him.

Had he ever intended anything other than getting me to give him the dagger? And like a trusting fool, I'd handed it over in exchange for empty promises. I pulled harder, throwing my whole being into the task of clawing back what I'd lost. What he'd stolen from me.

Something rushed into me, and new strength flooded me. But it didn't have the familiar feel of the dagger's powers. This was something deeper, older even than Ni'ishasana. No matter how hard I pulled, I couldn't seem to get hold of any of Ni'ishasana's power. The dagger itself was working against me, now.

Fine. I would sever the link instead, and keep the last vestiges that still clung to me. But when I tried to cut that bright cable, nothing happened. I may as well have hit it with a dead fish. The power continued to pour from me.

Umarenthe's doing, I was sure. She openly smirked at my struggles. Sweat sprang out on my forehead and under my arms, though the fight was all internal. I swayed a little, then found that odd new strength again and steadied myself.

The revenant stood quietly between us, waiting for Fallon's orders. Her skeletal arms hung at her sides; her head drooped forward, her stringy hair hiding her face. That was probably a good thing. I could feel my father's essence animating her, but nothing of my mother—not a single scrap of her soul remained.

How did I know that? I had no idea, but apart from that spark of borrowed life burning deep inside her, there was nothing there but rot and death. I was certain of it. There was no way this could become a real living body again—there was simply nothing left to work with.

The strain of our one-sided battle was showing on Fallon's face. A flicker of his surprise and alarm came through our connection, diverting my attention from the pitiful revenant between us. The creature should have been left to sleep.

"Give it all to me," Fallon snarled, and I forgot the revenant as he and the dagger renewed their attack.

There wasn't much power left in me now, but I still struggled against their pull. I wouldn't let them take it without putting up a fight. They didn't deserve for this to be easy.

"Give it to me, or you won't leave here alive."

27

"You never meant to raise Mama, did you?"

A knife appeared in Ash's hand as I spoke.

I sagged as the last of Ni'ishasana's power drained away, but motioned him to stand down. I was light-headed, but better than I had been in a long time. My mind had cleared, and all my thoughts were my own, without the dagger's poisoned persuasions twisting everything.

Fallon stood triumphant on the other side of the grave, surrounded by dozens of shadows—the ghosts of Ni'ishasana—with the dagger clenched in his fist. He looked menacing, but I felt safe enough. If he'd wanted me dead, he could have taken Ni'ishasana by simply killing me, without all this circus. Clearly, the faithless dagger would have helped him. Between us, the revenant waited amid a scatter of earth and broken tulips.

"Sadly, all my travels and poking into dark corners of

the world only proved to me that it is impossible to truly bring a person back from the dead. Raising revenants is easy, you don't even need a ritual—"

"You don't?" I gestured at the black candles and the discarded drum. "Then what was all this?"

He shrugged. "Window dressing. You were expecting a show, so I gave you one. As I was saying, raising revenants is easy, though it's taxing to sustain for a long time. But getting people back, fully alive, in possession of their original soul? Impossible. I accepted that long ago."

"So you lied to me." That was crystal clear, but I was surprised how much it hurt. I'd wanted so much to believe in the dream of our family, reunited.

"To get the dagger, I would have done far more than lie. You were a means to an end."

Had any of it been real? "What about all your talk of being a father to me? Was being Serpent of the Vipers so important to you that you'd throw away any chance of reconciliation with me?"

He laughed in genuine amusement. "Don't be ridiculous. You think this is about the Vipers? And you're a grown woman—what need do you have of a father?"

The shadows pressed closer at his back, Umarenthe at his right hand, Celebrach at his left. I was surprised I could still see them. Must be some lingering effect of having been the dagger's wielder—I certainly couldn't access any of its powers now. Or perhaps they wanted me to see them. Umarenthe wasn't above enjoying a little gloating.

"Now," Fallon said, "get out before I regret letting you live."

Ash's hand was on my arm, urging me away. Fine. I could take a hint. My father didn't love me—so what else was new? But what the hell did he plan on using the dagger for, if not to take his place at the head of the Vipers? The very thought of a man like Fallon with that much power at his disposal made me want to puke.

But that was a problem for later. Right now, the priority seemed to be getting out of here before Fallon regretted his leniency and decided to end the pair of us. We backed away, Ash still brandishing his knife, though he knew perfectly well it would be useless against the powers of Ni'ishasana.

Back on the road outside, Ash wasted no time in finding a place where two trees leaned together at the side of the road and opening a gate into the Wilds. I didn't realise how tense I'd been until I stepped through and my shoulders crept down from somewhere up around my ears.

I stood for a minute, just breathing. I was alive. I was ... free.

Ash stopped on the Greenway, turning to me with anxious eyes. "Are you all right?"

I nodded. I felt curiously numb, as if the shock of Fallon's betrayal and the dashing of my hopes of seeing my mother again, combined with the release from the dagger's control, were all too much to take in. Too many competing emotions trying for space in my heart at once.

"I can't feel the dagger anymore." Until it was gone, I hadn't realised how deeply it had invaded my mind.

"Not at all?"

"No. Can you?" What if my release of him hadn't survived the transition of power to Fallon? It would be a horrible irony if, after being his own father's servant for so many years, he ended up as a prisoner of mine. But he shook his head, and I breathed a sigh of relief. "The Vipers will have felt the transfer of power. They'll think I'm dead."

Half of them would probably be throwing a party at the thought.

"But you're not." He moved closer, drawing me gently into his arms, as if he was afraid his touch would hurt me. "Are you well?"

His eyes searched mine. What was he looking for? Was he afraid I was still under the dagger's influence somehow?

I smiled up at him in reassurance. "I'm fine. Better than fine, actually. I'm myself again."

All this time, I'd thought I was the one in control, when actually the dagger had been walking me around like a puppet. Had I had a single thought that was truly my own in all these weeks? I could hardly remember some of the things I'd done, and the ones I did remember didn't make me proud of myself. My time as wielder of Ni'ishasana was obscured by a dark haze.

"I feel clean. Like I can think again, now I'm the only one inside my head."

He broke into one of those rare smiles of his that lit his serious eyes with warmth. "I was afraid that you were gone forever."

I grinned. "I'm not that easy to get rid of."

"So you're not upset by your father's betrayal?"

My grin faded. My dream of a family reunited was

gone, and that was devastating—but I had gained my freedom. "Let's just say I'm not surprised. I realise now that the dagger has been pushing me towards Fallon ever since he came back into the picture. It kept trying to cut me off from you and Willow and my friends, making out that he was the only one who cared for me. I would never have trusted him, but under Ni'ishasana's influence ... it was as though I forgot all about what he did to Willow. The dagger was leading me on with this shiny picture of the perfect family and it was all I could see."

"I think the dagger has been pushing you towards Fallon since long before he approached you," Ash replied, frowning. "I suspect that's why it chose you in the first place. For its own reasons, it decided that Lord Celebrach wasn't enough for it anymore, so it started looking around for a suitable replacement. Then along *you* came, the daughter of a powerful necromancer, so it used you as a stepping stone to get to him."

"I guess that explains why it was ever interested in someone with so little magic." That had always puzzled me—and it had certainly puzzled the rest of the Vipers, who'd not always been successful in hiding their outrage at being ruled not only by a mere apprentice but by someone who wasn't even a full-blooded fae.

"At least you still have the Spring magic your father stole from you. You do, don't you?"

I sent green shoots from the side of the path winding playfully around his ankles, and he laughed.

"I guess that answers that question."

Yes, my Spring magic still burned bright within me,

along with that deeper strength I'd noticed earlier. It didn't feel like any of the powers I'd wielded with Ni'ishasana. Probably just my imagination. I couldn't remember the last time I'd had a decent night's—or day's—sleep.

"So, where are we going?" I asked. Behind him, the path simply stopped, blocked by the dark, forbidding trees of the Wilds. The shifting Greenways of the Wilds unspooled according to the will and magic of those who walked them. Clearly, he hadn't yet decided where the path should take us. "You're free now, too. You could go anywhere."

"Could I? I'm not sure an ex-Viper would find a welcome in many places."

"People will welcome you if I tell them to," I said fiercely. Just let anyone try to turn him away after all he'd done for me. I slid my arms more firmly around his back.

His face softened. "So determined. And yet wishing cannot always make a thing so."

"Seriously, Ash, you need to lighten up."

We could go to Willow's. She would welcome me back now that I was no longer the dagger's puppet. Allegra would accept him—she was still looking for people to help her rebuild Illusion. King Rothbold would pardon him, surely, once he heard our story. He could even go home to Winter. What was the name of that little village?

"You could return to Kelvarus," I said softly. I'd figured out that that must be where he'd lived with Hattah, his lost love.

He shook his head, a sharp, decisive movement. "There's nothing there for me now."

"Then what do you want?"

"I think you know what I want." His arms tightened around me, and a shiver ran through me at the intensity in his eyes. His heart was there, laid bare for me to see, in an uncharacteristic display of vulnerability.

Oh, God. Was this what *I* wanted? I'd come to know him very well over the last few weeks, better than any of the Vipers who'd known him for years. I liked what I knew. More than liked, if I was honest. I'd come to depend on him. And there was no denying the spark of attraction between us. Even now, his nearness had goosebumps breaking out on my arms and a molten heat swirling in my depths.

My glance fell on his full lips, and suddenly, I couldn't look away. The sound of the wind in the leaves faded, and I forgot the Wilds looming all around us, forgot the dagger and my father. Forgot everything except his mouth and the question in those cool grey eyes.

A crow landed in a tree behind his head, jerking me out of my trance. It stared at me with coal-black eyes for a long moment, before beginning to fluff and preen its feathers. It wasn't a raven, but still, my head filled with memories of Raven and a pair of midnight eyes. Black wings cradling me. A warm mouth on mine.

I'd given my very soul for Raven, taking on the poison of the dagger to save him. Now that I was free of its taint, I could return to my friends. To Willow and Rowan. To whatever it was I shared with Raven. But then, what about Ash?

How could I care so deeply for both these men? They

were so different. Ash would never be comfortable in Raven's glittering Court world, just as Raven would stand out like a sore thumb in the Nest.

The Nest—oh, shit.

"We forgot about Kel!"

28

We emerged from the Wilds into a freezing London dawn. The sky beyond the trees of the park was tinged a faint peach, and the air had that crisp quality that promised a cold, clear day.

I held Ash's hand in mine all the way through the quiet streets, half afraid he would disappear on me. This whole thing still felt rather like a dream. Any minute, I would wake up in my own warm bed in Willow's sith and assassins and daggers and revenants would dissolve like any other nightmare.

We stopped outside the police box that hid the entry to the Nest. The news stand beside it was still locked up tight against the night. Hardly anyone was around, though a homeless man huddled in the doorway of the eatery next to the station entrance. But his head drooped sleepily, and he paid us no attention.

"Wait here," Ash said. "Let me go. There's no need for both of us to go in there."

My hand tightened convulsively on his. He was still trying to protect me, only now I saw it as the gift it was and not an insult. But some part of my subconscious was convinced that if he went in there without me, I'd never see him again. "They're probably all at dinner anyway. I'll come with you."

"But they know you're not the Serpent anymore. It's too dangerous. You have few friends among the Vipers."

Didn't I know it. I lifted my chin in defiance. "I have Spring power to burn. They won't find me defenceless. Don't bother arguing—I followed you in there once, and I'm doing it again, whether you like it or not."

A gleam of amusement sparkled in his eye. "You remind me of a Chihuahua barking at Great Danes."

"Are you calling me short?"

"Of course not. Why would I do that? You are above average height for a woman."

"That's right, buddy, and don't you forget it." Why did I get the impression he was still laughing at me?

He opened the door, and mist swirled around our feet as we stepped through. Threshold magic tickled its way across my skin, and then we were on the other side. Before us, the main building of the Nest rose, its towers and turrets backlit against the peach sky.

"Welcome to Evil Hogwarts," I said.

He gave me a puzzled look before leading the way down the path. Right. He probably hadn't spent enough time in the human world to discover *Harry Potter*. I would have to put that right.

We went around the side, past the herb gardens to a more formal section of the garden where archways in high stone walls linked a series of courtyards, each one having its own characteristics. The first had a Japanese quality to it: a grouping of three large black rocks stood in solitary splendour among a carpet of white pebbles. Through the adjoining arch, a huge fountain of leaping dolphins could be seen, with paved paths leading away from it like the spokes of a wheel. Roses grew in the wedges between the paths. I knew these gardens well, as they were visible from the windows of the Serpent's apartment. I glanced up at those windows now, wondering when—or if—Fallon would claim those rooms.

Ash stopped outside a small side door. "At least stay out here in the gardens where your Spring magic can be useful. I can go in and find the cat."

"Okay. I'll look around out here." There was no guarantee Kel would still be in my chambers. Who knew what had happened when the Vipers felt the bonds dissolve?

Ash slipped inside, closing the door behind him, and I strolled through the minimalist sparsity of the Japanese-style garden into the one with the fountain. This was where I had apprenticed Atinna to Nuah after she'd tried to kill me. The air was heavily scented with rose perfume, and I took a deep breath. Water from the dolphins' mouths pattered down into the circular pool of the fountain. The smells and sounds reminded me of Spring, and my power stirred in response.

At least Fallon had left me that. He didn't need it, of

course, with the powers of Ni'ishasana at his disposal, but when had that ever stopped a man like him from taking things? Perhaps he did still feel something for me, however small.

Had he taken on the ties that bound the Serpent to the other Vipers? I wasn't certain, given how dismissive he'd been of the assassins, as if my suggestion that he wanted anything to do with them was utterly ridiculous. Yet passing on those bonds had always been part of the dagger's function. And being in command of a force of trained killers was its own kind of power. Fallon didn't strike me as the kind of man to pass up power—which made me wonder how the Vipers were taking it. Did they even know who their new Serpent was? The place must be in an uproar.

Booted feet crunched across the pebbles, and I turned. That was quick—Kel must have been in my rooms after all. But it wasn't Ash who appeared in the archway.

Atinna stood framed by the worn grey stone, regarding me without surprise. If anything, I would have said she appeared pleased to see me. And if that was the case, she must have had a complete personality transplant. I reached for my Spring magic, and the scent of limes rose around me as I held it in readiness.

"I thought you must have been close by when I saw your lapdog creeping around."

"If you mean Ash, he is an Adept and you're a mere apprentice. I'd watch my mouth if I were you."

"Of course, my Serpent." She bowed deeply, but there was mockery in it. Did she know I wasn't the Serpent anymore or not? "I only came to tell you I'd carried out your orders."

I tried to remember what she and Nuah had been working on. Wait—Sharis had said they'd finished their job two days ago. Had they helped Mezzi with his? "The hit on the Spring minstrel?"

"No." She smiled with such evident self-satisfaction that a deep foreboding lodged itself in the pit of my stomach. "Older orders. You did tell me when you punished me that I should obey every one of the Serpent's commands, did you not?"

That smile was spreading as she observed my unease.

"What have you done?" Where was Ash? If she had hurt him, I'd tear her apart. "What commands are you talking about?"

"Night has a new Lord," she said.

It took me a moment to realise what she meant, but when I did, it was like being hit by a freight train. Horror filled me. "You killed Lord Nox?"

"Of course." Her eyes gleamed with delight at my pain. "It was my duty as a Viper."

My chest felt so tight that I could hardly breathe. This couldn't be happening. She must be lying. "But *I* was supposed to kill him. Celebrach gave that hit to *me*."

And therefore, I had never countermanded the order. It wasn't as if *I* was going to kill him. Raven's face flashed into my mind, tight with anxiety as he begged me to call off the hit on his father. And I'd assured him that I would. That I *had*.

"True, but he also told Evandir and me to do it if you

faltered. And you most certainly faltered, wouldn't you say?" She laughed. "Oh, did you mean I should obey only the *current* Serpent's orders? Dear, dear, what a terrible misunderstanding. You should have been more specific."

"What I should have been was less merciful." I clenched my fists, the scent of limes growing stronger as my power rose in response to my anger. "I should have killed you after you tried to murder me in my sleep, you bitch. The world would have been a better place."

And Lord Nox would have been safe. Lord Nox, with his kind eyes and his courtly compliments at the ball in Spring. Lord Nox, standing with his wife and three strong sons at Allegra's ascension, his pride in his family clear to all. What must those sons be feeling now? What would Raven think? He must be assuming that this was my fault. That I'd purposely attacked after giving my word that I wouldn't.

That I was his enemy.

"I'll kill you." My voice was steady though my heart raced. She dared to stand there, smirking at me, after killing one of the best rulers in the Realms just so she could throw it in my face? I would *end* her, the petty bitch. "I hope you gave Lord Nox a merciful end, because yours won't be."

She raised a cynical eyebrow. "You don't have Ni'ishasana to back you now, you pathetic half-breed. I'll kill you with no more effort than swatting a fly." She cracked her knuckles. "But I'll enjoy it a lot more."

"I won't need Ni'ishasana to deal with a worm like

you." I had to remember to thank Ash for getting me to wait for him in the gardens. Such a good idea. So many possibilities. The plants all around me throbbed with life and potential.

"Did the Blade finally get sick of answering to someone so clearly inferior?" Atinna jeered. "I'm surprised it didn't just kill you."

"It was more that *I* got sick of *it*," I said flippantly. "So I gave it away."

She frowned. "You're lying. If someone else had taken it, you'd be dead."

Couldn't she feel a bond with the new Serpent? Was my father up to something or was it only that she was still an apprentice, tied more tightly to her Adept than to Ni'ishasana and the Serpent?

I shrugged. "I guess you'll have to wait and see when your new boss comes calling."

Without warning, she flung a spear of ice at me. A rose bush surged up, trebling in size in the blink of an eye, and tangled the ice in its thorny branches before it ever reached me. Atinna's eyes widened, but I had no time to enjoy her shock. My Spring magic was no longer a secret, so I went on the attack.

The roses nearest her lashed out, winding themselves around her. She shouted in surprise as they dragged her out of the archway and onto the grass, but she didn't lose her head. A blast of Winter magic froze them to death. I felt the life leave them as their green stems hardened and withered.

There were trees through the next archway, tall robinias with smooth bark and bright green leaves. I summoned their roots, and they burst out of the ground and twined around Atinna's legs, dragging her down into the soil. Willow had done something similar to the assassins that had attacked us the night of Nevith's death. I'd been taking notes.

In fact, I'd been watching people use Spring magic all my life. I knew all the tricks. Atinna struggled against the roots, but it soon became obvious that she couldn't freeze them the way she'd done with the roses.

Instead, she froze the ground. Being a Winter fae, the cold didn't bother her, but she was trapped hip-deep in frozen ground, which was a serious drawback in a fight. I grinned and pulled a small knife from a hidden sheath in my boot.

She snarled and unleashed another storm of ice spears. The rose garden came alive, branches thrashing through the air, catching the spears in their thorny grip. I poured life into the roses at the same time, so they wouldn't suffer the same fate as the first bush, now icebound and dead. I didn't want to run out of ammo.

A blizzard sprang up out of nowhere. She must be trying to freeze me to death, but she'd forgotten how useful bad visibility was to an assassin. In the face of her snowy onslaught, I couldn't regulate my body temperature forever, but I certainly wouldn't die of cold before I got to her. A knife in the heart would end the blizzard long before it became a problem for me.

I crept through the snowstorm, knife at the ready. But

she wasn't where she'd last been. Even as I realised the iced-over earth where she'd been trapped was all churned up, she came out of nowhere, knocking me to the ground.

We went rolling through the snow. I had to drop my knife to grab her wrist, because she had the longest knife I'd ever seen in one upraised hand. Much longer and it would have been a short sword. Whatever you called it, it made my little blade look like a child's toy, and I strained to keep her from plunging it into my heart.

The snowstorm eased as we struggled. Clearly, she was after the satisfaction of the up close and personal kill, without the use of magic. I had no such compunction, and continued to pelt her with rosebushes. Their thorns tore at her skin as she wrestled me to the ground. I sent one of them round her throat like a garotte, choking and squeezing. Her eyes bulged, and the hand holding the knife trembled.

Then, she collapsed on top of me, unmoving. Snowflakes clung to my lashes, and I blinked them away, knowing before I shoved at her that she was dying. The spark of her life dwindled within her and quietly went out.

How the *hell* had I felt that?

I rolled her dead body away and sat up.

Ash strolled across the snow, Kel cuddled protectively against his chest in one arm. His knife stood up from Atinna's back. It must have pierced her heart for her to die so quickly.

I stared down at the body, troubled. Spring magic gave the wielder the ability to sense the life within plants, but not people. I certainly hadn't sensed the life in her when she was alive; I'd only felt it depart. Was this some kind of residue of the bonds the dagger had forged between us? I certainly hoped I wasn't going to feel every one of the damn Vipers die. That wasn't a moment I wanted to share with anyone, much less a whole bunch of enemies.

I stood up, brushing snow off my clothes. The back of my shirt and jeans were soaked through from rolling around in it. "Thanks. I think I had her, but it never hurts to have back-up."

"You're not angry that I stole your kill?"

What a weird thing to say. "Why would I—"

Oh. Shame heated my cheeks as I remembered how I'd reacted in the forests of Summer, when he'd killed the deerkin instead of me. I'd tortured him for his "presumption" then. The dagger had turned me into a monster. Now, I was just grateful that the fight was over and I was still breathing.

"I'm sorry I was such a bitch to you before. The dagger had me all twisted up so I couldn't think straight. No, of course I'm not angry. Did anyone see you inside?"

"Only the servants in the kitchen. He was in there, looking for food. I don't think anyone's fed him since we left."

"Oh, poor boy." Thank goodness we'd come back for him. He could have starved to death before the servants fed him. Those poor slaves of the dagger didn't do anything unless they were commanded to do so. I reached out for the cat, and Ash put him in my arms. His fur was soft against my cheek as I hugged him. "Are you hungry, baby? Let's get out of here and give you some food."

Ash led the way, and we slipped out of the sith as quietly as we'd entered, leaving the Vipers short one apprentice. I wondered what would happen to the servants now the dagger was gone.

Not my circus, not my zombies.

29

———

By mid-morning, we were standing on the street outside the house that hid the entrance to Willow's sith. The sunlight glinted on its smeared windows and lit up every cobweb that clung to its sagging gutters. I still carried Kel, his furry weight warm and comforting in my arms.

He wriggled a little, and I realised I'd tightened my grip. I was worried that Willow had been as good as her word and changed the wards to lock me out, in which case we could spend the rest of the day walking in and out through the rusty gate in the low brick fence but would never arrive in the flowery meadow of the sith. I relaxed my death grip on the cat and rubbed under his chin in apology.

"What if we can't get in?" I muttered, staring at the unprepossessing house as if I could force it to let me in through sheer willpower.

"Then we wait here until they come out. Or we go to

that pub they all frequent and leave a message. But why not try it and find out? You could be wasting time worrying about a problem that doesn't actually exist."

I shifted uneasily from foot to foot. "Don't come at me with your damn logic."

He regarded me steadily. "It's not just the wards that have you on edge. What's wrong?"

I sighed. Those grey eyes saw far too clearly sometimes. "I'll have to tell them about Lord Nox." And Raven would hate me. "I took that damn dagger to save Raven, and now it's cost him his father. Atinna only killed him to spite me. His whole family is suffering for a stupid, petty revenge that should never have happened."

"How were you to know what Atinna was going to do? You can only be responsible for your own actions, not those of everyone else. Besides, as you say, if you hadn't taken up the dagger, Raven would have died. Whatever you did, one of that family would be dead. Who is to say that Lord Nox wouldn't have preferred that one to be himself rather than his son?"

"That's a weird way of looking at it."

"No weirder than assuming you are personally responsible for saving the whole world. Other people have agency, too, and you are not responsible for their choices."

"If I'd killed Atinna when she tried to assassinate me ..."

"If you'd killed Atinna, you would now be second-guessing yourself for judging her too harshly and taking her life unnecessarily." He moved closer and stroked my hair in a gesture so intimate it made me shiver. "This is why you could never have been an assassin. Stop beating yourself up. You did what you could, and that's all anyone can ask."

"Except that what I did put the dagger into Fallon's hands. A powerful necromancer in possession of the most feared dagger in the world—what could possibly go wrong?"

"Hush." His hand still on my head, Ash pulled me closer, careful of the cat in my arms, and planted a soft kiss on my hair. "You will wear yourself out with maybes. None of this is your fault. Ni'ishasana manipulated you. You never stood a chance against its power. I doubt even the king himself could resist its seduction once it had set its heart on him. You should be proud that you never craved its power as so many have done over the centuries. Instead, you took it up in an unselfish act of sacrifice to save your friend. And that unselfishness, that lack of craving, saved you in the end."

"How do you mean?"

"The fact that you never wanted it in the first place made it possible for you to let it go when you found some higher purpose for giving it up. You picked it up for selfless reasons, so you were able to lay it down again for selfless reasons."

"I would hardly call wanting my mother back a selfless reason." Plus, I more than half-suspected that it would have been much harder to give up the dagger if Ni'ishasana itself hadn't been so keen to be rid of me. Perhaps I should have mentioned that, but he was saying such flattering things about me, and it would have been rude to interrupt him.

"You know what I mean." Ash stepped back as Kel wriggled in protest. "There was no greed involved. You didn't want the power for its own sake, despite your own apparent lack of magic. Those who want that power become ensnared by it, because they can never let the dagger go once they've tasted its gifts. Fallon will end up as a miserable soul trapped inside it forever, like all its other wielders have done. Except you. Will he still think it was worth it then?"

"Maybe not. But I'm more worried about what he'll do with it in the meantime." I sighed. "Why was he pursuing it, if not to resurrect my mother?"

Ash shrugged. "Doubtless for the same reason all its other wielders have. For the power it bestows."

"But all those other wielders wanted to be the Serpent of the Vipers. He doesn't."

"So he says."

"But I think it's true. Atinna didn't seem to know there was a new Serpent."

"Well, not even you can solve all the world's problems at once." He looked at the rusty gate. "Why don't we start with determining whether or not these wards will let you pass? Preferably before someone calls the human police to report two vagrants loitering on the footpath outside this house."

"Two vagrants and a cat. Don't forget the cat."

"As if anyone could forget this cat." He smiled, his whole face softening.

"You really like him, don't you?" I wondered if he'd ever owned a pet. The Vipers probably thought it was weak to care about a mere animal. "Here, why don't you hold him? I think he likes you better anyway, and it makes you look less threatening. If you have your arms full of fluff you can't be reaching for a knife."

"I wouldn't be reaching for a knife in the house of your friend," he objected. "Probably."

I rolled my eyes as he took the cat. "But you *look* like you would. Try to look less ... menacing."

I really wanted him to make a good impression. He needed to smile more; it changed his whole face, making him less hard. I was right about the cat, too. Who could feel threatened by a guy holding an adorable bundle of fluff? Especially when that guy looked so comfortable, as if he toted his cat everywhere with him.

"Okay," I said, squaring my shoulders. "Let's do this."

Before I could lose my nerve, I strode forward, thrusting the gate out of my way so hard it banged against the brick wall.

My whole body sagged with relief as the familiar tickle of threshold magic washed over me. Willow hadn't changed the wards after all. She wouldn't have *forgotten* to do it—her threat to lock me out must have been a ploy, trying to scare me into giving up the dagger when entreaties had failed. That would be so like her. She had a ruthless streak a mile wide.

The flower-dotted meadow with its vista of distant trees greeted me. Ash stepped through behind me and gave me a look that said *I told you so* without having to open his mouth.

Butterflies danced across the sun-warmed meadow, flitting around our heads as we walked through knee-high grass towards the trees. Kel eyed the butterflies with interest, but evidently decided he was too comfortable in Ash's arms to bother chasing them. Or perhaps he'd learned from experience that they weren't as easy to catch as they looked.

At this time of day, Willow might still be awake, so I headed first for the pavilion that housed the common areas. There was no one there, but I paused in the doorway to the dining room.

A faint scent of roast meat and rich gravy hung on the air, and my stomach rumbled in response. It had been a while since I'd eaten. We'd have to fix that soon. Maybe Zinnia had some leftovers in the kitchen—or some of those light-as-air lemon cakes that she used to make because she knew they were my favourite. I debated taking a detour via the kitchen but decided that it was more important to find Willow first, much to my stomach's disappointment.

She wasn't in her library, either, so I headed down the hall to her bedroom, the carpet of grass soft and yielding beneath my booted feet. She was passed out face down in her bed.

So was someone else.

With a little jolt, I recognised him as the changeling guy—the new guitarist. Christian. I stood beside the bed, staring down at them like some creepy stalker until Ash, who'd stopped in the doorway, cleared his throat.

Right. I should wake them up. It had just shocked me to see her with someone I didn't even know. It wasn't as if I'd never known her to take a guy to her bed before—but I wasn't used to feeling like the stranger in her life. I'd only been gone a little over two months, but it was a reminder that normal life hadn't stopped without me.

I shook her shoulder gently. "Hey, sleepyhead. Wake up."

She cracked one bleary eye, then jolted into wakefulness when she saw it was me. Her face closed in, becoming watchful and suspicious as she dragged herself into a sitting position. "What are you doing here?"

"I took your advice and gave that dagger the flick."

"Really?" Her face lit up, then she caught sight of Ash in the doorway and frowned again. "Then why is he here?"

I glanced at Ash, doing his best to look less menacing, as instructed, with the cat cradled against his broad chest. It wasn't altogether convincing. "He's left the Vipers."

Her eyebrows rose in obvious disbelief. Her gaze never left Ash as she poked her companion into wakefulness. "I don't trust you, assassin."

"That's fair," he said calmly.

"Well, I do," I said, beckoning him into the room with a jerk of my head. "He's saved my life more times than I can count."

Kel sniffed doubtfully at my elbow as Ash came to stand at my side.

Willow eyed him with obvious misgiving. "I'm guessing there's a story here. Lily should hear this, too."

"I'll go wake the others," Christian said, and slid out of bed. He was wearing boxers, but he quickly pulled on a pair of jeans that had been lying on the floor and left the room, shirtless and barefooted.

What "others"? Was he bringing Zinnia and Yarys as well as the princess? Not that I wouldn't be thrilled to see them again, but Willow didn't normally include them in discussions of affairs of state. Nor, for that matter, her current bedmates, who were usually temporary. Was this guy something more?

Willow, clad in a long waterfall of green silk that clung to her curves and matched the colour of her eyes exactly, got out of bed, too. "Perhaps you could wait in the library while I get changed."

I was turning to leave when she grabbed me in a fierce hug.

"It's good to see you again."

She'd only seen me the day before, but I didn't point that out. I knew what she meant. She was happy to see me as myself, without the dagger's poisonous influence. "It's good to be home."

She didn't keep us waiting long. I'd barely sat down in one of the big, squishy chairs in her library when she strode in wearing faded blue denim jeans, biker boots, and a charcoal T-shirt with a tear in one sleeve. The brightest thing about her was her flaming red hair, which tumbled around her shoulders. She slid an elastic off one wrist as she walked in and dragged it all back into a messy ponytail.

Ash, still holding Kel, had been inspecting her bookshelves. He turned as she came in, and she looked at the cat with undisguised loathing.

"Did you have to bring that creature back with you? I was so excited when I realised you'd taken it. Finally, I'd gotten rid of it."

Ash's face took on a stony expression, and he stroked Kel's head as if in apology. The cat rubbed his head against Ash's chin and started purring.

I laughed. "It's all right. You're not getting him back. As you can see, he's found someone he likes better."

"Aren't you a little busy murdering people to have time for a pet?" Willow asked Ash, tilting her chin in a combative gesture I was only too familiar with.

"Business has been slow lately," he said dryly.

I choked on a laugh, then abruptly sobered as I remembered Atinna's very successful business and the terrible news I had to deliver.

Did Raven know yet? I assumed his father's body must have been found by now. I'd had the impression that Atinna had been returning from the kill when she had found me in the garden. But perhaps Raven had been away from home at the time. He might still be blissfully unaware of the tragedy that had fallen on his family.

I shivered. I knew what it was like to lose a parent unexpectedly.

Christian wandered back in, this time wearing a T-shirt even more ragged than Willow's. Had they been dumpster-diving together? It wasn't as if Willow couldn't afford decent clothes. Were her unusual fashion choices meant to make him feel more at home, less overawed by sharing a bed with the heir of Spring? She'd never bothered to make such allowances for a lover before.

In the daylight, the changeling looked older than I'd first thought him, and I rapidly revised my estimate of his age closer to thirty. Now that I had a better look at him, I could see crow's feet around eyes that held that air of loss so common among changelings. Willow patted the lounge next to her, and he sat down.

"They're coming," he said.

"Good."

Kel began wriggling, and Ash set him down. The cat wandered out through the open fourth wall of the room into the garden, where he found a sunny spot on the grass and curled up, narrowing his eyes into blissful slits against the sun's glare. Ash watched him the way an anxious parent watches a toddler.

"He won't go far," I said. "He likes to hang around the pavilions in case food miraculously appears."

Lily appeared in the doorway, her long dark hair unbound and swirling around a pale pink concoction of chiffon and frills that was probably meant to be a dressing gown but looked as though it would blow away in the slightest breeze, like something a film star would wear. Her regal gaze snagged on Ash, then travelled to me.

"I could hardly believe it when Christian said you were back." Her face broke into a smile that transformed her normally haughty features, making her look a lot more like her royal father than usual. "Thank the Lady."

I stared at her in astonishment. If Kel had started speaking, I couldn't have been more surprised. She actually looked pleased to see me. Surely there must be some mistake—the princess and I hadn't exactly seen eye to eye before I had left. In fact, I distinctly remembered threatening to murder her in her sleep and almost halfway meaning it.

"Willow has been so worried about you," she added.

Well, that sounded more like her. "I notice you don't say *you* were worried."

She frowned, as if my stupidity disappointed her. "Of course I was worried. Do you think I wanted someone so impetuous in charge of a guild of assassins? And not only that, but in possession of one of the world's most dangerous artefacts?"

So, she hadn't cared what happened to me, personally, only how it might affect the Realms she would one day rule. I smiled, oddly reassured by this return to normalcy.

Then Raven burst into the room, and my heart sank. What was *he* doing here?

Joy filled his face and shone from his midnight eyes as he hurried towards me, arms outstretched. That wasn't the face of a man who knew his beloved father was dead. I leapt up, my own hands out to ward him off, as if I hoped to push away the bad news that weighed so heavily on me.

Ash moved to my side, and Raven's headlong plunge towards me slowed as he saw how very close Ash was standing. He came to a stop in front of me and took my hands in his, his wings fluttering in and out of sight in a sign of the turmoil of his emotions.

"Sage," he breathed. "What a sight you are for sore eyes."

"W-What are you doing here?" I managed to choke out.

God, why did *I* have to be the one to break the news to him? And he looked so happy to see me. This was a nightmare. Guilt lay on my chest like stone, crushing me, and I couldn't draw a proper breath.

"Willow sent word yesterday that you'd visited, so I came at once, hoping you would return." His eyes searched my face, and his brows drew together in a crease of worry. I must have looked pale; I felt utterly sick with shame and horror that I had to deliver such terrible news. Knowing what pain I must inflict. All his joy in seeing me again would turn to ashes. "What's wrong?"

I drew a deep, shuddering breath. *Don't be such a bloody coward. Putting it off won't make it any easier.*

"I'm sorry, Raven," I said softly. "I have some bad news for you."

The room stilled, as if the others sensed the gravity of the moment.

His glance slid sideways to Ash for a moment, then back again. "You got drunk in Vegas and married some guy you met in a bar?"

I gripped his hands harder, trying to convey support through my touch. "You need to go home at once. Your father ..." I bit my lip as the light went out of his face. Somehow, he sensed what I was going to say. I swallowed hard. "I'm so sorry. Your father is dead."

His hands slipped from mine, and he stepped back. Shock and horror flitted across his face, his heartbreak clear for all to see. Then, his expression hardened. "You said you called off the hit."

"I didn't need to, because—"

"You didn't *need* to?"

"Raven, I'm sorry." I took a step forward, hands held out entreatingly, but he recoiled. "I—"

"You're *sorry*? My father is dead because of you, and you think *sorry* is good enough?" Tears ran down his cheeks, but his eyes burned with such fury I doubted he even knew he was crying.

"It's not like that! Please, let me explain."

"Let you lie to my face, you mean? How dare you stand there and act as though you care? As though you're my *friend*? You betrayed me!"

And with a shriek of pain that dissolved into the harsh croak of a raven, the man became a black bird that launched itself into the air and disappeared among the trees.

30

Some hours later, at Lily's insistence, the four of us—Lily, Willow, Ash, and I—stood outside her father's gates. Raven had never reappeared. Presumably, he'd taken my advice and gone home.

Every time I thought of him, the sick feeling in my stomach intensified. Though I'd explained what had happened to the others, I hadn't had a chance to tell Raven the story. Perhaps this wasn't the time, but it hurt to know that he was out there with such rage in his heart, believing that I'd turned against him. That I'd gone through with murdering his father after I'd promised him I wouldn't. It hurt that he thought I was capable of that.

On recognising the princess, the captain of the gate had sent a messenger ahead and a pair of guards to escort us straight into her father's presence. Of course, I would have reported to the king eventually, but my first instinct had been to go after Raven. Ash had talked me out of it.

"Raven and his family need time alone to grieve," he'd said. "It's not a time for outsiders."

So, I'd started filling them in on what had happened and how I'd won free of the dagger, but I hadn't gotten far into the story before Lily had announced that her father needed to hear this *right now*. Willow had instantly agreed —since when had these two gotten so chummy? So here we were, being ushered into the king's private apartments to await his pleasure.

He didn't keep us waiting long, although judging from the state of his hair, he'd been in bed before we'd arrived. We all leapt to our feet, even Ash, as Rothbold strode in wearing a long blue coat that set off the famous Brenfell eyes his daughter had inherited. The sun pouring in the large windows sparkled on a plain gold circlet nestled in his rumpled dark hair. He waved us all back to our seats— grey leather lounges so deep you could lose a small child in them—and took one himself, crossing one booted leg over the other.

"I seem to remember telling you that you were not to return until I summoned you," he said to his daughter, who shrank a little in her seat.

Willow immediately leapt to Lily's defence. "The occasion warrants a little disobedience, sire. Once you hear what Sage has to say, I'm sure you'll agree."

"Will I?" The king's dry tone suggested that Willow's sureness was presumptuous, but he turned to me. "So, you have returned from your mission with the Vipers. I'm pleased that you survived the experience. But who is this you've brought with you?"

"This is Ash, sire. A former Viper." I made sure to lay the emphasis on *former*.

Piercing blue eyes examined Ash. "And how long ago did you cease to be a Viper, young man?"

"In my heart, I was never one," Ash replied. "But technically, yesterday."

The two guards who'd accompanied the king stepped forward in alarm, but the king waved them back.

"That is very recent indeed," Rothbold said, turning his frown on me. "You had better explain."

So I did. The explanation went on for long enough that the king called for food and wine partway through, and I fell on the little pastries the servants brought as if I hadn't eaten in a week.

When I'd finished talking, the king stared into his wine glass as the minutes ticked by. I waited in silence for his verdict, too tired now that I had it all out to care what he thought of me or the mess I'd made. My stomach comfortably full, all I wanted was to sleep somewhere uninterrupted. Preferably for about three weeks.

"So, in essence," Rothbold said at length, "the Vipers are in turmoil and perhaps engaged in a civil war to see who will lead them, unless Fallon Domani chooses to. And he has the dagger, but we don't know what he plans to do with it."

"Whatever it is, it can't be good," I said. "He and the dagger have both been manipulating me in order to get together."

"So, a dangerous necromancer is in possession of the most powerful weapon in all the Realms."

"Yes." I felt like such an idiot. How could I have been so taken in by both of them?

"I can't deny, that could be catastrophic. If your father's goal was to become leader of the Vipers, things may continue much as they always have. But if he has some other end in mind, we could be in for a very difficult time. That dagger contains immense power."

"Yes," I whispered. No one knew better than me how much power Ni'ishasana bestowed on its wielder.

"And Lord Nox is dead." The king covered his eyes with his hand for a moment, and I remembered belatedly that Lord Nox had been one of the king's greatest allies. This could cause problems for Rothbold's hold on his kingdom, which still wasn't as sure as he probably would have liked after his return from his long imprisonment. "I'll have to send one of my Chosen to Night to ascertain the situation there and give my condolences to Lady Fiana and her sons. Quinn will be Lord of Night now."

"Yes." I'd seen Quinn at Allegra's ascension. He looked a lot like Raven, though I had the impression he was a steadier personality from some crack Raven had made once about his boring older brother.

The king dropped his hand and took in my guilty expression. "And you think it's all your fault."

This time, I couldn't even speak. I stared at the carpet and nodded. Poor Quinn had probably been preparing all his life to take his father's place one day, but he never would have expected that sad day to come so soon.

"Sage had nothing to do with Lord Nox's death," Ash said hotly.

"I'm aware," the king said, cutting him off with a single look. "I heard what happened. Sage, none of this was under your control. The Thief of Souls is far too old and powerful for someone of your age and experience to stand any chance against. I grant you that things look dire, and the loss of Lord Nox is a terrible grief, but instead of blaming yourself, consider the situation from another angle."

What other angle? How could he possibly find any good in this mess?

"First, the Vipers are at least temporarily headless and uncoordinated, which makes them vulnerable."

"We could strike at them now, while they're in upheaval," Lily said, thoughtfully.

"And thus remove a menace that has plagued these Realms for centuries." The king smiled gently at me. "Just as you wished to. Only now we have the expertise and inside knowledge of you and Ash to make our job easier."

"You'll finally get what you wanted," Willow said to me.

It seemed so long since I'd set out to avenge Nevith. So much had changed since then, but justice for Nevith—and for Lord Nox and all the others the Vipers had killed—was still a worthy goal.

"You and Ash can lead my knights on a raid of the Nest," Rothbold said. "If we are quick, we may be able to destroy them before your father establishes himself, thus removing part of the threat he poses. That would leave only the problem of the dagger to be dealt with. Secondly, don't discount the fact that you are back, unharmed. Your loss would have been felt by many."

That was nice of him to say, but wildly inaccurate. Very few people beyond Willow and Rowan and maybe one or two regulars at The Drunken Irishman would have noticed I was gone.

But Willow was nodding—and, hey, so was Lily. I glanced suspiciously between her and Willow, as if Willow had pushed her into it, since they seemed to be getting on better now. But Lily smiled at me with no sign of coercion. How odd. Her time in the human world had made her almost bearable.

"Oh, sire—speaking of knights." In my haste to get to the important part of my tale, I'd left out who had paid for Lord Nox's death and jumped straight from realising I could use the dagger to help raise my mother to the actual ceremony. Now, I cringed at what I still had to reveal. "There's one other thing. Sir Ebos is a traitor."

"What?" The king sat up straight, his eyebrows shooting up toward his golden circlet.

"I left out that part of the story. Sorry."

Before I'd finished recounting the tale of my infiltration of the palace and the abortive attempt on Sir Ebos's life, the king was on his feet, roaring to have the Dragon summoned. The unfortunate page who was given the job was gone a long time, during which the king paced back and forth from the door to the windows like a caged lion.

"Well?" he barked, when the boy finally reappeared.

"I can't find him, sire. No one's seen him since the princess arrived."

A troop of guards was dispatched, but in the end, they had no better luck than the page. Sir Ebos was gone.

If we were going to look at everything from a glass-half-full perspective, then that could be point three: a traitor in our midst had been revealed. I didn't say that out loud, however. I wasn't sure the king was quite ready to view it that way. He looked gutted.

Lily suggested making a thorough search of Ebos's quarters, and watching him nod thoughtfully, I figured there might even be a fourth point buried in all the bad news: Rothbold looked impressed by his daughter. I was guessing her exile wouldn't last much longer. Somehow, while I'd been gone, Willow had managed to smooth over her most abrasive edges.

"I can't believe that was you who attacked the palace," Willow murmured as the king issued instructions to another set of guards. "You've been busier than a one-armed wallpaper hanger."

"Busier than a ...?" I stared at her, my mouth open.

Oh, how I had missed this. Willow and I had been trying to outdo each other with the most outlandish pieces of human slang we could find ever since we'd arrived in the mortal world. She smirked at me, confident I couldn't beat this one. I snapped my mouth shut, then grinned at her. She didn't care that I'd been possessed by an evil magical dagger. She didn't care what I'd done. We were still friends.

"You made that up," I accused.

"Did not." Her shit-eating grin widened. She knew I hadn't been in the human world enough lately to find anything half as good.

"What even *is* a wallpaper hanger? Surely that's not a real job?"

Ash watched us, bemused, as our argument continued in fierce whispers while the business of the kingdom went on around us. For the first time in weeks, something coiled tight inside me unwound.

Maybe the king was right, and there was hope that the future wasn't as dire as it seemed. Sure, Fallon had that damn dagger, the Vipers still had to be dealt with, and the Lady alone knew what Sir Ebos was up to—but for the moment, I was content eating the king's extremely good pastries and indulging in a pointless argument with my best friend.

I smiled at Ash around a mouthful of cake. Point five: the world might be going to shit, but I had people who were prepared to wade through it with me.

THE END

Don't miss the next book, *Assassin's Bane*, coming soon! To be informed when it's released, plus get free stories, special deals and other book news, sign up for my newsletter at www.marinafinlayson.com.

Reviews and word of mouth are vital for any author's success. If you enjoyed *Assassin's Dagger*, please take a moment to leave a short review at Amazon.com. Just a few words sharing your thoughts on the book would be extremely helpful in spreading the word to other readers (and this author would be immensely grateful!).

ACKNOWLEDGMENTS

Thanks again to my lovely writer friend, Jen Rasmussen, for her support. She is a great beta reader and an even better cheerleader.

For cheerleading on the home front (and cooking of meals and other helpful acts of love), plus once again providing his sterling beta-reading services, I am indebted to my darling husband, Mal.

ABOUT THE AUTHOR

Marina Finlayson is a reformed wedding organist who now writes fantasy. She is married and shares her Sydney home with three kids, a large collection of dragon statues and one very stupid dog with a death wish.

Her idea of heaven is lying in the bath with a cup of tea and a good book until she goes wrinkly.